Winter Fire
By Jess Dee

Guilty pleasures can heat the coldest winter night...

There's never been any question in Rachel Ashberg's mind. Jackson Brooks is *the one*, and they both know it. The problem? Thanks to his unbreakable rule—never date his twin sister's friends—he's completely off-limits. Even if they can't imagine being with anyone else.

It's been over two years since their last encounter, when they gave in—just once—to their passion. Now, as the Brooks twins' milestone birthday approaches, Rachel and Jackson are about to meet again at a gorgeous mountain resort. Needing something to take the edge off the desire that has never faded, she indulges in a fling with sexy stranger Garreth Halt. He even makes her forget Jackson for a while. Or...maybe not.

When she mentions Jackson's name in passing, Garreth picks up on all the hidden undertones in her voice. And he brings Jackson into their bed, if only in a fantasy they play out together. Funny thing about Garreth's fantasies, though. Even the most improbable, *impossible* ones have a way of becoming reality...

Warning: Enough heat is contained within these pages that you won't even notice the winter cold. You might fall in love with Jackson—the real-life hero, determined to protect his sister from further pain—but it's the handsome stranger, Garreth, who'll take your breath away.

Triple Dare
By Lexxie Couper

Two men, one woman, one momentous dare.

Serious and determined, Joseph Hudson isn't Australia's businessman of the year for nothing. So now he's asking himself, how did he get lost on the side of a mountain in the Colorado Rockies—in the middle of winter—with night fast approaching? Three simple words. *I dare you.*

Fear isn't in Rob Thorton's vocabulary. Life is for the taking, and Rob uses both hands. Challenging his best mate to take an impromptu snowboarding trip to the U.S. is just the latest in a lifetime of dares. Besides, he has an ulterior motive for the trip. And a plan...

Park Ranger Anna McCarthy knows what trouble looks like, and it's written all over the two Aussies she first encounters in the ski lodge. Instinct has her following them onto the mountain, and sure enough, they end up needing her winter survival expertise. But not even her skills can stop her body from responding to the sexy muscles she finds beneath their ski suits.

Stuck in a remote cabin until the storm passes, the temperatures rise until all bets are off. And a double dare turns into a triple threat—to their hearts.

Warning: Contains lots of scorching boy on girl on boy action, a heroine who knows what she wants and two sexy-arsed Australian heroes to really work up a sweat over. Oh, and a soul-deep love story with a revelation that may make you cry.

True Heart
By Delilah Devlin

Two men plus one woman equals three bodies on fire...

True Wyatt's hands are going to be full enough keeping the herd alive through the dead of winter. The last thing he needs to hear is that his brother Lonny has rented out their isolated hunting cabin to a reclusive writer—especially a sassy, disaster-prone brunette. Who has time to babysit a city girl until spring?

With a deadline looming, erotica writer Honey Cahill is looking forward to six distraction-free weeks to finish her next book. However, between Lonny's flirty sensuality and True's hard-edged intensity, the Wyatt brothers set the stage of her imagination for a winter of wicked delights.

The fire that destroys the cabin, though, is as real as it gets. Forced to seek a bed under True and Lonny's roof, the temptation to experiment—all in the name of research, of course—is overpowering. One night in their arms doesn't feel like enough; it feels like *more.* Particularly with one cowboy who fires all her cylinders...

Warning: It's a Devlin ménage—expect men with stamina and not an ounce of mercy to behave like sex gods, and the lucky woman to love every minute of it. A little domination goes a long, long way...

Red-Hot Winter

Samhain Publishing, Ltd.
11821 Mason Montgomery Road, 4B
Cincinnati, OH 45249
www.samhainpublishing.com

Red-Hot Winter
Print ISBN: 978-1-60928-340-7

Editing by Heidi Moore
Cover by Kanaxa

Winter Fire, ISBN 978-1-60928-323-0
First Samhain Publishing, Ltd. electronic publication: January 2011
Triple Dare, ISBN 978-1-60928-322-3
First Samhain Publishing, Ltd. electronic publication: January 2011
True Heart, ISBN 978-1-60928-324-7
First Samhain Publishing, Ltd. electronic publication: January 2011
First Samhain Publishing, Ltd. print publication: December 2011

Contents

Winter Fire

Jess Dee

Dedication

With special thanks to Lexxie Couper, for reeling me into this anthology and keeping me here. Oh, and for her invaluable insight into this book. Twisted as it may have been, it was spot on every single time.

To the Down Under Divas: Every writer should have a chance to brainstorm their ménages in a hotel lounge, with a strange man sitting opposite them listening spellbound to every word.

And of course, thank you to Heidi Moore for taking a chance on me. Ayzeh yoffe, boet, it's been lekker. I've had a jol and a half (And seriously? I don't think there's another editor in the whole world I could say that to).

Chapter One

Heat radiated from the stone fireplace, warming the room. The temperature in the cozy, modern hotel lounge was a welcome contrast to the frigid wind outside. Mesmerized, Rachel Ashberg stared into the flames, watching as they danced around the logs, consuming the wood with hungry licks.

She sipped the last of her wine, relishing the tranquility that settled over her. Tomorrow that peace would be stripped away like old paint.

It had been a good idea to drive up to the Blue Mountains from Sydney a day early. The ninety-minute car trip through winding roads and national parkland had given her a chance to decompress a little. Twenty-four hours of rest and relaxation, away from the stress of work and failed relationships, was proving to be a much-needed tonic. Plus, she was building up her energy reserves for the weekend. She was going to need them.

The walk down to Wentworth Falls earlier had helped too. All that crisp, wintry air, lush eucalyptus forest, calming birdsong and getting back to nature had either cleared her mind of any remaining despondency or frozen her brain and heart enough that those issues no longer worried her. So what if things hadn't worked out with Paul? She'd known from the beginning he wasn't the right guy for her, but she'd tried anyway.

Just like she'd tried with James and Ethan and a whole host of other men who hadn't quite cut it. Hell, none of them were the right guy.

How could they be, when she'd already met the right guy—

and he was the one man she couldn't be with? Of course, fate dictated he was *also* the man she was about to spend two days and two nights with, in a romantic boutique hotel.

He, his sister and ten of their closest friends.

God, it was going to be hell. Torture to the *nth* degree. How would she ever make it through to Monday?

Rachel shook her head, chastising herself for her negativity.

She would make it through to Monday. Her strength and her resistance had been fortified today, and she'd be fine. The weekend would pass without her once pining for Jackson Brooks. Without accidentally brushing up against him. Without sneaking outside in the blistering cold to steal secret kisses as they once had.

Rachel fidgeted with the cover of her book, considered opening it, but in the end just wasn't in the mood for reading.

"Mind if I join you?"

The question registered, but Rachel didn't respond. Since she was here alone, whoever had spoken must have addressed someone else. Pity. The voice held appeal. It was a deep rumble, smooth as old scotch. And accented. American?

She smiled to herself. Her relationship skills may be shot to hell, but her body still worked just fine. It didn't matter that yet another relationship had failed as a result of her feelings for Jackson. Her sex drive obviously hadn't suffered for it.

Proof in point? A few words from an unseen man with a sexy accent, and her pussy stirred. After all, sex was a wonderful way to temporarily forget her woes and heart-ache.

The evocative voice spoke again. "Okay, I won't join you, but could I at least share the fire?"

Rachel blinked. Share the fire? Maybe the unseen man with the sexy-as-sin accent *was* talking to her after all. She turned in the direction of the voice and had to stifle a gasp. An absolutely gorgeous man gazed down at her, awaiting her answer.

Not staring at him was an impossibility. He was movie-star beautiful, with chiseled facial features and eyes the color of a crystal-clear emerald. His lips, full and lush, made Rachel want to sample them with her own. They made her want to sink her fingers in the silken brown locks of his stylishly cut hair, pull his face close to hers and kiss the living daylights out of him.

He had to be a model. No other profession suited a man of such defined beauty.

Her spine tingled.

Oh yeah. Definitely nothing wrong with her sex drive.

"Would you let me sit down if I swore not to say another word and spent the entire time looking anywhere but in your direction?" he asked with a charming smile.

She broke into a smile of her own, belatedly realizing she hadn't answered. She'd been too busy ogling him. Rachel held out her hand in invitation. "Of course you can share the fire."

He flashed her a huge grin and settled his towering frame into the chair beside hers with a relieved sigh. "For a moment I thought you might blow me off before I even found out your name."

She raised an eyebrow. So he'd come to talk to her, and not to be close to the fire? Okay. She could live with that. "And for a moment I thought you'd just sit here and not say another word," she said with a straight face.

He smiled impishly. "I lied."

Oh, Lord, what a smile. "Ah, so you do intend to speak then?"

"Hell, yeah. A stunning woman sitting in front of a fire, all alone? Damn straight I'm gonna speak. I'm gonna say whatever I can to get her attention."

Sexy devil. She tilted her head to the side. "Are you flirting with me?"

He frowned. "That depends."

"On what?"

"On whether there's a Mr. Beautiful who might get upset."

"And if there's not?"

He met her gaze and grinned. "Then I'm flirting."

She laughed at his audacity, even as her breath quickened. "How about those plans to look anywhere but in my direction?"

He nodded gravely. "Yeah. I kinda lied about those too."

She suppressed a smile.

"So is there?" he prompted.

"Is there what?" His eyes were so exquisite she got lost staring into them.

"A Mr. Beautiful?"

She shook her head. "No." Well, there was, but as much as she might wish it were different, Jackson wasn't her Mr. Beautiful, and aside from that one illicit afternoon, he never would be. Didn't change the fact that her heart belonged to him and always would.

"Lucky for me then." He held out his hand. "I'm Garreth Halt."

"Rachel." She deliberately left out her last name, enjoying the anonymity of chatting with a stranger who knew nothing about her. When she placed her palm against his and his fingers curled around hers, shivers rocked her hand. Dear God, could she please drag him to her room and have her way with him?

Er, probably better to stick around and make small talk. She'd known him all of five minutes. Jumping him now would hardly be appropriate. Or maybe it would be? Maybe if she jumped Garreth she wouldn't have to think about Jackson.

She chose the small-talk option. "You visiting from the States, Garreth?"

He shook his head. "I'm Canadian. Heading back to Toronto in a couple of weeks."

See? She could do the light chatter thing and not feel compelled to haul him off to her chalet. "Enjoying Australia so far?"

His eyes glinted. "Well enough. Although I'm not a tourist. I've been living here for the last two years."

"In Leura?" she asked, referring to the closest village to the hotel.

He shook his head. "Nope. Brisbane. This is my first trip to the Blue Mountains."

"Brisbane, huh? I lived there almost my whole life."

"It's a small world," Garreth said thoughtfully. "Where do you live now?"

"Sydney. Been there over two years. It's good to escape

from the city for a while though. Isn't it beautiful here?"

He grinned at her. "Let's just say the mountains became a whole lot more interesting in the last few minutes..."

She laughed out loud. "You really are flirting, aren't you?" And was she ever responding. A tingling awareness flowed through her, an open recognition of the energy that crackled between them.

"Is it working?" he drawled earnestly.

She pretended to think about her answer. No need for him to know just yet that her belly was already quivering in anticipation. "I'm not sure. Maybe you should try a little harder."

"You know, we could skip the flirting part altogether and head straight into heated kisses beside a roaring fire."

Damned if her heart didn't miss a beat. "We could." But she couldn't be that easy. Could she? She and Paul had only split up six weeks ago. "Or I could read my book and pretend you're not really here."

"You could." He nodded. "But heated kisses beside a roaring fire would be a lot more entertaining for both of us."

Entertaining? Hell, forget the fireplace, the two of them would probably ignite flames of their own together. "For all the other hotel guests too. I bet they'd get a kick out of watching."

Humor sparkled in his eyes, and something else. Desire? Hunger? Or maybe raw lust?

Nah, the raw lust was radiating from her, not him.

He lowered his voice. "If it's privacy you're wanting, there's a fireplace in my chalet."

Heated kisses beside a roaring fire in the privacy of his hotel room? With a Canadian she'd never see again? A man she could spend her passion with and move on. Damn, there was very little that appealed more.

Okay, so maybe there was something that appealed more. Jackson.

Yeah, didn't matter how much Jackson appealed, nothing else could ever happen between them. Not without causing Jackson's sister untold heartache.

"If I'd wanted privacy, I'd never have invited you to sit

here," she pointed out logically.

"Tell me you're not regretting the invitation?"

She nibbled on her lower lip. "Well, you do talk a lot..."

He shot her a purely wicked look. "Not when I'm in the middle of a heated kiss."

"You talk a lot about kissing." She didn't mind one bit.

He nodded. "I've been thinking about it a lot. Since I first spied you in the lobby earlier."

"You saw me earlier?" How could she not have noticed him?

"While I was checking in. You were on your way out. Dressed for a blizzard I might add."

He'd noticed her attire? "I went for a walk. It was so cold there may as well have been a blizzard brewing."

He shook his head. "You Australians have no idea about cold and blizzards."

She let her gaze slide away from his face and down to his chest and shoulders. "We have no idea? Mate, you're wearing a T-shirt." A T-shirt he filled out beautifully. It hugged his broad shoulders and ended halfway down his upper arms, showcasing muscled biceps and golden flesh. "It's three degrees Celsius out there, the mercury's plummeting, and you're wearing a T-shirt."

"We're indoors. There's a fire. It's warm."

Was he nuts? "It's warm here and now. But the sun's going down. Soon as it sets, the temperature will drop below freezing."

"Not a prob. I have a sweater for when I go out."

"*A* sweater?" One sweater? She had two jackets, an assortment of jumpers, three sweaters and a cardigan—and those were just for a three-day trip.

"It's enough."

"You're crazy." Gorgeous, ridiculously sexy and crazy.

"You're cold?"

"I'm always cold in winter." God, she missed the sun-drenched days of summer.

"You know, in Canada we have a brilliant system for keeping warm."

"Ducted heating. I know."

"Actually, I was talking about sex."

His answer was so unexpected she laughed out loud. "Sex, huh?" Dear Lord, she wanted to keep warm with Garreth, Canadian style. For sure it would take her mind off Jackson's imminent arrival—and their checkered past. "Nope, sorry. We don't have sex in Australia."

He looked aghast. "Not even in the Blue Mountains?"

"Especially not in the Blue Mountains."

He nodded gravely. "Ah. That's a damn pity."

"Don't let it worry you. You're going back to Toronto in a couple of weeks. I'm sure you'll have plenty of sex then—even if it is summer and there won't be any need to keep warm."

"Maybe, but I was hoping to have sex with you, here in the Blue Mountains."

Again she laughed, enjoying his witty repartee. Enjoying it almost as much as she enjoyed the tantalizing sparks that flickered between them. "Would you settle for a drink by the fireplace?"

He considered her question. "Depends which fireplace."

"This one, right here."

"How about the one in my room?"

She shook her head. "Nah. Too risky. I might have to fend off your heated kisses." Yeah, right. If anything, he'd be the one fending her off. The longer they chatted, the more appetizing his lips became.

He grinned devilishly. "No might about it. Another red wine?" He motioned to her empty glass before signaling to a waiter.

She nodded and he ordered wine for her and a scotch for himself. "So, Rachel," he said as soon as the waiter had left, "what is it you do when you're not seducing men into kissing you beside roaring fires?"

For a couple of seconds she hesitated to tell him. If he knew about her job, she'd lose some of her anonymity. And if she were to entertain ideas about kissing Garreth beside the fire, she knew she'd have to maintain that sense of them being strangers. A fling appealed no end. A brief affair with a stranger to take the edge off before Jackson arrived. A little something to distract her from her obsessions about the man she could never have.

A one-night stand.

Garreth was the perfect stranger. Gorgeous, charming and sexy to boot. He'd be a perfect distraction. Exactly what she needed.

But then she forged ahead. She'd never see Garreth again after tonight. He lived on another continent. What could it hurt to tell him a few things about herself?

Answering his question in the same light he'd asked it, Rachel revealed a little of herself. "I seduce gold into forming intricate pieces of jewellery."

His eyebrow shot up. "You're a jewellery designer?"

"You look surprised."

For a good few seconds he didn't answer. "I am," he said finally. "See, I thought you might be a model."

She laughed out loud. "I thought *you* were the model."

"Me?" He gave a boisterous snort then eyed her speculatively. "I'm a journalist."

"Newspaper?"

"Uh huh."

Damn. Seemed she had a thing for journos from Brisbane. "I have a friend who's a journalist." Her heart twisted beneath her ribs. "He'll be here tomorrow." Ridiculous. Here she was chatting to a gorgeous guy, and she'd found a way to introduce Jackson into the conversation. Ridiculous and pathetic.

He peered at her curiously, as if trying to establish the depth of her and Jackson's "friendship". "You're meeting him here?"

Hah. He should only know. Meeting Jackson and doing her best to avoid him at the same time. "Uh huh. It's his thirtieth. He and his twin sister are celebrating in style." She gestured to the hotel lobby with her arm. "A weekend in a boutique hotel in the Blue Mountains."

"Nice birthday celebration. You friendly with the sister also?"

"BFFs," Rachel told him with a smile. She and Jenna had been friends since their last year in school. Now that they lived in different cities, Rachel missed her like the devil.

In truth, Rachel was in the mountains to celebrate Jenna's birthday, not Jackson's. She and Jackson had no business celebrating together. They had no business being together in any way. They'd tried that once and the guilt had left them both unsettled and ashamed.

The waiter returned with their drinks, and Rachel sipped hers slowly as they spoke.

"So what, you came up a day early? Before the celebrations begin?"

She nodded. "I needed a break."

"From the stressful world of jewellery design?"

Was he mocking her?

Nope. Teasing, not mocking. "Among other things."

The light from the flames hit the tawny liquid in his glass. It glinted, just like the russet strands in his hair. The man was beautiful enough to make her chest ache.

"May I?" He reached over and lifted her arm, holding it up so he could see the bracelet that hung around her wrist. His touch burned her skin, licking at her flesh like the flames on the logs.

"Did you design this?" he asked.

"Uh huh." It was one of her favorite pieces. An intricately woven gold chain with tiny diamonds embedded along its length.

"Impressive." He gave an appreciative nod. "I've never seen gold quite that color before."

Rachel smiled, enjoying the feel of her arm in his hand. How would her breasts feel in that same hand? "Copper gives it the pink tinge."

He looked up, clearly surprised. "You mix gold with copper?"

"Uh huh. Mixing gold with different metals creates the different shades of gold."

"You're an alchemist," Garreth murmured.

"Hardly." Rachel chuckled. "I don't make gold. I simply alter its color a little."

Garreth flashed her a seductive grin. "Same difference."

The wine settled in her belly in a pleasant puddle. Her

limbs relaxed and her muscles loosened. She didn't try to pull her arm away. She was more than content with it in Garreth's hand. He had long, slim fingers. Fingers she could easily imagine trailing up her arms and over her shoulders, leaving goose bumps in their wake.

"So, what else did you need a break from?" he asked.

Ah. Back to that conversation. "Life in general. Nothing specific." No need to mention her spectacular failure at building romantic relationships, or the little issue of spending the last twelve years in love with a man she could never have—no matter how much they might want to be together.

He raised an eyebrow. "Not even a man? A certain journalist friend perhaps?"

She gaped at him. How on earth had he singled out Jackson so quickly?

"You blushed earlier," he said.

"When?" Her free hand flew to her cheek. Was she still blushing? Flushed at the thought of Jackson?

"When you mentioned your friend. Your cheeks turned pink. Just like your bracelet. A most alluring color on you I might add." His gaze settled on her face. "It's a damn pity."

"What is?"

He smiled at her ruefully. "That there *is* a Mr. Beautiful out there."

Rachel's jaw dropped. Good grief. Just how much had he determined about her feelings for Jackson. She couldn't be that open a book, could she? She licked her very dry lips. "Jackson's a friend. Nothing more." They could never be anything more, and they both knew it. No matter what they felt for each other, they'd had to shove it aside and pretend it didn't exist.

History had taught the Brooks siblings that terrible things could happen if they dated each other's friends. And Rachel was Jenna's best friend.

"I had to ask," Garreth said, and then smiled his devilish smile. "I had to check out the competition."

Rachel arched an eyebrow.

"If I have any hope of getting you into my bed tonight," he explained, "I have to know exactly what I'm dealing with."

"You're hoping to get me into bed tonight?"

"Kissing beside a fire is nice. Making love in a king-size bed is sensational." The smile was gone. His eyes burned with the intensity of his words.

She tilted her head. "So if I climbed into that king-size bed with you, there wouldn't be any kissing?" She gave him a pouty frown. "Pity. I've been fantasizing about those heated kisses beside the fireplace."

"And I've been fantasizing about making love to you in the king-size bed in my chalet."

"Hmm." She tapped her finger on her lips, pondering the quandary. "Seems we've reached an impasse. I want one thing, you want another."

"Seems we have," he agreed.

"What to do, what to do?" she wondered out loud.

"You big on compromise?" he asked.

"Depends on the terms of the compromise," she answered.

His green eyes sparkled. "What if the king-size bed were beside the fireplace?"

Chapter Two

It wasn't.

His bed was on the other side of the luxurious chalet. Flames leapt behind an iron grid in the fireplace, which sat against the opposite wall of the large room, facing a double couch. The giant, wooden sleigh bed, covered with snow-white linens, overlooked a wall of windows. The sunset outside cast a pinkish-orange glow over the trees and mountains.

The chalet was identical to hers, only a mirror image.

"You have a choice," he said as he kicked the door closed behind them. "I can spread a blanket on the floor beside the fire, and we can do this the slow romantic way." His eyes gleamed with desire, with a fire hotter than the one across the room.

Her heart picked up speed. "Or?"

He kicked off his shoes. "Or I can toss you on the bed and fuck you until we both pass out."

She slung her jacket over the couch. As if there was a choice. Sensual, dreamy and romantic, or hot, hard and ruthless. "Option two." Dreamy and romantic were stored away for Jackson.

His lips twitched. "I had you picked for the heated-kisses option."

"And I had you picked as a model. Apparently we were both wrong. Now you gonna keep talking, or you gonna fuck me until we both pass out?" Oh, yeah, when she met Jackson tomorrow, the last thing on her mind would be jumping him. She intended to fully satisfy herself on the delicious man before her.

His T-shirt was off before she finished the question. "Option two." His smile scorched her all the way through to her bones.

She stared at him, dumbstruck. With his shirt on he was beautiful. Without it, he was panty-wetting, tongue-drooling gorgeous. Sex on legs.

Her hands shook as she unbuttoned her cardigan and let it drop to the floor.

"Bed?" he rumbled.

"Lead the way," she concurred and pulled her shirt over her shoulders.

Garreth fiddled with his button and seconds later his jeans gaped open. Rachel forgot to breathe.

He tugged at her thermal silk undershirt. "Any more layers I should know about?"

"Just two."

He shook his head. "No blizzards in Australia."

"I told you, I hate the cold." She lifted her arms and let him dispose of the silk.

His thumbs grazed over her covered nipples, making her tremble. They beaded instantly.

"Too many clothes," he grumbled, and the cami she wore disappeared.

He gazed hungrily at her bra-clad breasts. "God, you're beautiful."

"Look closer," she urged, and reached back to dispose of the black satin-and-lace bra. Her breasts sprung free, feeling heavier than usual under the close scrutiny of those emerald green eyes.

"Jesus, fuck," he swore hoarsely, and then she was in his arms, pressed against the glorious wall of his muscular chest.

His full, lush lips took hers in a blistering kiss. A kiss so wicked it shook her very foundations. It burned off the cold, replacing it with a fierce heat that seared her from her mouth right through to her feminine core.

He tasted of scotch and man and sex—every bit as scrumptious as she'd anticipated.

Better.

She tunneled her fingers through his hair, holding his head

close, molding her lips to his, pushing her body against his.

Ah, that erection. It felt good against her belly. A solid mass pressing into her softer flesh. She wanted it in her hand. In her mouth. Fuck, who was she kidding? She wanted it buried in her pussy. And in her ass. Hell, she just wanted it inside her.

She slipped her hand inside his open jeans and cupped it over his cock.

He moaned into her mouth, rocking against her hand.

Or maybe that was her moaning. He was thicker than she expected. And harder. She struggled to find breath. If he felt so good in her palm, covered by his boxers, how would he feel driving into her pussy?

Garreth broke the kiss to kick off his jeans and boxers. Toned, muscular legs were revealed inch by endless inch. His freed cock jumped up, slapping against his stomach.

"Yours too," he said as his boxers hit the floor. "Take 'em off."

She shook her head. "Can't. Sorry. My hands are full."

"Yeah? Of what?"

"You." She wrapped one hand around his shaft, closing it around the silken steel of his erection. The other she used to cup his balls.

He threw his head back with a hiss, and she experimentally slid her hand up and down, testing his girth and his length. Both were impressive, yet neither overwhelming. He'd be a good fit inside her.

"Ah, Christ," he groaned. "Just like that."

For a long moment he stood stock still, letting her explore, feel, play. And then his patience snapped. He picked her up and tossed her on the bed.

"Carry on like that, Rachel, and it'll be game over before we even begin."

"What, no staying power?" she ragged as he tugged at her zipper and pulled her jeans over her hips.

"What the devil…?" He stared, dumbstruck, at the lower half of her body.

He'd found her leggings. "They're my thermals," she explained with a grin.

He shook his head. "You wouldn't last a second in a Canadian winter."

"Then we're even 'cause you hardly lasted a second in my hand."

His eyes gleamed as he pulled off her boots and her knee-length, woolen socks. "Is that a challenge?"

God, who would have thought disposing of sixteen layers of clothing could be sexy? Yet, with each item he removed, Rachel squirmed more and more on the bed. "You up to a challenge?"

"Woman, I've been up since I saw you in the lobby this afternoon."

She eyed his impressive erection. "Hope it feels as good up as it looks."

Her thermals vanished, leaving her lying in nothing but panties. "It'll feel better buried inside you."

She shuddered in anticipation. "Now about that challenge..."

He dipped his hands under the elastic of her panties and slowly rolled them over her hips and down her legs. "You think I can't last longer than a second?"

"See, that's the thing..." It was getting harder and harder to talk and tease. Her nudity left her exposed to his gaze, and his gaze left her smoldering. "...I'd at least like you to try."

He gave her a quirky grin. "I'll see what I can do."

She grinned right back, thoroughly enjoying herself. Garreth was fun. He made her smile. When she'd made love to Jackson, neither of them had smiled. The ride had been too intense, too emotional and too shadowed with guilt to be fun.

Garreth covered her body with his and kissed her. His lips were so seductive, his tongue so alluring, so sensual, desire trickled through her belly like syrup. There was something sinfully erotic about making love to a stranger. No strings, no history, no emotional complexities. No secrets, no failings. And possibly the most important aspect of all: no future.

They were just two people intent on pleasuring and satisfying each other here and now.

Garreth tucked his leg between her thighs, using it to grind against her pussy. How he unerringly knew to position his thigh just so, so her clit benefitted from the full attention of his movements, she had no idea. She simply spread her legs and gave his thigh free access.

He dipped his head to draw a nipple into his mouth. As his lips closed around the supersensitive flesh, cream spilled from her pussy, coating his skin.

She raked her nails over his back. If this continued much longer, she'd come. On his leg, with her nipple in his mouth.

"Garreth," she whispered.

"Mm hmm," he mumbled around a mouthful of her breast.

"I thought you were going to fuck me 'til I passed out."

He released her nipple to cup a breast in each hand, pushed them together and ran his tongue from one nipple to other. "And I thought you wanted me to last more than a second."

She instinctively arched her back, pushing her chest higher, pleading silently for more. She also ground down against his thigh, seeking relief from the pressure building in her clit. "I want both. *Now.*"

Lord, it was good to live in the *now*. To not worry about the future or the past.

He chuckled. "A lady who knows what she wants. I like that."

"And I'd like it if you'd replace your leg with your dick, and fuck me like you promised."

"Getting impatient?" He licked her nipples again, moving his leg torturously against her pussy.

"Getting hornier by the second," she sighed. "Carry on like that and I'm going to come on your leg."

He stilled completely, then sat up. "Not my leg. My hand."

"Huh?"

He swept a finger over her clit and when she shuddered, did it again. He pushed her legs wide open to swirl his finger around and around, slipping it deep between her folds.

The breath left her lungs with a shudder.

"I want to watch you come. I want to see every tremor, every spasm that hits your pussy as I touch you."

"O-okay," she answered, because there was very little else

she could think of to say in this position.

He trailed his finger lower, exploring between her butt cheeks, making her ass clench in helpless anticipation.

A groan escaped him, and he closed his eyes, grabbing his cock with his free hand and squeezing hard. His other hand continued to seduce her ass and pussy. He dipped his finger back inside her channel.

A fierce wave of pleasure began to crest over her. “Open your eyes,” she demanded.

“Why?”

“Because if you want to see me come, you better look now.”

His eyes opened as the first spasm hit, rocking through her body.

Garreth drove his finger in and out, and rubbed circles around her clit as waves of bliss washed over her. His gaze held firm, watching her pussy convulse, exactly as he’d promised.

The simple eroticism of the act, of his scrutiny, increased the intensity of the spasms, stretching the orgasm out. Garreth’s death grip around his cock must have slackened marginally, because as she came he pumped his shaft, timing his movements to coincide with hers. As her muscles clamped around his finger, he stroked down, and as they relaxed he pulled up again.

Her breath was gone. Ripped away by the force of her orgasm. Rachel collapsed against the bed covers, panting as the last waves of pleasure ebbed away.

“Don’t move an inch,” Garreth whispered and the mattress shifted.

His footsteps echoed over the wooden floor. A door creaked, and something scraped, like the hinges of a drawer being pulled opened. *He must be looking for a condom.*

His absence gave Rachel a minute to breathe, to think. And her thoughts instantly wandered to Jackson.

Making love to Jackson had been so different from sex with Garreth. With Garreth it was hot, hard and fun. No complications of any kind.

With Jackson their pleasure might have been compounded exponentially by their love for each other, but the strings and the history had left them both feeling wretched afterwards.

Damn it. She needed to shove Jackson from her thoughts. He had no place in her head. She was here with Garreth to cleanse her mind of her past. To take away the edge she always felt around Jackson. She was here, now, intent on having as much sex and as much fun as possible—because tomorrow when Jackson arrived, sex had to be the last thing she craved. Especially when she was in close proximity to the man she loved.

She pushed herself up on her elbows and watched as Garreth walked out of the en-suite bathroom, his cock standing proud, erect and fully sheathed. Christ, the man was indeed sex on a stick. She gave him her full attention, deliberately pushing Jackson to the far reaches of her mind.

Garreth placed one hand on her hip and pushed her gently. "Roll over, onto your stomach."

She didn't need to be asked twice.

"Spread your legs for me, sweet thing."

Moisture pooled in her pussy as she shifted slightly on the doona, spreading her thighs wide. "Sweet thing?" Movement behind her told her he'd climbed onto the bed and knelt between her legs.

"Mmm. You taste sweet enough to eat." He licked her at the point where her butt cheek met her thigh, surprising the heck out her. She'd expected his hips to be there, not his face.

Not that she was complaining. Oh, quite contraire. "Bon appetite," she offered with a delighted sigh. Shivers raced up her spine.

Something grazed her pussy. His thumbs?

No. His tongue.

The realization made the liquid that gathered between her legs spill from her lips, and he licked at it with a low growl. Her breath caught in her throat. Exquisite tingles raced through her groin.

"The thing about this position," he said in a hoarse voice, "is that it lets your imagination run wild."

Rachel tried to respond, but honestly, she was too horny to speak. Her imagination was already going wild, showing her snippets of all the things his tongue could do to her in this position.

"You can't see me behind you," Garreth said. He swept his hot, wet tongue over her pussy lips, making her sigh with bliss. "You can't see what I'm doing. So it's easy to close your eyes and imagine I'm anyone you want me to be."

Her eyes were already closed, and all she saw was the devilish stranger who'd insisted on sharing her fire. It excited her no end.

"I could be me, a man you've never met before." He punctuated his sentence with a devilish swirl of his tongue. "Or I could be someone else altogether. The man of your dreams, perhaps? Mr. Beautiful."

Ah, which one did she want more? A handsome stranger or a man she'd loved her entire adult life? Depended on which dreams she wanted fulfilled now. A night of anonymous sex, or a lifetime of wretched, impossible love.

Garreth parted her butt cheeks and licked her from her pussy all the way up the cleft between her cheeks and back down again, making her shiver uncontrollably. Holy hell, he had a talented tongue.

"I could even be your journalist friend," he said, then added in a soft whisper. "Jackson."

Jackson?

He'd said Jackson's name?

Holy crap. He had.

The man was no fool. No matter how much she might have denied her feelings in the hotel lounge, he'd seen straight through her. And now he'd brought Jackson up in the middle of their sex play.

Damn it, she didn't want Jackson interfering in their love making. She wanted him as far away from her thoughts as possible.

Too late. Goosebumps erupted over her flesh and her pussy fluttered. Jackson was in her head again.

"Mmmm." Garreth gave a satisfied groan and licked her from her clit to her ass again and again. "You like that idea, don't you?"

No, she hated the idea.

Shit, not true. She loved it. Imagining Jackson knelt behind her was not only easy, it was second nature.

She whimpered, too embarrassed to answer truthfully. She didn't need to. Her body told Garreth everything he needed to know as she squirmed on the bed, desire whipping through her in a dizzying coil.

"I like the idea too," he murmured before dipping back in and treating her pussy to a stupendous licking.

Good God, he was aroused at the mention of Jackson's name? White noise roared in her ears, and her eyes closed of their own accord. An image of Jackson burned her eyelids. Jackson kissing her, Jackson licking her, Jackson making love to her.

Not Jackson. Garreth. Garreth was behind her. She didn't want Jackson here.

With her eyes closed, it was all too easy to envisage Jackson as the one who now tugged on her hips, pulling her up into a crouching position and lifting her ass higher in the air.

It wasn't as if the fantasy was a new one. How many nights had she dreamed about just this? Fantasized about Jackson taking her—even though they both knew it couldn't happen a second time?

Rachel thought she might never breathe again. Her chest heaved uselessly, unable to obtain the oxygen it sought as Jackson's—*no, Garreth's*—wet tongue delighted her with its expertise. Sensation spiraled through her as he swirled it around her folds.

God, Jackson.

Garreth.

The sensation was utterly exquisite. Tender and tempestuous all at the same time. Rachel was on fire, burning with desire. She could explode just like this, with his tongue in her pussy. Jackson's tongue. Or Garreth's. Either one.

Garreth licked his way up the crease of her butt and found the tight bud hidden there. Rachel nearly hit the roof as he feathered his tongue over it. Around it. Tantalizing, teasing.

And then not teasing. He pressed his tongue inside her,

pushing in maybe a centimeter.

She exploded around him, the unexpected orgasm blindsiding her.

Low groans echoed from Garreth as she came, telling her the pleasure was just as arousing for him. Within seconds of the orgasm, he got to his knees and lined himself up between her legs. The sensation of his cockhead rubbing at her highly sensitized and slippery folds had her gasping. Rabid hunger ripped through her once again.

Again? She'd just come. She couldn't possibly take anymore.

"Know what else you can imagine in this position?" he asked, his voice a low rasp across her spine. He didn't wait for her response. "That there are *two* of us behind you. One taking care of your pussy. Me." He pushed his cock inside her an inch, just enough to tease and not nearly enough to satisfy. "And one tending to your ass." Something cool and slippery slid up the crease of her butt cheeks and touched her anus. A finger, probably covered with lube. "Jackson."

Her eyes popped open. He'd brought up Jackson. *Again.* Holy crap. Was Garreth here in her head? Sharing her fantasies?

He pushed his cock inside her an another inch. At the same time, the finger that had been massaging her hole slid inside unobstructed, straight past the tight ring of muscle. "You okay with that?"

No, she wasn't okay with it. She didn't want Jackson here.

But then why was her body shivering with delight? And why did she ache all over, desperate to come with Garreth *and* Jackson inside her? "I'm okay with that." Her words rasped through her throat.

Garreth thrust once, hard, and embedded himself deep inside her with a low moan.

Dear God, he felt good. Thick and long, he reached all the right places. Rachel moved on instinct, rocking her hips, swaying forward and pulling off his cock a few inches, before pressing back and engulfing him once again.

"Oh, yeah. Just like that," Garreth growled.

The finger in her ass slid deeper, and deeper still, until her pussy was filled with Garreth's cock, and her ass with Jackson's finger.

Jackson.

One of Garreth's hands clasped her hip, and he pulled his cock back before plunging inside her again. Rachel threw her head back with a cry. The sensation of his cock sliding in her pussy while a finger filled her ass was...unbelievable.

He did it again. Only this time, when he plunged back in, the finger was withdrawn.

Jackson and Garreth developed a rhythm, one filling her, while the other withdrew, then vice versa. Each stroke felt better than the last. Exquisite tingles filling first her pussy then her ass, until she could no longer determine where the tingles began and ended. They simply overwhelmed her.

God, yes, she knew it was only Garreth with her. Jackson wasn't here. He would never be here. But the imagination was a powerful tool, and with her eyes closed and sensation building within, it was easy to pretend.

All too easy. And made even easier when Garreth changed the rhythm. Jackson pumped in time with Garreth's movements, filling her ass as Garreth filled her pussy, and withdrawing as Garreth drew back.

She could spend an eternity like this. With Garreth and Jackson behind her. Garreth in her pussy, Jackson in her ass. Pleasure rolled through her, utterly delicious.

"Christ, sweet thing," Garreth moaned. "I want your ass. Wanna come there."

The finger felt good there, but the thought of a cock, a real long, thick cock in her back passage had Rachel's knees quivering.

Garreth withdrew from her, as did Jackson. The loss was overwhelming. Too much. She couldn't bear it. Acting purely on instinct, she burrowed her fingers into her pussy.

Jackson.

A deep rasping groan sounded behind her. "Jesus, that is so fucking hot. Leave your hand there. Don't take it away. Fuck your pussy while I fuck your ass."

"Garreth."

She pumped her finger into her channel, in, out, added a second finer, pumped faster.

"Oh, yeah." His breath was uneven, his words jerky. "Your fingers could be his cock," Garreth whispered. "Jackson can fuck your pussy while I take your ass."

Oh, sweet, heaven. Had he just suggested…?

Yes, he had, and the very comment sent her hurtling into another orgasm, one so intense it brought tears to her eyes.

God, when had she ever been this aroused, this desperate? When had she ever fantasized about two men at the same time?

He gave her all of five seconds to recover before something cold and wet dripped onto her ass. More lube. She clenched her cheeks as Garreth used the tip of his condom-covered cock to massage it in.

He thrust once, a quick, short thrust, and penetrated her an inch.

Rachel froze. "More," she demanded.

Garreth pushed forward, penetrating her farther. Sweat beaded on her forehead. Damn. That stung. Burned.

"Rub your clit, sweet thing," Garreth urged, and she did, removing her fingers to play with herself.

Ahhh, better.

Garreth slid in deeper, stretching her back passage, hurting her, delighting her. Pleasure mingled with pain as he pulled out, easing the tension, then pushed back in.

Damn, how good did that feel?

Jackson slammed his cock back into her pussy.

Garreth seated himself to the root in her ass with a lusty moan.

She couldn't keep still, couldn't not move. She wanted Garreth driving into her, fucking her for all he was worth. Wanted Jackson pleasuring her pussy as Garreth took her ass.

She swung her hips forward, almost displacing Garreth's cock, then drove back, engulfing him completely.

That was all it took. Garreth's hands found her hips, and using them to steady himself, he began to fuck her in earnest. Long, slow, drugging strokes, followed by short, quick, carnal ones, then back to the drugging ones.

Time lost meaning. All that existed was her and Garreth and Jackson. The three of them. Or the two of them at any rate. Every inch of her skin was covered in goose bumps. Pleasure soaked deep into her bones.

She couldn't hold back the ecstasy. It swept through her, over her, unbridled bliss exploding inside. Her climax hit with force, starting in her pussy and spreading in shockwaves through to her ass.

She clamped her muscles around Garreth's cock, squeezing him, clenching around him.

He let out a roar, thrust hard through her wild orgasm, and froze. Seconds later he too erupted, his cock pulsing in her ass, emptying itself as it beat rhythmically inside her.

With Garreth in her ass and Jackson in her head, Rachel continued to come, one wild undulation following another. Her orgasm was explosive. Fierce. All-consuming.

When the force of her release finally subsided, she was left wasted. Utterly exhausted. She dropped onto the doona, spent, and Garreth followed, collapsing on her back in a massive heap of heated male bulk.

Jackson was nowhere in sight.

Chapter Three

Rachel leaned on the railing at Echo Point and stared sightlessly at the Three Sisters. The natural rock pillars stood majestically before her, demanding her attention. She knew she should give them their due and concentrate on the incredible beauty of the panoramic mountain formations before her, but thanks to Garreth and their evening last night, her mind was too full to focus on anything besides Jackson.

She shoved her hands into the pockets of her jacket and tried not to shiver from the cold.

Just a few more hours and Jackson would arrive. Two and a half years had passed since she'd last seen him. By mutual consensus they'd decided the path of no contact whatsoever would probably be the wiser one.

God, she missed him. Every day she thought about him, wondered about him. Imagined his kisses, imagined making love to him. And every day she quietly told herself that her living in Sydney was the best thing for them. They couldn't be together, so why torture themselves?

Problem was, since Garreth had made Jackson a part of their sexual play last night, Rachel was no longer thinking about him every now and again. She was pretty much obsessing about him all the time. Counting down the minutes 'til she saw him. Or she would be if she had an ETA.

"You're looking pensive," a familiar Canadian accent drawled in her ear.

A flash of heat ripped through her belly at the unexpected voice. She turned to him with a smile. "Garreth." Once again, she was struck by his beauty.

"Fancy meeting you here," he said.

She laughed. As if visiting the Three Sisters wasn't the number one tourist attraction in the Blue Mountains. "I thought you'd have left the mountains by now."

He shook his head. "Nope. I'm here for the rest of the weekend. Just like you."

Rachel did a double take. For some reason she'd been under the misguided impression he was checking out of the hotel this morning. "Oh...uh..."

He frowned. "I hope that's surprise on your face and not horror."

She laughed. "Definitely not horror." A hot tug on her pussy verified her response. Oh, yeah. No horror anywhere in sight.

"Relieved to hear that. You know, I almost didn't recognize you," he said.

She stared up at him. "What? You forget what I looked like already?"

He tsked. "Woman, an image of you, naked and coming, is forever seared in my brain." His voice was low and a little hoarse. His emerald eyes sparkled with desire, which in turn triggered her own lustful hunger.

She licked her lips.

"It's the toque," he explained.

Huh? "The what?"

He touched her head. "Your hat."

"My beanie?" For a minute there she wondered if he'd been speaking English. "What about it?"

He moved his hands to her neck. "Between it and your scarf, they hide your hair." He wrapped his hands around each end of the scarf and tugged on it, pulling her closer.

She closed the distance between them voluntarily, so they stood pressed together. If she didn't have on another sixteen odd layers of clothes, they would have been touching. "It's cold. I need to keep warm." At least he wore a sweater today.

"It's cold, for Australia, I suppose," he acknowledged. "But as I told you last night, we Canadians have a good way of keeping warm."

Rachel's knees went weak. Last night. Hell, last night had been up there with the best sex she'd ever had. She whimpered softly as desire, fierce and heated, shot through her. Garreth had left her sated and satiated in ways she'd never dreamed. He'd also left her with a burning need for Jackson. A need hotter than it had ever burned before.

Yesterday she'd thought about Jackson on an emotional level, blocking out the attraction they'd once shared. Today all she seemed able to concentrate on was sex. Sex with Jackson. Sex with Garreth too. Sex with both of them.

By the time Garreth had finished with her last night, her head and heart had been so full of Jackson, she suspected if she'd fallen asleep in Garreth's bed, she'd have woken up expecting to see Jackson. As it was, she'd dreamed about Jackson the whole damn night. Dreams even more erotic than usual.

Garreth looked at her now with troubled eyes. "You've got that pensive expression on your face again. Wanna talk about what's bothering you?"

"You read me too easily for comfort." It was uncanny how he'd picked up on her feelings for Jackson.

"I don't need a degree in psychology to see something's on your mind." He rubbed his thumb over her cheek tenderly. "It's Jackson, isn't it?"

She gaped at him. Damn it, psychology degree or not, he was far too astute for his own good. "How do you know?"

"It's the sighs you keep emitting. They're a dead giveaway."

She slapped her head. "Oh, God, I'm so pathetic."

"Pathetic? Hardly." He snorted in derision. "Sexy, beautiful and about the most fuckable woman I've ever met? Definitely."

Was he crazy? "Garreth, I'm standing here, sighing about another man, and you still think I'm fuckable?"

"I don't think. I know. Last night you were supremely fuckable. Today? Even more so. I would dearly love to get you back to my room so I can get rid of that jacket, and the four hundred sweaters you have on beneath it, and have my wicked way with you."

Goosebumps skittered up her spine. "Even knowing there's another man on my mind?"

He brushed a tender hand over her cheek. "I'm leaving Australia in two weeks," he said. "Never coming back. Does it bother me that the woman I want to spend a dirty weekend with has someone else on her mind? No, sweet thing. Not in the least. Now tell me about him."

She hesitated.

"Will it help if I tell you there's a woman on my mind too?" he asked, as though sensing her reluctance to talk honestly.

She raised an eyebrow.

He gave her a sad smile. "I'm not feeding you a line to make you feel better. I just want you to know you can talk to me."

"Tell me about her." If he could talk about his woman, perhaps she could tell him about Jackson.

He shrugged. "There's not much to tell. She's the one. I fell for her the first time I laid eyes on her."

"And yet you're not together?"

He shook his head. "She says she loves me too, but won't act on it. She apparently has her reasons."

"Is she mad?" Rachel asked before she could stop herself. "You have to be the catch of the century."

He brushed her cheek again, and a shivery tingle shot through her face and neck. "I'd like to think so." He smiled, but there was a melancholy in his eyes that belied his gentle humor.

"I'm sorry," Rachel told him. "If I wasn't already in love with another man, I'd fall for you like a ton of bricks."

"You're just trying to making me feel better."

"Is it working?"

He looked thoughtful. "It would work better if we were both naked and you said it around a mouthful of my cock."

She laughed. Oh, God. There went her pussy, gushing like a waterfall all over again. "Garreth?"

"Uh huh?"

"You wanna head back to the hotel so we can both be naked?"

He leaned in real close. "Damn, woman. I would love it." He

meshed his mouth to hers, jerking her body to life in a mad rush, then pulled away, leaving her crazily aroused. "But until you spill your heart, I ain't leaving this place."

She gaped at him. "You'd leave me like this? Teetering on the brink of no return? Wet and wanting? You'd actually refuse to fuck me, just so I'll talk about *him*?"

"You mean Jackson."

She froze. "Wh-why do you keep bringing him up?" Her heart banged against her ribs.

"You brought him up first, sweet thing. Last night in front of the fire. And when I said his name in my room... Let's just say your reaction told me everything I needed to know."

"God, I'm sorry," Rachel said, suddenly mortified. "I didn't mean to react like that. Didn't mean to get so...turned on." Heat burned her cheeks and for the first time since she'd been outside she didn't feel the cold. If anything, she was way too warm. She must be blushing crimson.

He shook his head with disbelief and hauled her into his arms, pressing her close against his body. His erection was clearly evident, even through the numerous layers of their clothing. "You're apologizing? For acknowledging your real feelings? Don't. You think your reaction didn't get me so fucking hot I almost came on the spot?"

She gaped up at him.

"Know the only thing that would have turned me on more?" he asked, his voice a whisper, a way of ensuring his words didn't carry through the crowds, or worse, echo through Echo Point. "If he'd been in that bed with us. Making love to you at the same time as me."

She swallowed. He liked that idea? Seriously? "I... I thought you were just weaving a fantasy for me last night."

He shook his head, his eyes blazing with green heat. "Not just for you, sweet thing. For me too. I would love to take your ass while your guy—Jackson—takes your pussy."

Her knees trembled.

He pulled her close, as though instinctively realizing she needed the support. "Do you love him?" he asked in her ear.

God, what was the point of denying it now? "I do." She

always had, and she always would.

"Does he love you?"

"He did." But after more than two years, who knew? Out of choice they hadn't spoken in all that time.

"You break up?"

"No. We were never together." Damn it. There came the cold again, sneaking through her jacket, creeping into her bones.

"Why not?"

She sighed and buried her face in his shoulder, absorbing his warmth. "His sister."

"Your BFF?"

He didn't miss a trick. "Uh huh."

"What does she have to do with it?"

"Jenna has rules."

"About her brother?"

"About them being twins."

"What kind of rules?"

"Their friends are off-limits to each other."

"You mean you can't be Jackson's friend?"

"Oh, I can be his friend. Just not his lover."

"Excuse me?" He sounded shocked. "Jenna decides who her brother can or can't sleep with?"

She tried to pull away from him, but he kept his arms around her, holding her tight. "No. Not at all. Jenna's just forbidden Jackson from having relationships with her friends."

He rubbed her back, and she felt oddly comforted. "Why?"

"Experience."

"Jackson's had a lot of relationships with her friends?"

She sighed. The story was complicated. Too complicated to tell Garreth the full version. "He had his share. Problem was, when Jackson was through with them, they no longer showed interest in being friends with Jenna."

"Sounds like school issues, not adult ones."

"They were school issues," Rachel agreed. "But even school issues have a way of spiraling out of control." They had a way of destroying people's lives. And one such issue had brought Jenna—and Jackson—close to the brink.

"Did something happen?"

"You could say."

"Tell me."

Rachel shook her head. "It's not my place." Jenna's life had changed forever. As had Jackson's. Their experience had given both her and Jackson sound reason to never date each others' friends again. Reasons Rachel understood, even though it killed her not to come out and confess to Jenna how she really felt about her brother. "Suffice it to say by the time Jenna and I became friends, she'd placed a strict, off-limits sign on her friends as far as Jackson was concerned. And a strict, off-limits sign on Jackson as far as her friends were concerned."

"How about Jenna? Can she date Jackson's friends?"

Rachel snorted. Her friend did not have double standards.

"I'll take that as a no," Garreth surmised.

"Both of them were badly hurt. They came to a mutual understanding."

Garreth was silent for a while, as though absorbing what she'd told him. When he spoke he pulled away slightly so he could look into her eyes. "You've been in love with him how long now?"

"Twelve years."

"Twelve years? And you've never slept with him, in all that time?"

Rachel didn't answer.

"So you have slept with him," Garreth guessed from her silence.

"Just once," she admitted.

"And?"

Her stomach turned to mush just remembering. "And it was the best and worst time of my life."

"The best?"

"You ever made love to someone you've loved and desired since you were seventeen?" As awkward a conversation as this was to have with a man she'd just slept with, it felt good to speak about it. To get it out in the open.

"Can't say I have." He shook his head.

"It's almost worth the wait. The sex is that good." It had

been the most incredible hour of her life. A culmination of almost ten years of loving Jackson, of him loving her. The desire that burned between them was so hot, so thick, the room itself had practically glowed.

"And the worst?"

"Guilt is a terrible thing. The entire time I was with him, I felt like I was betraying Jenna."

"By being with the man you love?"

"We did it in secret. Took advantage of her absence. We betrayed her trust. Both of us." The guilt had been so bad Rachel had come to the conclusion she needed to resist seeing Jackson again. The best way? Leave Brisbane. Within a month she'd moved with her brother to Sydney to open their jewellery store, Ash Diamonds.

He frowned. "Ever thought of telling Jenna how you feel?"

"I'd never do that to her." Jenna still had nightmares. Over twelve years later, Rachel refused to give her reason to have more.

"She must be a good friend."

"The best." A girl could not ask for a more loyal, better friend. They were closer than friends. More like sisters. Rachel hated living in a different city from her. Hated keeping such a huge truth from her. "Why are we discussing Jenna and Jackson anyway?" she asked.

"Because you needed to discuss it. Needed to get it off your chest."

She gave him a sad smile. "I bet now that you know the full story you're not so keen to get back into bed with me. With me or Jackson."

He snorted. "You're kidding right?"

She sighed. "I never kid about Jackson. It hurts too much."

"Ah, sweet thing. I want to climb into bed with both of you now more than before. I'd show Jackson what he's missing out on. Show him you're a woman to be treasured, not denied."

"We denied each other," she told him. "We had no choice."

"Circumstances may have kept you apart, but he still denied you. I'd simply remind him all over again just how damn desirable you are."

She smiled up into his eyes. "You're good for me, Garreth Halt. A balm to my soul."

He smiled back at her, a smile that warmed her all the way through to her toes.

Then he pulled up his sleeve and checked the time. An unreadable expression crept across his face before he grinned at her. "I can be a balm to your entire body. Come to the hotel with me. Let me show you and Jackson what he's missing out on."

Chapter Four

Garreth spent all of three minutes freeing them of their clothes, teasing her mercilessly as he stripped layer upon layer from her body. With each inch of flesh he revealed, Rachel became more and more aroused.

She cupped his balls in her right hand and palmed his shaft with her left as he moaned raggedly. God, so hard, so smooth. Like silk and steel. But warm. She couldn't wait to taste him, couldn't wait to consume him whole, every delicious inch of him.

A knock on the door interfered with her intentions.

"Shit," Garreth complained, his voice rough as sandpaper.

"Ignore it," Rachel urged and dropped to her knees.

His cock jumped in her hands, and she licked his slit.

He growled low in his throat. "It might be housekeeping, and they have a key."

Frustration shimmied through her, and she stood back up.

"I'll get rid of them," he promised.

"Hurry," Rachel urged.

Garreth donned his jeans and went to open the door as Rachel ducked into the bathroom. It was easier to step out of the room then pull on her clothes.

Shit. Talk about an inconvenient interruption. She was primed and ready for another epic session in bed. She wanted to wrap her lips around his dick. Wanted his tongue on her clit, his cock in her pussy. Wanted images of Jackson floating through her mind as Garreth made love to her body. Damn it, she wanted to come.

Deep voices sounded on the other side of the door. Housekeeping?

Rachel spied one of Garreth's T-shirts hanging on a towel hook. Perfect. She slipped it on, taking the time to inhale the masculine scent that clung to it. The shirt smelled of his aftershave, spicy and sexy. It was enormous, reaching way past her knees. She spared herself a glance in the mirror. Color touched her cheeks and her mouth looked swollen and pouty, compliments of Garreth's incredible kisses. Her hair was a tousled mess. It fell in dark, wild curls around her face. Her eyes were a good shade darker blue than usual.

All in all, she looked like a woman disturbed in the heat of passion. Which she was. A woman more than ready to pick up where they'd left off.

She opened the door, stepped into the room and almost fainted from shock.

Standing beside Garreth, watching her exit the bathroom, was a beautiful, blond-haired man. A man whose face she pictured every night before going to sleep and every morning upon waking.

His jaw dropped. "Rachel?"

"Jackson?" Had he come looking for her? "Wh-what are you doing here?"

He stared at her with wide, baffled eyes. "What are *you* doing here?"

"She's with me," Garreth said quietly. He folded his arms across his massive, shirtless chest.

Jackson swung around to glare at the other man. "What the fuck, Gazza?"

Gazza? Her eyes popped. Gazza?

There was only one reason Jackson would call Garreth Gazza, and the comprehension almost knocked Rachel sideways. "Y-you two know each other?"

Jackson nodded slowly. "He's my housemate."

It was Rachel's turn to gape at Garreth. She rubbed her ear, certain she'd misheard. "I'm sorry. What?"

Garreth looked her dead in the eye as he nodded. "We share a house."

She closed her eyes and prayed to God she didn't pass out. "You share a house, in Brisbane, with a journalist named Jackson, who just happens to have a twin sister, Jenna?" Her heart pounded so hard she couldn't catch her breath.

"I do," Garreth answered.

"That's why you're in the mountains? For their birthday?"

Garreth nodded.

Rachel knew her jaw hung open, but she couldn't seem to shut her mouth.

"You knew Rachel was here for the same reason and you never told her?" Jackson asked, sounding as stunned as Rachel felt.

She should open her eyes, should look at them both, but she couldn't. She didn't have the strength or the courage.

"I would have," Garreth said with quiet conviction. "You arrived before I could."

"You knew?" Rachel asked on an airless gasp. "You knew all along?" He'd encouraged her to fantasize about Jackson. Made her tell him all about them, about how much she loved him and why they couldn't be together. And all along he'd known exactly who Jackson was. Had he known who she was? Had Jackson ever told him about her?

"I put two and two together when you told me you were a jewellery designer," Garreth said.

Which would explain why he'd looked so surprised at the time.

Rachel put her hand on her chest, struggling to breathe. She felt utterly betrayed. Deceived. Garreth had known Jackson all along, had even known who she was, and he hadn't bothered to mention the connection.

"You slept with her?" It was Jackson's voice demanding an answer. "You fucked Rachel?" Fury and disbelief echoed through his words.

"We made love." Garreth said calmly.

Rachel began to tremble. First her hands started to shake, then her legs, and soon her entire body shuddered. Her teeth knocked together as though she were freezing.

She had to get out of here. Had to get to her room and

escape the madness. Jackson's housemate had seduced her. She'd voluntarily slept with him and never been the wiser.

Clothes. She needed to dress. Needed to leave. Now.

She opened her eyes and dropped to her knees, scrambling around the floor, grabbing her jeans, shirt and boots. They'd do. So long as she had on some clothes she could always come back later for the rest.

"Rachel—" Before Jackson could finish his sentence she escaped to the bathroom again.

Pulling her pants on was virtually impossible. Her hands shook too violently, and she couldn't balance on one leg. But she did it somehow, perched on the edge of the spa bath. She even managed to button up her shirt, although it hung crooked and out of synch. She didn't care. She'd sort it out back in her room.

What on earth had Garreth been thinking? How could he do this? Had he acted out of malice? Dislike? Did he have something to prove to Jackson—or her?

Instinct told her that wasn't the case. Garreth was a decent man. A good man. No way had he been out to hurt anyone. No way could they have shared such explosive, hot sex if there'd been any negative undercurrents to his words or actions.

Oh, dear God. Realization burst like shattered glass through her heart. He'd included Jackson in their sex play. He'd brought up Jackson's name. He'd even told her he wanted to make love to her at the same time as Jackson. It hadn't been a wild fantasy of his—or one he'd spun for her. He knew Jackson. He *did* want to sleep with her at the same time as Jackson.

So why keep his friendship with Jackson secret? She didn't understand it. And at this moment, she didn't want to try. She just wanted to get the hell out of Dodge.

No way could she stay in his room another minute.

Angry voices sounded on the other side of the wall. Raised voices, one Canadian, one Australian. She couldn't listen. Didn't want to hear what they said. She donned her boots and without acknowledging the men's presence, walked into the room again, grabbed her jacket and bag and dashed for the door.

"Rachel, wait!" Jackson caught her arm before she could

get away and twirled her around to stare into her face.

He looked as tortured as she felt. His familiar blue eyes were dark with distress and disappointment. Haunted.

Her stomach plummeted. Two and a half years she'd waited to see him again. Longed for him. And now, this. "Let me go, Jackson. Please."

"We need to talk. Don't go."

She shook her head. "I have to."

"Rachel."

"Jackson." This was sheer hell. Agony. Looking into his eyes, every iota of emotion she'd ever felt for him came flooding back. Nothing had changed. Nothing. She still loved him every bit as much as the day she'd left Brisbane. As much as the afternoon they'd made love. Their forced time apart had done nothing to extinguish her feelings for him.

"Talk to me, Rach, please."

"Talk to him," Garreth said from across the room.

She looked over Jackson's shoulder at him. He stared back, his gaze intense and focused. And warm. So warm. Again her gut told her there'd been no malice in his intent.

Just looking at him reminded her what she was doing in his room. Whatever had attracted her to him in the first place still held a magnetic pull over her.

Confusion turned her brain to sludge. Without saying another word she pulled away from Jackson and disappeared from the room, running as fast as her legs would carry.

Jackson turned to Garreth, rage blooming in his chest. He was going to fucking kill the man. "Just what the hell where you thinking?" he demanded.

Garreth leaned against the back of the couch, his arms still folded over his chest. "I'm thinking you're an idiot."

"What the fuck? You slept with her. *You* slept with *Rachel* and you think I'm the idiot?"

"You're not just an idiot, Jack. You're a dumb fuck."

Jackson took a deep breath and counted to ten. Instinct told him to hurt the man. To inflict deep, endless pain. Common sense told him Garreth had good rationalization for his actions. "Explain."

"You let her get away."

Gazza's perfect calm pissed Jackson off even further. "And that's reason enough to fuck her yourself?"

"You're a moron for letting someone that perfect slip through your fingers."

Was he fucking crazy? Rachel was the one woman he wanted to hold on tight to. Wanted to never let go. He hadn't let her slip through his fingers, he'd been forced to release her.

He clenched one hand into a fist and pointed at his friend with the other. "You, more than anyone, know what Rachel means to me. You know I had to walk away. So don't fucking tell me I let her slip through my fingers. And don't even try to use that as an excuse for screwing her."

"I make no excuses for screwing her. She's a damned beautiful woman. The second I laid eyes on her—before I knew who she was—I wanted to sleep with her."

"And discovering she's the woman I love didn't stop you in your quest?"

"No. It inspired me."

Jackson stared at him in disgust. "You're a sick fuck."

Garreth raised an eyebrow. "I am? Funny, I don't remember you thinking that when you slept with Sarah."

A muscle twitched in Jackson's cheek. Sarah. One of Garreth's girlfriends. "You invited me to sleep with her. Both of you did."

"And Rebecca?"

Jackson's girlfriend. Not even a girlfriend. A woman he'd dated a few times. A woman he'd slept with. He and Garreth. At the same time. "She wanted it."

"We all wanted it. Just like we all wanted it when it was Deanne. And then Shirley."

"You gonna list every woman we ever slept with together?" There'd been several over the last year. Sarah had been the first. The experience had been an eye opener for Jackson, but it had been so damn good, he'd looked forward to the next time, and then the next.

In fact, he and Garreth had kind of gotten into a pattern.

They'd begun dating women who showed interest in both of them. Women who were more than happy to accept them both into their bed.

Ménage sex was a turn on Jackson had never expected. After Rachel had left he'd been hell bound and determined to get over her. He'd tried so damn hard to find another woman, someone he could have a deep and meaningful relationship with. He'd never succeeded. Rachel was the only woman he wanted.

The one thing he had found was a bone-deep satisfaction in sharing women with Gazza. The sex was always mind blowing, and it kept his mind off Rachel. It also kept him from ever having to commit to another woman.

"I'm just making a point," Garreth told him.

"Point taken." He'd slept with Gazza's women, Gazza had slept with his. Neither had minded before. "But Rachel's different."

"Why? Because you love her?"

"Yes, God damn it. You have no business being with her."

"Ah. So now you're placing restrictions on who I can and can't sleep with?"

"There are rules, asshole. Unspoken rules. You don't fuck your best mate's girl."

"Just like you don't fuck your sister's best mate?"

Garreth's words hung in the air between them.

"Your rules are screwing up your life, Jack. You don't wanna mess around with Jenna's friends, fine. I get it. You're being a good brother. But when you let the best thing that ever happened to you get away, you're being an asshole."

"Letting her get away doesn't give you permission to sleep with her."

"She wanted it. As much as I did."

Jackson snapped his head back as though Garreth had punched him. Fuck. Who'd have thought a couple of words could hurt so bad? "Nice, mate. Why not stick a knife in the other side too?"

"I'm not trying to fuck you over. I like Rachel. You love her. I thought, with her approval, the two of us could show Rachel how we feel."

"Over my dead body." The answer shot out of his mouth before he could think.

Garreth looked at him with a deep frown. "You don't want to share?"

"You don't fucking get it, do you?" Jackson grit his teeth. "Rachel isn't like the women we've shared. She isn't someone I can fuck and forget. She's the one, mate. She's in my head." He thumped his chest. "In my heart."

"Yeah, but she's not in your life. That's a choice you've made. So what, you can't have her, no one can? Is that your game?"

"You think I wanted to walk away from her?"

"I think if I were in your shoes you couldn't have dragged me away from her."

Jackson glared at his house mate, a bad feeling stirring in his stomach. "You falling for her, Garreth? You falling for my woman?"

Garreth didn't answer for a long time. He stared thoughtfully at Jackson. "You make her your woman, and I swear to stay away from her. Until such time, Rachel's fair game."

"Fuck you, Halt."

Garreth smiled at him. "I'm happy to share."

"And I'm happy to slam my fist into your nose."

"Give her the choice, Jack. Let Rachel decide if she wants to sleep with us both."

"You make it sound like a rational choice." Fuck. After two years he'd have thought Garreth understood. Obviously he was wrong.

"It is."

"There is nothing rational about sleeping with her. She's off-limits to me, and from this second on she's off-limits to you too."

"Tell me the idea of holding her between us doesn't appeal. Tell me you don't want to slide inside her sweet pussy while I take her ass."

Jackson saw red. And white. White stars. Jesus, the image

made him instantly hard. It also made him so fucking angry he thought he might seriously injure his friend. Garreth talking about Rachel's pussy? His Rachel? Uh uh. That pussy belonged to him. No one else.

Fuck. No, it didn't.

"You thinking about it, Jack?" He lifted a scrap of material off the back of the couch. A bra. A black satin-and-lace bra. Rachel's black satin-and-lace bra.

He glared at Garreth, hating him.

"You are, aren't you? You're wondering how she'd feel wrapped around your cock. You're wondering if she can take us both at the same time." Garreth used the bra to palm his cock over his jeans. "I am. The thought has me ready to blow."

Jackson's balls tightened, pressing close up to his dick.

"Know what I'm picturing now?" Garreth pressed on. "Rachel on her knees, wearing this bra—and nothing else. She's bent over you, sucking your shaft. I'm behind her, fucking her while she blows you. Christ, Jack, she's gorgeous. So beautiful it almost hurts to look at her. You can barely contain your orgasm. She's licking you, sucking your balls. Taking you in all the way to your root."

Jackson's ribs compressed his lungs. He couldn't breathe. Against every instinct, the images Garreth painted clamored through his mind. Fuck, yes, he could picture Rachel doing everything Garreth said. It was so real he could almost feel her mouth on his dick, her warm tongue lapping his balls. Could hear her soft moans as Garreth pumped into her.

It made him despise Garreth. And desire Rachel even more.

"Rachel is off-limits," he ground out.

Garreth shook his head. "I'm not backing off, my friend. If Rachel will have me, I intend to spend the rest of the weekend with her. My gut tells me you should spend that time with us."

The quiet conviction in his voice had Jackson shaking his head in incredulity. "You truly believe that, don't you?"

"I wouldn't push it if I didn't."

"I won't share her."

"So you've said."

"Don't do it, Gazza. Don't fuck her, and don't fuck with our friendship."

"Give me a good reason not to."

"I love her. It's reason enough."

"Then quit living in the past."

"I have no choice. She's my sister's best friend."

"So what?"

"So, I can't do that to Jenna."

"Because of some childish demand she made years ago?"

"Childish?" Jackson glared at him, feeling murderous. "You know fuck all, Halt."

"I know Jenna got hurt because you messed around with a couple of her friends."

Thunder roared in Jackson's ears. "Jenna didn't just get hurt. She damn near killed herself."

The color leeched from Garreth's face. "What did you say?"

Jackson forced a deep lungful of air into his chest. "I never told you the full story."

Speechless, Garreth shook his head.

Jackson stiffened his spine and straightened his shoulders. It was time Garreth knew. Time he understood the real reason Rachel was off-limits to Jenna's twin. In a twisted way, he understood why Gazza had seduced Rachel. Why he'd thought a threesome might be a good idea between them. Gazza believed it was time to get over the *immature* barriers that had kept Jackson and Rachel apart. Garreth was pushing him to take a stance, to make Rachel his. But Garreth had acted without knowing all the facts.

"I had a fling with one of Jenna's so-called friends when we were seventeen." She'd been pretty, she'd been popular, and she'd been interested. She'd also been about as fascinating as an empty can of tuna. After a few dull dates Jackson had told her they wouldn't work out. "When she realized I didn't return her interest, it pissed her off. She decided I needed to be taught a lesson. So she told fifty of her closest friends that I couldn't get it up."

Garreth opened his mouth, but Jackson pushed on.

"For her. She told them the only girl I could get it up for was my sister."

Garreth gaped at Jackson.

"The rumor spread. Within a day the entire school had heard it. Only by then it had morphed into Jenna and I having a heated sexual relationship. We were the talk of every teenager at South Brisbane High." The viscous bitch had destroyed Jenna's life. Had she kept her bitterness focused on Jackson, he'd have had no trouble laughing it off. But she'd targeted Jenna as well. Accused them both of hideous untruths.

Those untruths had taken root in the school grapevine and grown out of all proportion, destroying Jenna's and Jackson's reputations in the process. The talk and the gossip had not died down quickly. Over the weeks it had changed Jenna, turned her from the vivacious, confident sister he'd known, into a hollow shell of her former self.

"Jenna became depressed. I'm not talking sad and miserable. She suffered a full-on clinical depression. And she stopped eating. By the time my parents admitted her to hospital, she weighed barely thirty-five kilos. If she'd gone on like that she'd have starved herself to death." The memory still dredged up the same sense of uselessness, of helplessness, he'd felt back then. It left him as powerless now as he'd been at seventeen.

"She stayed in the clinic for the rest of the year," he told Garreth. "Three months passed before either Jenna or her doctors and therapists believed she was ready to be discharged."

At the beginning of the new year, Jenna and Jackson had transferred to a new school and a new life, leaving the scandal and the rumors far behind them.

"Jenna has every right to make the demands she now does. I couldn't stop the landslide that followed that bitch's assassination of her, but I'll damn well make good and sure nothing bad ever happens to my sister again."

"I-I never knew," Garreth whispered in a tortured voice.

"Jenna never wanted you to know. She doesn't want anyone to know."

Garreth nodded. He was quiet for a very long time, absorbing everything Jackson told him. "Rachel would never do anything like that," he said finally. "Even if things don't work out between you."

"Of course she wouldn't," Jackson agreed. That was a given. Rachel was the one who'd helped Jenna through her trauma. The girl who'd befriended her at their new school, who'd seen through his sister's pain and somehow accessed the real Jenna again. "But even dating Rachel would freak Jenna out. It would bring back memories she's put away and moved on from." He shrugged. "I made a promise to Jenna. I won't go back on it." No matter how much he wanted to be with Rachel.

Rachel spent the day in hiding. The shock of discovering Garreth was Jackson's housemate was too overwhelming to think about. She chose not to. Instead she went in search of Jenna, found her and hauled her off to the chocolate shop in Katoomba.

Sam, Jenna's boyfriend, opted out, choosing to read in the warmth and comfort of their hotel room rather than witness the choc orgy the women intended on indulging in.

Over creamy, rich, hot chocolate and brownies worth dying for, she and Jenna caught up on each other's lives. They spoke for hours, like they had when they'd shared a flat in Brisbane.

Rachel told Jenna about the jewellery store. Ash Diamonds had lived up to all of her and her brother's dreams and expectations, and was now a well-established, renowned business in the heart of Sydney. She told her about Paul and the dismal failure of yet another disastrous relationship. And she told her about life in Sydney in general.

In turn Jenna spoke about Sam and how they'd been together for almost three months. He was fun—but she couldn't really see any long-term prospects with him. She mentioned how her practice as a dietician was booming, and she caught Jenna up on all the goss from Brisbane, telling her about all their mutual friends. Rachel was more than aware that gossip to Jenna meant sharing only items that were factual and already public knowledge.

Nothing was news to either of them. They'd discussed it many a time on the phone. But going through it all again was an essential part of their friendship. And so much fun, she and

Jenna spent most of their time together laughing.

Rachel gave Jenna the birthday gift she'd brought along for her. Diamond earrings, handcrafted specifically for her friend. It was a day early, but Rachel figured with everyone else joining the celebrations this would be the last time they'd have alone. Jenna loved her present on sight, and they were in her ears two minutes later.

There were two subjects Rachel refused to broach.

She would not tell Jenna about Garreth, not just yet anyway. Her own thoughts about him were too scattered to share.

As for Jackson, well, she mentioned she'd seen him briefly and left it at that. Jenna did not seem to notice the way Rachel's spine straightened when she said his name, or the way her heart thundered so loud it almost deafened her. It was surprisingly easy to not say anything about her shock in Garreth's room. But then she'd spent so many years avoiding talk about Jackson with Jenna, not bringing him up now was simply second nature.

That didn't mean it was easy to be with her friend. Just looking at Jenna was reminder enough of the man she loved.

Like Jackson, Jenna had warm blue eyes that lit up with humor and delight as she spoke. Their expressions were so similar, every time Jenna laughed and her eyes crinkled, Rachel could imagine it was Jackson. They'd once had the same colored hair, the honeyed gold that still crowned Jackson's head, but Jenna was now a platinum blonde, thanks to her very expensive hair dresser.

The main difference, aside from their gender, was their size. Rachel could bury herself in Jackson's embrace and feel petite as a flower in his arms, which was quite an accomplishment considering she stood at a good five foot seven. Jenna on the other hand, was tiny. No taller than Rachel's shoulders and thin as a rake.

She knew when they got back to the hotel Jenna would make use of the gym to work off the four gazillion calories they'd consumed. Rachel would hop into a hot bath and read.

It had taken Jenna a long time to come out of her shell after they'd met at school, but sticking with her, persevering at their friendship had been the best decision Rachel could have made. Jenna was a first-class grade-A friend, and today she unwittingly did a fantastic job of helping Rachel escape from the anguish of her thoughts and the unfulfilled desire that still seeped through her body tormenting her with its persistence.

Chapter Five

He shouldn't be here. He shouldn't do this. He should walk away and talk to Rachel later. At dinner. When there'd be at least ten other people to buffer his feelings. To stop him from doing anything rash.

But when Rachel opened the door, dressed in a robe, with her hair piled on top of her head and her cheeks flushed, he knew there was nowhere else he'd rather be.

Without saying a word, she stepped aside, and Jackson walked past her into her room.

She shut the door tight and looked up at him with her enormous midnight-blue eyes. "I didn't know he was your housemate," she spluttered.

"I know."

"I'd never have let anything happen..."

He nodded. He knew that too. It didn't stop the jealousy from flooding his system.

"Do you hate me?" She could hardly look him in the eye. Her gaze was focused on his chest.

"What the—? Rach, I could never hate you."

"I slept with your housemate."

He scraped a hand through his hair. Jealousy tore a red streak through his stomach. "I hate that you slept with him. I don't hate you."

Color raced to her cheeks. "H-he spoke about you. We both did."

"When?"

"While we, uh, you know..."

Huh? "I thought you didn't know he knew me," Jackson said, perplexed.

"I didn't." She frowned. "It's complicated. When he told me he was a journo living in Brissie, I instantly thought of you. I mentioned you were coming up here. Garreth picked up on something in my voice." She blushed and turned around. "Later, when I was in his room, he kind of, well..." Her voice trailed off.

Jackson gritted his teeth. "He kind of what?"

"He, er," She cleared her throat. "He suggested I fantasize about you while making love to him."

Jackson absorbed her words with shock. Gazza had included him in his and Rachel's bedroom play. Even while Jackson had been in Brisbane, Gazza had brought him in on the action.

Rachel dropped her head into her hands. "God, I thought he'd been so insightful, picking up on feelings I'd tried to hide." She shook her head. "He wasn't perceptive at all. He knew the whole story."

"Don't judge him too harshly," Jackson said, striving to keep his tone neutral. "He had his reasons."

"He should have told me."

"You're right. He should have. And I suspect he would have. But I arrived early."

She turned to stare at him. "Y-you're defending him?"

He shrugged. "I understand him."

"Well, I don't. Maybe you could explain."

Uh uh. Garreth had dug this hole. He'd have to fill it in. "You need to ask him."

Rachel looked at him for a long time before sighing heavily. "I thought being with him would take the edge off. Would head off the attraction I feel for you."

Jackson rubbed a hand over his face. Fuck, this was going all wrong. He'd been so resolved about seeing Rach this weekend. So determined not to let their past interfere with his and Jenna's birthday celebrations. He was going to treat her like an old friend. Like Jenna's friend. Nothing more.

He was an adult. He could do it. He could hide the longing

and the lust that had lived with him since the first time Jenna had brought her new friend home. The lust that had sizzled and burned between them for twelve years, and the longing that drove him insane with frustration. They left him with blue balls every fucking time he saw her.

Instead, he'd been flung head first into a situation that demanded he sit up and take notice. Demanded he see Rachel in a sexual role rather than a platonic one. Demanded he see her as someone's lover. Gazza's lover. And Gazza wanted to share her. Wanted to bring him in on their loving.

Fuck it all, he'd insinuated the thought in Jackson's brain, and now Jackson couldn't get rid of it. Hard as he tried, every time he closed his eyes he saw himself taking Rachel's pussy as Gazza took her ass. And every time he saw it, he had an overwhelming urge to rip Garreth apart limb by limb.

"Did it take the edge off?" His voice was far too hoarse when he asked the question.

Rachel took a very long time to answer. "Nothing's taken the off the edge. Not in twelve long years."

Not for him either. Standing before Rachel was just as torturous as it had always been. She was just as impossible to resist. But resist he would, for he simply had no choice. Neither of them did.

He set his shoulders in determination. "You know what?"

"What?"

"We're going about this all wrong." Focusing on sex and lust and threesomes was not going to give either of them any peace this weekend. They needed to turn their attention to the other side of their relationship. To their friendship. To the mutual trust, the respect and the genuine affection each held for the other. They needed to focus on the non-physical aspect of their connection.

Rachel lifted an eyebrow in question.

"I haven't seen you in over two years. Can we do what any two normal people would do after all that time, and just say hello?"

She smiled then. A small, tremulous smile, but a smile nevertheless. "Hello, Jackson."

"Hey, Rach. It's good to see you again." He hadn't meant to hold open his arms, hadn't meant to invite her to step into them, but somehow his arms were stretched wide on either side of his body, and she was staring at him, indecision written all over her exquisite face.

"Just one hug," he said. "One plain old hug between two friends. That's all."

Her smile vanished for a second, and then it returned, a full-blown I'm-real-happy-to-see-you-again smile, and she stepped into his embrace.

She fit perfectly against his body. She always had. Her soft curves molded into his firmer muscle. His shoulder was just the right height to cradle her head. It was almost as if they'd been made to match. As if they were each one part of a two-piece puzzle.

Even as he buried his face in her hair, breathing in the scent of her shampoo—lemon and citrus—she inhaled deeply, as though breathing him in as well.

"Christ," he said with a soft groan. "I've missed you."

She clung to him, held tight, like she couldn't bear to let him go. "I've missed you too. So much."

"I miss our talks."

She nodded, her hair tickling his chin. "So many times I picked up the phone to call you. To tell you about my day, about something little that happened. But I couldn't do it."

"Ah, baby, I understand." He stroked his hand over her hair, cherishing the silky softness. "You don't know how many stories I worked on that I wanted to run by you. Wanted to get your take on before I wrote them up." Rachel had always been his sounding board. Before he'd sit down and put his article to paper, he'd discuss it with her, look at it from every angle, get her thoughts.

Since she'd been in Sydney, his articles had lacked something vital. Her insight.

"I have dozens of photos I've taken of my designs. Hundreds. I wanted to email them to you, find out your opinion." She never had.

Jackson had always been blown away by Rachel's talent,

by her ability to turn lumps of metal into fine jewellery. To choose the perfect stone to set into whatever piece she worked on. She was an artist, every design a masterpiece.

"You know what I missed the most though?" she asked softly.

"What?"

"Just hanging out. Just being with you."

His arms tightened around her. "Ditto, Rach," he whispered. "Ditto."

And then, because his cock was hardening at an alarming rate, and Rachel was pressed against it, her hips hugging his growing erection, he released her—although the effort nearly killed him. "Shit, baby, I'm sorry. I didn't mean for that to happen."

She gave him a sad smile. "No worries, I understand."

Oh yeah. She did. If anyone understood, it was her. "I better go. Before I can't pull away again." He pressed a tender kiss to her forehead. "I'll see you at dinner."

Rachel didn't answer. She nodded, her eyes filled with every bit of longing and sorrow he felt.

Damn it. She couldn't avoid him any longer. Now that Jenna had gone to the bathroom, she no longer had a shield. Jackson was chatting to some buddies across the table and Garreth was headed in her direction, looking pretty darned determined. He also looked as sexy as the devil.

Damned if her pussy didn't twitch just watching his approach, didn't remind her of what Jackson had interrupted when he'd knocked on Garreth's door.

Rachel had been aroused this morning. More than ready for some hot and heavy action with Garreth. She was aroused still—despite the trauma of discovering he and Jackson were housemates—and seeing him did nothing to calm her lust. Between the shocking—and unsatisfactory—conclusion to her and Garreth's morning activities, and seeing Jackson again, Rachel was wound tight as a coil, ready to go off at any second. She was aroused, she was horny and she wanted to be fucked.

She also never wanted to see Garreth again.

Tricky.

He took the seat Jenna had just vacated. "I came to your room earlier, to return your clothes. You weren't there."

The muscles in her shoulders knotted. "I was out. If it's okay with you, I'll come around in the morning and get them?"

"Of course it's okay." He frowned. "I'm sorry. For not telling you from the start that I share a house with Jack."

She furrowed her brow. "Yeah, about that... Why didn't you?"

He met her gaze with his beautiful green one. "If I had, would you have come back to my room with me?"

"No." She'd never have knowingly slept with Jackson's housemate.

He shrugged, as though to say *point made.*

"You knew I wouldn't sleep with you, so you kept it secret?"

"I swear, I'd planned on telling you. I was just waiting for the right moment."

Shit, she wanted to believe the worst about him, but couldn't. Somehow she knew he was telling the truth. Not that the knowledge lessened her anger any. "So when would the right moment have been?" She lowered her voice, making dead certain no one besides Garreth could hear her. "When I had my lips wrapped around your dick?"

A muscle ticked below his eye. "Actually, yes."

His response had her jolting backwards in shock. She gaped at him.

"We can't talk here." Garreth held out his hand. "Come and sit with me at the bar. There's no one around. We can speak more freely."

She eyed his hand warily.

He dropped it and stood. "You don't have to touch me. We do have to talk. Come with me?"

Against her better judgment, she nodded and followed him to the bar.

"You were saying?" she prompted once they were both seated facing each other.

"He was with us, Rachel. He was there the whole time, in

my room. In my bed. You can't deny it."

She shook her head. "I'm not. You brought him into bed with us."

His eyes turned dark. "You liked that, didn't you? Pretending he was in your pussy while I was in your ass."

She took in a quick mouthful of air. Yes, she'd liked it. Too much. The very memory made her nipples bead and her skin prickle.

"I liked it too." His voice was a whisper, even though no one was around. "I wanted you to know I knew him. But I wanted you to be fully aroused when I told you. I suspected that if I told you in the heat of passion, you'd be more open to hearing the truth."

She gave a cynical laugh. "So you figured you'd wait 'til I blew you to share the truth?"

"It's not that simple. Or that callous. I'd planned out a...more romantic, er, sexier disclosure."

She raised a dubious eyebrow.

"You don't believe me?"

She shook her head.

"Know what I would have done first?" he asked.

"No." Oh, Lord. Did she want to know? The way his voice had dropped, the way he now spoke in those bedroom tones wasn't going to do her libido any good.

"I would have asked you to close your eyes."

Keep your back up and your shoulders straight. Don't be seduced by him again. "Why?"

"Because that's how I'd have wanted you. Naked, on your knees, your mouth around my cock and your eyes closed."

She couldn't help it. She imagined herself in exactly that position, kneeling before him and working over his shaft.

He leaned in close. "Once I knew you were fully into the task at hand—when I could hear your moans and smell your desire—I would have asked you to imagine it was Jackson's cock in your mouth. Not mine."

The breath caught in her throat. She had no doubt whatsoever he would have done exactly that.

"And then I would have described him to you, bit by bit. I

would have told you that the man before you was not Canadian, he was Australian. A blond Australian, with blue eyes. And a body that you adored. Thinner than mine, but still well-muscled. That he was staring at you, desire burning in his blue eyes." He nodded. "I would have painted his picture in your mind so you had no doubt who you were tasting. Licking. And it wouldn't have been me."

Sweet Lord, on her knees, sucking Garreth and pretending he was Jackson. Shivers tingled down her arms. "You would have turned yourself into Jackson." The image was arousing, it drove her wild, but questions still nipped at her. She shook her head, trying to understand him, understand how his mind worked. "Why?"

"Because sweet thing, you love him. And he loves you. Two people who love each other should be together. You and Jackson should be together."

She stared at him, mystified. "And you and I sleeping together, while you get me to think you're Jackson, could achieve that...how?"

Garreth smiled then. A small, sexy smile. "There are things about Jack and I you don't know. Things bigger than the fact that we're roommates."

A bad feeling stirred in her stomach. She looked at Garreth aghast. "Oh, God. Please, don't say you're bedmates as well."

He shook his head. "We're not lovers. But we've shared a bed more than once. Making love to the same women—at the same time."

Her jaw dropped. Thoughts twirled in a crazy jumble in her mind. Jackson and Garreth shared women? Made love to the same woman at the same time? "So what? You honestly did intend for me to sleep with both of you—at the same time?" Christ, he'd told her that. He'd said he wanted to make love to her at the same time as Jackson.

Garreth took her hand and squeezed it. "It's a lot to take in all at once. I know. I never intended for it to come out this way. I wanted to introduce you to the idea slowly. One step at a time."

"That's why you suggested I think of Jackson last night? And told me you wanted Jackson in bed with us this morning?"

He nodded. His eyelids drooped sensually. “I loved watching how talk about him got you all hot and bothered. If a mere fantasy could arouse you—and me—so much, the reality of having Jackson in bed with us could be a million times better.”

The truth dawned on her then, like a light being switched on in her head. “You set it all up. This morning, with me in your room and Jackson knocking on your door. You set the whole thing up.” Rachel stared at him, utterly shocked. “You knew Jackson was already at the hotel, and you knew he’d come looking for you.”

Garreth held his gaze steady, not once looking away from her. “He said he’d come to my room at twelve.”

“And we got there just after eleven.” Jackson had been early. Garreth had never gotten the chance to tell her the truth. “Dear God! You wanted Jackson to find us together, in bed.”

He nodded. “Of course I did.”

“But…w-why?”

“Because Jackson needs to see you as a lover again. He needs to climb back into bed with you. And you need to climb back into bed with him.”

Rachel couldn’t help it. She gaped at him again. “If Jackson and I wanted to make love, we would. We don’t need you to help us into bed.”

“No, you wouldn’t,” Garreth contradicted her. “You do want to make love. Both of you. Yet neither of you is willing to breach the barrier Jenna set up.”

“So you decided to take the bull by the horns, so to speak. Breach the barrier for us.”

“If the only way to get him into your bed is to get you into my bed, so be it.”

She opened her mouth to argue, but he placed a finger over her mouth to shush her. “He loves you, sweet thing. The idea that I slept with you is tearing him in two. If you and I did it again, there is no way in hell Jackson could stay away. He’d come after you.”

She shook her head. “You are one twisted bloke. You think Jackson and I should be together, so you get me into your bed, sleep with me, and then wait for him to follow. And you believe that will work."

He puckered his brow in concentration, as though mulling her words over. "Yep. That's pretty much exactly what I believe." He smiled at her. "You and Jackson need to get into bed together again. You need to show each other your love."

Hysterical laughter bubbled in her chest. "You know, in your own warped way, I think you only mean well. I honestly do. But even if your plan had worked, even if you had gotten me and Jackson into bed with you, you're still overlooking one factor."

"What's that."

"Jenna."

Garreth's expression changed instantly. His face paled, and his eyes filled with grief. "Jack told me what happened to her. To them."

He had? Wow. She wondered what Jenna would have to say about that. "Okay, so now you understand the full story, you know that all your good intentions were for nothing. Jackson and I can *never* be together." And the bitch of it now was that thanks to Garreth, Rachel was craving Jackson's body more than ever. Lusting over him. Desperate to get back into bed with him.

Him and Garreth.

Garreth's grin was slow in forming, but once it appeared, his sorrow vanished. He was back with her, in the moment. "I'd hardly say a night of freaking fantastic sex was nothing. Besides, knowing what happened to Jenna and why she insists Jackson can't date her friends, doesn't change my thoughts. You may be Jenna's best friend, but you're not the stupid kid who fucked up her life, and it's not fair to assign that responsibility to you. I still think you and Jack belong together." He leaned in close. "And I still want you in bed, between him and me. I would love to fuck you while Jackson makes love to you."

Rachel swallowed. Now that he'd put it out there, she also wanted it. As much as she'd wanted it last night and this morning. Only now the idea aroused her even more, because Jackson was here. He was real. And if Garreth was to be believed, he'd come after them if they slept together again. He'd join them.

He'd join them. In bed. He'd make love to her at the same time as Garreth.

Her belly tumbled at the thought. Goosebumps covered her flesh and her breath vanished.

"You're thinking about it," Garreth whispered.

Shit. How did he know?

"Your cheeks just flushed. And your eyes have turned the same midnight blue they turn when you're about to come."

Rachel licked her lips. Perspiration spotted her forehead. "You read me too damn easily," she grouched.

"You're aroused. Like me." Garreth's voice was hoarse. "All I want right now is to get you back in my room. To strip away your clothes, and your anger, and sink into your depths. I want me *and* Jackson sinking inside you."

Moisture pooled between her legs, teasing her. "It's not going to happen," she negated his words, even as her body begged her to live up to them. "It can't. I won't do that to Jenna."

"This isn't about Jenna. It's about you and me and Jackson."

"Don't make it about me and Jackson. We can never be."

"You can, if you make love to me. He'll come after you."

"No." She shook her head fiercely. "I can't do that to Jenna. I won't."

"This isn't about Jenna. It's about sex. And love."

"And betrayal and guilt. Been there. Done that. I won't do it again."

"Even though you want it? You want me—and Jackson?"

She gulped. She did want them. Both. Garreth for another night of erotic pleasure. Jackson forever. "I..." I what? What could she say? "I..."

"I what?" he prompted.

"I..." She shook her head, at a complete loss. She couldn't answer. Wouldn't, because, God help her, she wanted everything Garreth had predicted to happen. She wanted to fuck Garreth, and she wanted Jackson to come after her, to make love to her. At the same time. And she wanted Jackson to openly declare his love for her. To stake his claim. To tell her she was his and they never had to be apart again.

She shook her head helplessly. "I, er, I need the bathroom. Please excuse me."

Jesus Christ and holy fuck. Rachel was aroused. Garreth, the stupid fuck, had pulled her away from the table and fed her some crock of shit. Whatever the bastard had told her had worked.

Rachel's cheeks were flushed and her nipples poked at the black stretchy top she wore. She looked as though she were about to jump Garreth right there, at the bar.

But she didn't. Instead she stumbled off her chair and walked away. Headed to...?

Jackson didn't stop to check. Acting on instinct, he got up and followed her.

She rounded a corner, in the direction of the kitchen. And bathrooms. And a door leading out to what had to be the back of the restaurant.

A second before she pushed open the door to the Ladies', he caught her back against his front and without saying a word, steered her towards the door leading outside.

She gasped and twirled her head to see who'd taken her captive. "J-Jackson? What on earth?"

He didn't respond. Couldn't. His blood boiled. Rage ran through his veins. It was one thing that she'd fucked his housemate when she didn't know who he was. It was another thing altogether getting aroused by Garreth, in front of him, when the truth had been laid bare.

The scent of rain hung in the air. Icy air ripped the breath from his lungs. It stung his cheeks and made his eyes water. He didn't care. The second they were outside, he swung Rachel around, pressed her flat against the wall and crushed his mouth to hers.

Holy smoke.

Dear God.

Her lips. Her full, ripe lips. Kissing him back. Pressing against his with the same urgency he felt. They did him in.

Stripped away whatever self-control he had left. He swept his tongue inside her mouth, losing himself to her taste.

Twelve years he'd loved her. Twelve years he'd tried to deny himself.

Why? What for?

So she could sleep with his housemate? Fall in love with someone else?

No fucking way. Rachel was his. They'd both known it from the start. They'd both tried to deny it and never succeeded.

And this here was the very reason they'd failed. The passion that flared between them was too real to deny. The love that blazed just refused to be extinguished.

He pressed himself against her, chest to chest, groin to hips, thighs to thighs. His cock, already hard from watching Rachel with Gazza, now ached with repressed desire. He burned for her. Burned for them. Bled for what they should have together—but never could.

Rachel was his. She was born to be with him. He was born to be hers. Distance and time had done nothing to dim that knowledge.

She moaned in his mouth, ground herself against his erection.

Frigid wind sliced over the back of his neck, but holding Rachel in his arms had him so fucking hot he barely felt it.

Something wet touched his lips. Wet and salty.

Tears?

Though it almost killed him, he pulled away from their kiss and rested his forehead against hers, breathing hard. The ache is his groin increased, but he shoved it to the back of his mind. He brushed his thumb against her cheek and found it wet.

"You're crying." The knowledge stabbed at his heart.

"We're resorting to this again?" she asked in a broken voice. "Stealing kisses out back? Where no one can see?"

Christ, this wasn't what he wanted. It wasn't what either of them wanted.

With all his heart, Jackson wished he could lift her up and carry her through the restaurant. Carry her openly, for everyone to see. Carry her back to the hotel and into his room.

Make love to her without the guilt of knowing he was betraying his sister.

"The way you were looking at Garreth… Fuck, Rach. You're ripping my heart out."

"H-how was I looking at him?"

He growled low in his throat. "Like he was breakfast."

Rachel swallowed audibly before murmuring something so soft he couldn't hear her. "What did you say?" he was forced to ask.

"Garreth wants to have a threesome," she whispered. "Him, me and you."

Jackson groaned out loud. He couldn't fucking believe Gazza had told her. He also couldn't fucking believe how hard his dick was.

"I-I said no. We couldn't do that. Not to Jenna."

Jackson took a very deep breath. "You said no. But is that what you want?"

Rachel didn't answer. But her shaking body gave her away. Her breasts heaved against him, her nipples torturing his chest.

"You want it, don't you?"

Her breath quickened, but she still didn't answer.

Something twisted in his chest. "You want to sleep with him and with me."

"I do," she said at last. "God help me, but I do."

Fuck, how could more blood fill his dick? There wasn't space. The pain was excruciating. "Do…" The words wouldn't come out. He cleared his throat. "Do you love him?"

She laughed, although the sound was not humorous. "I hardly know him."

"You know him well enough."

"We've slept together. I'm attracted to him. I don't love him."

"But you want to fuck him. Again."

She caught her breath then released it with a hiss. "Yes."

"Alone? Just you and him?"

"No." There was no hesitation whatsoever in her answer.

"You want me there too?"

A soft moan escaped her mouth, as though she'd tried to contain it but couldn't. "Yes."

"You want to fuck me and my housemate at the same time?" He didn't know if he was angry beyond measure, or aroused beyond control. Probably both.

She shook her head. "I-I want to fuck your housemate. I want to make love with you."

"Fuck it!" Frustration swamped him and he slammed his hand against the wall beside her head. "Fuck, fuck, fuck."

She cringed. "I shouldn't have told you," she said, instantly contrite. "I should just have kept my big mouth shut."

"No!" He shook his head fiercely. "No secrets between us. Ever. There are enough damned secrets in our lives."

She wrapped her arms around him, held him close. So close he had no hope of hiding the effect she had on him. He didn't try.

"I'm sorry, Jackson. So sorry. I wanted so much for this weekend to go smoothly. To pretend nothing had ever happened between us. That we were no more than friends." She shook her head. "But I can't do that. I can't act like I don't feel all of these things. Can't pretend I don't want to fuck Garreth again. Can't pretend I don't want to make love to you. Or that I don't love you. Because I do. I love you. I am quite hopelessly in love with you." The tears were back, falling down her cheeks. "And now I am going to walk away again, before we do anything stupid. I'm going to drive back to the hotel and lock myself in my room."

He wanted to stop her. Wanted to refuse to let her go, but knew better than that. Rachel was doing the right thing. She was walking away. She was doing it for Jenna's sake.

"Please, give Jenna my apologies. Tell her I had a headache or something." She disentangled herself from his embrace. "Tell her I'll see her in the morning."

With that, she fled back inside the restaurant, leaving Jackson empty and hollow. And so fucking aroused he ached.

For several moments he remained where he was, rooted to the spot. Waiting desperately for his erection to subside. The freezing air helped, forcing blood away from his dick and to his heart in an effort to keep warm. His hands were blocks of ice and his toes almost too cold to wiggle.

His mobile phone buzzed in his back pocket, and he fumbled taking it out, his frozen fingers barely able to hold the phone, let alone press the necessary buttons.

A text message? At this time of night?

And then he saw the sender's name. And the message.

"I'm going after her. Tonight. Coming?"

Chapter Six

It was past midnight when the knock came, loud enough that had she been sleeping it would have woken her.

But she wasn't sleeping, she was curled in a ball on the couch in front of the fire, desperately trying to get rid of the chill. Rain had begun to fall outside, the drops pelting the roof, dropping the temperature even lower. Wind howled around the windows.

Her silk pajamas gave her no protection from the cold. Funny that she needed the warmth of the flames, because inside she burned. Heat flowed through her, a persistent reminder of the arousal that would not quit. Of the lust she felt for Garreth and the love she felt for Jackson.

Yet on the outside she shivered. Her skin was covered in prickles. She simply could not shrug off the cold. No, it wasn't physical. It was an emotional chill. One that told her all her hard work, all her efforts to get over Jackson had come to naught.

God help her, she still loved him. So much it hurt just to breathe around him. So much that had he been anyone else's brother she would have thrown caution to the wind and gone after him. Chased him until she wore down his defenses and made him hers.

But he wasn't anyone else's brother. He was Jenna's, and Jackson would never hurt his sister. No matter how much he might love Rachel, his first duty would always be to Jenna. Yes, he'd slipped more than once, even slept with her. But he'd rectified that mistake. They both had.

Garreth had said something earlier in the evening that left Rachel with food for thought.

You may be Jenna's best friend, but you're not the stupid kid who fucked up her life, and it's not fair to assign that responsibility to you.

Never had truer words been spoken. Rachel wasn't that kid. But she was Jenna's friend, and somehow, because she and Jackson were involved, Rachel now had the potential to become that kid. The person with the power to hurt Jenna. Which was of course nonsense, since Jenna was the last person in the world Rachel would ever hurt.

Not for the first time, Rachel wondered how Jenna would react if she just came out and told her the truth. If she just confessed her love for Jackson. She'd be upset, no question about it. But would the hurt and disappointment persist? Would Jenna be able to overcome that initial burst of panic? Would she believe that no matter what happened, Rachel would always be her friend? Could she trust Rachel and Jackson enough to know they had no intention of hurting her, that they simply wanted to be together?

It was a useless debate to have with herself. Jackson would never allow her to speak openly to Jenna.

The knock came again.

Rachel knew who it was. And she knew she was going to open the door.

When she did, Garreth raised an eyebrow. "I wasn't sure you'd answer."

Good grief, he was gorgeous. "I'll always answer when you knock. I'm just not sure I'll let you in." Rain fell steadily behind him, and the wind cut a path into the chalet, chilling her to the bone.

"Let me in, sweet thing. You know you want to."

Shit, he was right. She did. She wanted to haul him inside, rip off his clothes and fuck him mercilessly. She also wanted to get the damned door closed so she could trap the heat inside and the cold out. "You sure you want to come in? Knowing I love Jackson this much?"

"I told you this morning, it doesn't bother me at all. And knowing it's Jackson on your mind just turns me on more."

Her pussy jumped. Damn, did he say all the right things or what? "He's not with you, is he?" She knew the answer would be no. As hard as she tried, she couldn't hide the disappointment.

"No." Garreth shook his head. "I'm sorry. I was so sure he'd come after you."

She gave him a sad smile. "He has to put his sister first." Rachel chewed on her lower lip. "Garreth?"

"Yeah?"

"I can't do this." She hadn't been sure what her answer would be until this second, but now she'd voiced it she knew there could be no other choice. "I think you're wonderful. I do. I also think you're about the sexiest man I've ever laid eyes on." She smiled a small smile, telling him in her own way that he was forgiven for keeping the truth from her.

"But?"

"But I can't make love to you again. Not without Jackson. Not knowing who you are and how you fit in with Jackson's life."

His eyes filled with the warmth she'd come to associate with him. "Ah, sweet thing. I never expected you to sleep with me without him."

"You, uh, didn't?"

"You and Jack are supposed to be together. I told you that. There's no way you'd be disloyal to him with me now."

God, his insight was truly astounding. "Then why did you come here?"

The wind shrieked around him. "Because I thought he'd follow."

Tears rushed to her eyes. He'd done that for her? For Jackson? "Damn it, Garreth. If I wasn't already in love with Jackson, I'd fall for you like a ton of bricks. Even if your logic is somewhat twisted."

"Yeah, and if I wasn't in love with someone else, I'd fall for you too."

They smiled at each other, a sad smile born of mutual compassion. If two people ever understood each other, it was her and Garreth. "Would you like to come in anyway? I have wine and scotch in the bar fridge. We can drown our sorrows together."

Garreth nodded. "I'd love to." He stepped inside and walked over to the couch.

Rachel pushed the door shut and headed to the fridge. Before the door had a chance to latch, it was shoved open again, so hard it slammed against the wall.

A furious Jackson stormed into the room, looking menacing. Water dripped from his hair and jacket. His cheeks were scarlet, and his chest heaved as though he'd run all the way here from the restaurant. His eyes blazed with fury.

"You are not fucking doing this," he roared. "No way. No how. Do you understand me?"

"Jack," Garreth nodded at him, calm as anything.

"You," he pointed at Garreth. "You don't get to touch her one more time."

Rachel gasped.

"And you—" He turned to glare at Rachel "—You don't get to fuck him. Ever again."

Rachel gaped at him. "What—"

"I told you," he raged. "You are not fucking doing this. *Not without me!*"

"Not without..." Rachel let the words trail off as their meaning registered. She lost her breath.

"Finally come to your senses, asshole?" Garreth asked.

Jackson tore off his jacket. It landed in a wet pile on the floor. "Don't asshole me, you prick. I told you all along. She's mine." He yanked his sweater over his head and shook his hair out. Droplets splashed around him.

Rachel blinked. "I am?"

His hands stilled on the buttons of his shirt which he'd begun to open, and his expression softened. "You know you are, Rach. You always have been."

Her heart pounded.

Garreth stepped up behind her and pressed himself to her back. "She wasn't yours last night," he told Jackson. "She was all mine. Every last naked inch of her." His cock, which he'd strategically positioned snugly behind her butt, shifted. It grew with every word he spoke.

Jackson's eyes flashed dangerously.

Garreth wrapped an arm around her waist and pushed her pajama top up, exposing her belly. He dragged his hand over her stomach, igniting all sorts of fires inside her. She looked at Jackson, felt Garreth's touch on her naked flesh and groaned.

Garreth had been right. Jackson, thinking Garreth intended to sleep with her, hadn't been able to stay away. He'd come after her. She could have kissed Garreth.

She *did* kiss him.

She twirled around his arms, held his face in her hands and pressed her mouth to his. His lips parted to meet hers instantly. Even with his tongue sweeping into her mouth, she could feel his lips curving into a smile.

She smiled right back.

Until Jackson interrupted the kiss with one furious word. "Enough!"

Garreth pulled away an inch. "Go to it, sweet thing," he whispered. "Make him yours." He gave her a gentle push, and she lost her balance and toppled over.

Jackson caught her, spun her around and kissed her. So forcefully she couldn't breathe. But that was okay. What was a little life-saving oxygen when the man she'd loved forever kissed her as though his very life depended on it?

He kissed her and he kissed her and he kissed her. And when Rachel began to think she might pass out from the sheer pleasure his mouth induced, he kissed her some more. And she kissed him back, cherishing every second.

An eternity passed before Jackson pulled away, before he looked over her shoulder at Garreth and nodded. "This is it. The last night we share. Ever."

"Then we best make it worth our while. And Rachel's."

Rachel smiled. Oh, this was going to be worth all of their whiles. She put her hands on Jackson's shirt and finished off the task of opening his buttons for him.

Jackson shivered beneath her touch, and his hand tightened in her hair. "Enjoy it, Halt. After this you don't get to touch her again."

Let the men argue it out. Let them iron out all the creases. She just wanted to touch them. Both of them. Rachel pushed Jackson's shirt off, showing his lean, muscled chest. She pressed her lips to one of his nipples and then the other, making him groan out loud.

She smiled at the knowledge she and Garreth shared. They'd already accepted the fact they wouldn't touch again. Tonight, now, was simply an added bonus for both of them.

Rachel turned to face Garreth, still smiling, and he winked at her. She went to work on the buttons of his shirt too. The six-pack covering his stomach made her mouth water. Both of them, Garreth and Jackson, looked ridiculously good shirtless. Two hot-blooded males, filling her room.

She could hardly wait for them to dispose of their pants.

She leaned in to lick one of Garreth's nipples and he brushed his hand through her hair. "Oh, yeah, sweet thing. Just like that."

Rachel sucked the nipple into her mouth, making Garreth shudder.

"Christ," he rasped. "I need to see you naked."

Rachel grinned as she released his flesh. "Then get rid of these pajamas."

"I'll let Jackson do the honors," he said, and turned her in his arms so she faced the man she loved.

He stood less than a meter away. His eyes were dark as night and heated breath escaped his parted lips. When he stepped forward and lifted his hands to undo her buttons, they shook.

It probably didn't take long to open her pajama top, but it felt like forever. His hands worked torturously against her. They were icy cold, making her nipples bead instantly, but it was the soft flicking of his fingers over her breasts that drove her wild. It had her moaning in Garreth's hold. The cold prickles that had covered her skin vanished. Goose bumps took their place, erupting all over her arms and shoulders. Her nipples were tight buds, desperate for Jackson's touch. For Garreth's mouth.

Wet heat pooled in her pussy.

Jackson heaved in a deep breath as her top fell open. "Dear

God." His voice was dry as grit, and he spent several seconds just staring at her.

Her breasts grew heavy beneath his gaze. Needy.

"Damn, Rach." Jackson swallowed hard. "You're beautiful."

Garreth's arms reached around her, and he cupped her breasts. One he massaged gently, and the other he brushed with his thumb, running it over her erect nipple.

Rachel let out a squeak. God, that felt stunning.

Jackson leaned in and kissed her. She drank from his lips thirstily, dying for another taste of his mouth, his tongue. His hands found her hips and he stepped even closer, holding his lower body snug against hers. His erection ground into her stomach through his jeans.

Behind her, Garreth nuzzled his nose through her hair to nibble at her neck. He pressed his cock between her buttocks.

Rachel had trouble remembering to breathe. How could she, when every sense was inundated by these beautiful men? When Garreth, the gorgeous stranger she'd grown so fond of, tantalized her neck with tiny kisses and tormented her breasts with perfect strokes of his hands? When Jackson, the man she'd loved forever and given up hoping for, kissed her like he might never kiss another woman again?

Guilt licked at her subconscious. This was wrong. They shouldn't be here. Shouldn't be doing this.

She pushed it away, refusing to think about it. Later there'd be time for self-doubt and recrimination. Later she could face the consequences of her actions. And Jackson's. Now she just intended to luxuriate in those actions. To relish every second spent in Jackson's and Garreth's arms.

As Jackson had said to Garreth, this was a one-off thing, the last night. She wasn't about to waste a second on shame and remorse. Not now. Tomorrow. But not now.

Garreth's hands left her breasts and his cock left her ass. He moved against her back, lowering himself to his knees, dropping light kisses all the way down her spine, making her tingle. He steadied himself by holding her around her hips, just like Jackson.

And then slowly her pants were sliding over those same

hips. Whether Jackson was pushing at them, or Garreth was tugging them down, she couldn't tell. She just knew they were coming off, and the knowledge had her chest squeezing in anticipation. The liquid pooling in her pussy oozed from her lips and slid onto her inner thigh.

As Garreth nuzzled her buttock, Jackson dipped his head forward and drew a nipple into his mouth.

Rachel's head fell back as sensation and lust tore through her.

Garreth inserted his hand between her thighs, pushing her legs apart. Jackson suckled on her nipple, the action sending a dart of pleasure rippling through her, deep into her pussy.

When Garreth swiped a finger over her slick, wet folds and found her clit, Rachel lost it.

She came. Just like that. With Garreth on his knees behind her, and Jackson latched onto her breast.

Her knees gave way as waves of bliss crashed over her. Jackson caught her before she fell and carried her to the couch, where he lay her down. She barely had time to breathe before he crouched and buried his face between her legs.

Rachel's eyes popped open. Jackson was licking her pussy. She stared at Garreth in disbelief.

He grinned at her. "Told you," he mouthed silently.

Rachel tried to smile back, but Jackson lifted her leg up high and tongued her clit as he slid a finger inside her, making her howl almost as loud as the wind outside.

Garreth stripped off his pants and headed to the couch, his erection bobbing proudly before him. "You and me have unfinished business," he told her. "This morning, when Jackson walked in on us, he disturbed us. Remember?"

She nodded. God, how could she ever forget?

He gripped the base of his cock. "Wanna try again?"

"God, yes." She licked her lips. Her pussy in Jackson's mouth, Garreth's cock in her mouth? Damn straight she wanted to try again. Jackson moaned out loud as cream gushed from her pussy. He licked up every drop, still using his finger to fuck her.

Garreth placed his hands on the back of the couch and

leaned over her, bringing his balls to her lips. She dragged her tongue over them.

The sac pulled tight against the base of his dick and he threw his head back. “Oh, yeah!”

Jackson paused to look up and watch them. His expression was black, as if seeing them together hurt physically.

She drew a testicle into her mouth and sucked it gently.

Jackson inhaled a sharp breath and his eyes darkened, lust lurking in their depths. His finger moved rhythmically inside her. In, out. In, out.

She released the testicle and repeated the process with Garreth’s other one.

Using his free hand, Jackson palmed his shaft. He grimaced, as though this was the last place he wanted to be, and the only place he could be.

Rachel palmed Garreth’s shaft, pulling him down at a different angle so she could place her mouth over the tip of his cock.

Jackson stroked himself as his finger caressed her channel.

Rachel swallowed the drops of precome that beaded on Garreth’s tip. She closed her mouth over his cock and took him in as deep as she could.

Garreth’s groan echoed through the room.

With a growl, Jackson lowered his head back to her pussy and licked her from her clit, over her lips and around his finger, and between her butt cheeks.

Then he did it again.

Rachel broke. She came in his mouth with a loud cry.

Garreth’s cock slipped from her mouth as the orgasm continued. God, she was coming. On Jackson’s face. With his finger buried in her pussy.

Jackson.

She moaned his name out loud.

He continued to lick her. Even as the spasms subsided, he licked her. Relentlessly. Refusing to stop. He licked her all the way back into another orgasm, which ripped through her, leaving her winded and breathless.

Only when the ripples of that climax faded did he give her a break.

Still shuddering in the aftermath of her pleasure, Rachel rolled over. Garreth had knelt on the floor, and because he was so tall, he was at the exact right height. She took his cock back into her mouth. Knowing Jackson watched every move, his gaze both disturbed and aroused, she hungrily sucked Garreth off. And she would have kept on going if Garreth hadn't pulled back.

"Easy there, sweet thing," he muttered. "My staying power is about zero right now." He looked at Jackson. "Switch?"

A muscle worked in Jackson's jaw. "Oh, yeah." He ditched his jeans.

Rachel stared at Jackson's erection, entranced. God, it looked delicious. Long and hard and weeping.

He and Garreth swapped places, but Jackson did not kneel. Instead he took her hand and drew her upright into a sitting position. All Rachel need do was lean forward and part her lips.

"Love me, Rach," he urged with a groan.

She did, licking off his spilled semen, and Jackson growled his pleasure at the contact. She opened her mouth wide and swallowed him down.

Dear God. She had Jackson's dick in her mouth. Jackson's. Yes, she'd tasted it once before, but the guilt associated with the act had dulled the memory. She'd forgotten how easily he slid over her tongue. How greedy she'd been to get him in deeper, to take him all the way down her throat. The memories flooded back now. His taste, his length, delighted her.

"Ah, fuck." Jackson's entire body tensed. "God, baby. That feels so good."

She took him in as far as she could and used her hand to cover the rest of his dick. Then she bobbed her head up and down, loving him with her mouth.

Garreth squeezed in behind her on the couch, placing a thigh on either side of hers and pushing his cock against the small of her back. Rachel edged forward, closer to Jackson, to give him more space.

She nearly hit the roof when Garreth's hand found her

pussy.

She'd just come three times in quick succession. She wasn't sure if she could bear the sensitivity of being touched again.

But Garreth must have been wise to her mood, because his touch was not designed to arouse. It was designed to soothe. And soothe her he did, sliding his fingers gently over her pussy, using her cream to prevent his hand from abrading her delicate skin.

The soothing lasted mere seconds before she began to squirm. Before need slammed into her once again, and she no longer wanted his gentle touch. She wanted more. So much more. And she wanted it as much as she wanted Jackson in her mouth.

"You ready?" Jackson asked, his voice lower than she'd ever heard it before. He sounded both resigned and aroused. Resigned to Garreth's presence—and aroused by it.

Ready for what? She couldn't ask. Her mouth was full.

"Fuck, yeah," Garreth answered.

Jackson put his hands on her head, stilling her movements. "Stand up, Rach. Just for a minute."

She pulled off him reluctantly, and he swore, as though the loss of her mouth might kill him. It might kill her as well. Now that she had him where she wanted him, she hated for him to draw away.

Garreth pushed her hair aside and nibbled on her ear. "I'm going to fuck you, sweet thing," he whispered. "While you blow Jack. I'm going to slide my cock deep into your pussy, and you're going to ride me while you suck him. You okay with that?"

Was that a trick question? "Hell, yeah." The walls of her pussy constricted, as if searching for his dick. "Do you have a condom?"

"Already on."

"Then what are you waiting for?"

"For you to stand up."

"Why?"

"So that when you sit back down I'll be ready for you."

A fresh gush of juice trickled from her pussy.

Jackson took her hand and pulled her up, straight into his arms. He didn't give her a chance to say anything. He simply kissed her.

God, he kissed like a dream. Like a beautiful, wonderful dream. She got lost in his kiss, lost to the gentle delights of his mouth. Lost in his arms.

Jackson.

"I love you," she whispered when he released her lips.

He stared at her with intense eyes. "You're mine, Rach. Always. Remember that when you're fucking him."

And then there was a pair of hands on her waist, urging her down. "Straddle my legs, sweet thing," Garreth said in a voice wicked as night.

She did as he requested, and he pulled her down. He'd moved, closed his legs and shifted down a little on the couch. With his guidance, Rachel lowered herself onto him, and her pussy met the tip of his cock.

They moaned together. Liquid seeped between her legs.

"Take me in, sweet thing. Take me in all the way."

Slow as could be, she seated herself on his lap. For long seconds neither of them moved. They simply sat, joined together like one. She inhaled, relishing the sheer pleasure of holding him inside her.

"Know what the good thing about this position is?" Garreth asked. "Neither of us has to move. Jackson's gonna do all the work."

"He is?" Her voice was virtually non-existent. "How?" She looked up at Jackson. He stood before her, slowly pumping his dick. His gaze was rooted to her face.

"You're gonna lean over him, just like you did before, and lick his dick. He'll do the rest."

She was higher than before, and had to lean forward a little more this time. She opened her mouth wide and sucked Jackson back in.

A hoarse cry rent the air. Jackson's? Garreth's?

Jackson began moving almost immediately, rocking his hips, pumping into her as she sucked him. Every time he pumped, Rachel was driven back slightly. Not too much, but enough that her hips moved as well, making her pussy clench over Garreth's dick with every thrust of Jackson's hips.

It was a subtle delight. Nothing too vigorous, nothing that would make either her or Garreth come, but delicious enough that they both gasped for air.

With her hands clutching the firm, round cheeks of Jackson's ass, she gorged on him, relishing the fluttery sensations in her groin as she did. Long, delicious moments passed.

"Christ, this is better than I imagined," Garreth gasped.

Jackson growled low in his throat and took a step back, making Rachel lean over farther. Garreth's response was instantaneous. He drew his finger between her butt cheeks to play with her anus. Light, feathery strokes at first, strokes that took her breath away and forced her to concentrate on Jackson's dick harder. Then firmer ones. Wetter ones.

Garreth must have squeezed lube onto his finger, because he eased it past the tight ring of muscle, all the way up to his knuckle with no difficulty.

She groaned around Jackson's shaft. Christ, that felt good. So unbelievably good her pussy began to spasm.

Garreth withdrew his finger immediately. "Uh uh, sweet thing. You come, I come. And I'm not ready."

Frustration grabbed hold of her and she clenched her ass cheeks together, over and over. She wanted his finger back. Now.

She got what she wanted. Only this time it was more than one finger, and although they slipped inside her easily enough, the unexpected stretch was enough to bring tears to her eyes. The need to come shriveled.

"Breathe through it, Rach," Jackson urged. "It'll be worth it. I swear. Just breathe deep." He ran his hands over her shoulders, soothing her.

Rachel had no doubt it would be worth it. Even though the pain persisted, the pleasure was now back, twofold, because Garreth filled both of her holes.

Garreth behind her, and Jackson in front.

"My fantasy is about to become a reality," Garreth whispered, his breath fanning up her spine. "I'm going to take your ass now, Rachel. And when I do, Jackson's going to make love to you. Just like he's been wanting to do since the day I met him."

Rachel whimpered. Liquid gushed to her pussy.

"Oh yeah," Garreth rasped. "You like that idea, don't you, sweet thing?"

"I can't wait, Rach." Jackson said hoarsely. "Can't wait to make love to you."

Rachel released his dick. "Now," she demanded. "Do it now." She lifted herself off Garreth with a wet squelch, then thrust her hips forward, so instead of his cockhead touching her pussy, it now pressed into her ass.

Garreth grabbed his dick, holding himself firm. "Oh, fuck. Christ, and holy shit."

She lowered herself onto him. Slowly, ever so slowly, gritting her teeth because as freaking good as it felt, and as smooth as the lube made the path, it also burned like hell.

Jackson moaned out loud. "I could come just watching you."

"*No.*" No way was he coming like that. "Inside me." Okay, so she wasn't big on words right now, but he got the general idea. After waiting for him all this time there was no way he was coming anywhere but inside her pussy.

The breath left her lungs as she sat down. Garreth was seated all the way in her ass.

He panted behind her and spread his legs wide. "Put your feet on my thighs." His voice was barely a whisper, as though talking was impossible. He placed his hands on her hips, balancing her as she pulled her knees up, and rested her feet on his thighs. She put her hands on the couch on either side of Garreth.

Dear God, in this position, she was totally exposed. Jackson, who could not seem to tear his eyes away, had a bird's eye view of everything. *Everything.*

His hand was on his cock again, stroking. "Touch yourself, Rach. Rub your clit."

She shook her head violently. "C-can't. I'll come." With Garreth's shaft in her ass, her pussy stretched wide for Jackson, and Jackson's gaze between her legs, she wouldn't last a second.

Jackson reached over to the coffee table and grabbed a condom she hadn't known was there. "I want you to come. I want to watch you climaxing." He ripped the package open without taking his eyes off her.

"Touch your clit, sweet thing," Garreth wheezed. "Do it for all of us."

How could she resist? Her clit throbbed, aching for the contact. As she reached down and stroked her finger over the stiff bud between her legs, Jackson sheathed himself.

He massaged his balls as she rubbed tiny circles around her clit.

Too much. Way too much. She didn't make ten seconds before the sensation overwhelmed her. She climaxed with Garreth buried in her ass.

Cream spilled from her pussy as her muscles clenched rhythmically.

"Oh, fuck." Garreth groaned. "Jesus fucking Christ." He froze beneath her, not moving an inch.

Jackson dropped to his knees with a loud moan, and before the orgasm subsided, licked her pussy thoroughly. She came again and again. Perspiration beaded on her forehead. Shivers shook through her body, and her pussy undulated in pleasure.

"Jackson, fuck, I can't take much more," Garreth yelled at him. "Do it. Now!"

Rachel dropped her head back against Garreth's shoulder, absolutely shattered. Her eyes were closed. She couldn't breathe. Couldn't move. Tremors raced up her spine and down again.

And then Jackson stood. What he did, she didn't know, but something touched her thigh. A foot? A knee? The cushions on the couched shifted, and he was there. Leaning over her. Into her. His cock was centered at her pussy—and he pushed.

Rachel cried out as he drove into her. Her pussy, still pulsating from her orgasms, jumped at the intrusion. Holy crap.

She was full. So full she couldn't breathe. Couldn't think. And Jackson was only halfway in.

He thrust again, and a long, low rasping *aaahhh* escaped his mouth.

"God. Fuck, yes!" Garreth ground out behind her.

"Rachel?"

She opened her eyes. Jackson gazed at her from inches away. "I love you, baby. Always have, always will."

He gave one final thrust and was in all the way.

Rachel came again, at the exact same minute that she burst into tears.

This, here, was the single most intense experience she'd ever had. Physically she was so aroused she thought she might simply implode. Yes, there was pain. But damn it, the pain only made the pleasure better. More exquisite. And yes, she was stuffed full to overflowing. But that fullness was about the best damn thing she'd ever felt.

And emotionally? This weekend probably topped the scales. She'd met a stranger and made love to him. And that stranger had done everything in his power to make her every fantasy come true. Which explained why, here and now, her fantasy half-stood, half-knelt before her, his cock in her pussy, professing his love for her.

Tears streamed down her face, even as her body writhed in ecstasy.

Jackson kissed them away as they fell.

"Don't cry, sweet thing," Garreth puffed in her ear. "Please don't cry." His hands rubbed her hips, soothing her.

She shook her head against his shoulder and smiled through the tears. "It's good crying," she told him. "Promise."

"You sure?" he asked.

"I'm positive," she said.

"You enjoying this?" He thrust up into her ass as he asked, and she clenched her butt in response. Jackson groaned out loud.

"Loving it." She sighed in pleasure. "Do that again."

He did. It was all any of them needed. Even as the remaining tingles of the orgasm fluttered away, Garreth and

Jackson began to fuck her in earnest. Jackson plunged into her and then withdrew, and Garreth bounced her on his lap, driving up her from behind.

Rachel couldn't hold still. When Jackson plunged into her again, she thrust back against his invading cock, and when Garreth drove up her back passage, she ground down on him.

Perhaps it was the men's past experience, but Rachel was surprised there was no fumbling, no misplaced body parts. The two of them worked in perfect harmony, bringing her such exquisite delight she thought she might die from it.

Perfect, passionate pleasure at the hands of two men.

Garreth and Jackson.

Jackson and Garreth.

So perfect was the pleasure, she couldn't deter the build to another climax. It spiraled down upon her, overwhelming her, usurping her senses, commandeering her desires. The sensation of two penises inside her was too powerful.

The orgasm hit, the most potent one ever. It tore through her, shattering her composure. Surges of satisfaction rocked her world. Her pussy and her ass clamped down around Jackson and Garreth, milking them both.

Garreth lost control. As Rachel exploded around him, he slammed into her one last time and howled. His dick beat rhythmically in her ass, telling her he was spurting stream upon stream of semen into his condom.

His release must have spurred Jackson's, because he froze, for just a second, before crying out in agony. He threw his shoulders back, arched his back and erupted in her pussy.

A more magnificent sight Rachel had never seen. A more incredible experience she'd never had. It was a night, a moment, Rachel knew she'd remember for the rest of her life.

Chapter Seven

They bathed together. All three of them, in the massive spa bath in the bathroom, with Garreth and Jackson soaping away every last trace of stickiness from her body. Then they climbed into bed and fell into an exhausted sleep.

In the wee hours of the morning, they woke again. Their love making was calmer this time, but just as gratifying. Rachel lay on Jackson, chest to chest, his cock in her pussy, and Garreth knelt behind them, his shaft buried in her ass.

"Last time," Garreth murmured, seconds before they came together in a heated rush.

When Jackson disappeared into the bathroom after lovingly cleaning Rachel with a warm cloth, Garreth stood, leaned over her and pressed a kiss to Rachel's lips. She sat up, satisfied but tender.

"Those were my marching orders," he told her. "It's time for me to go."

Rachel stared at him with wide eyes. "Now? In the middle of the night?"

He smiled at her. "My job here is done. The two of you need to be alone."

She frowned. "And you're okay with that?" He felt no resentment?

"More than okay. I told you, you and Jack are meant to be together. Not you, Jack and me."

She gave him a half smile. Sure, she and Jack were meant to be together, but a night of ménage sex hadn't changed anything. Jenna still stood between them like an impenetrable brick wall.

She laid a hand on her cheek. "Thank you, Garreth. For everything." He'd tried to give Jackson and her a start at something, and for that she would be forever grateful—even if Jackson chose to walk out of her chalet just minutes after Garreth left.

"My pleasure, sweet thing."

"You know, when we first met, you called me an alchemist. But you're the real alchemist here. You're the one who's striving to create gold where none exists."

"You and Jackson could become gold together. You just need to work out a few things."

She leaned forward and kissed his lips. "I hope that one day the woman you love comes to her senses and realizes what she's missing out on."

She must have caught Garreth off-guard, because his face fell. He looked at her with devastated, haunted eyes. "I do too," he said at last. "But it's not going to happen." His skin paled and his eyes filled with grief.

He'd looked just as broken when they'd spoken last night. When Garreth had told her he knew the truth about Jenna's past.

Oh, dear God. Could it be? Was it possible?

It was. And it made sense too. It would explain why Garreth was so desperate to get her and Jackson together: because he understood how they felt being forced apart. And he understood because, if Rachel's guess was correct, he'd experienced almost the identical torment.

"It's Jenna," Rachel said. "The woman you love. Isn't it?"

He blinked hard but didn't answer.

"That's why you're so intent on things working out between Jackson and myself. You understand it all too well because you've been through it too."

Garreth rubbed a hand over his eyes, looking suddenly bone-weary.

"She loves you too?"

He nodded.

"But she won't act on it because you're Jackson's friend."

Jenna staunchly believed that if Jackson could not date her friends, then his friends were strictly off-limits to her. Since the *incident*, she'd had a very strong sense of fairness and justice.

He gave her a sad smile. "I'm like you. Off-limits to the Brooks twin I love."

"God, Garreth, I'm so sorry." Her heart broke a little then. For him and for her. For the two people helplessly in love with the twins who refused to openly love them back—regardless of their feelings for them.

"Me too, sweet thing. Me too." He shrugged. "That's why I'm going back to Canada. I can't have her, and I can't bear to see her with anyone else. It's killing me." He gave her a self-deprecating smile. "Pathetic, huh?"

As pathetic as her being in Sydney. She suspected he'd deliberately used the very word she'd used yesterday. "No. Just sad. Just very, very sad."

And then, because she didn't know what else to say, she stood up and hugged him. He hugged her back, holding her tight.

"Make it work, Rach. Don't let Jackson walk away. You have him in your bed. Now keep him in your life."

"I'll try," she promised. And she would. But what could she do? Jackson had protected his sister for twelve years. He wouldn't stop now. Not even for her.

"Where's Gazza?" Jackson looked around the room, expecting to see him. Rachel was curled up on the couch by herself.

"He left."

"Voluntarily?" Would surprises never cease?

She nodded and bit her lower lip. "He said we needed to be alone. You and I."

Ah, that they did. He and Rachel, alone. Just the two of them. For the rest of their lives.

Not going to happen.

Fuck that. Jackson crossed the room to sit beside her. When he opened his arms wide, Rachel moved into them without hesitation. She crawled onto his lap and wound her arms around his neck. He held her close. Held her tight. Held her to him and refused to let go. Ever. A wave of love rolled through him, so powerful it made him shake.

Over two years ago he'd vowed to never touch her again, never make love to her again. He'd broken those vows. Smashed them to smithereens. Christ, he should have known it would come to this. Should have realized he'd never be able to hold back.

He and Rachel were meant to be together. They were interlocking pieces of the puzzle called love. What the two of them shared wasn't a passing whim. It wasn't a quick fuck when his sister wasn't looking. It was the real thing. Walking away wasn't going to make it less real. It wasn't going to make his feelings go away. They'd tried that route. Tried it for years, and look how successful they'd been.

Not at all.

"I love you, baby." The words were out before he realized he'd spoken them. "I love you so damn much it hurts just to be near you."

Rachel looked up at him, meeting his gaze. Her eyes filled with tears. "It hurts more when we're apart," she whispered. "I hate it. Hate not being near you. Hate not being able to talk to you. I h-hate not seeing you."

Christ, what a fucked-up situation. They couldn't be together, and they couldn't survive apart. With a frustrated groan, he crushed his lips over hers, kissing her with every iota of passion and love he felt.

If Rachel had sat lifelessly in his arms and merely accepted his mouth, the force of his kiss may have hurt her, but she wasn't passive. She kissed him back with just as much emotion. Just as much passion.

Frustration and dissatisfaction swirled around them, a couple supposed to be together and forced to be apart. Fuck, it wasn't right. Wasn't fair.

He pulled away to catch his breath, and her scent filled his nose. She smelled of him. And of sex. And of Gazza.

She smelled of Garreth. His woman smelled of his housemate.

No fucking way. Never again. Last night he'd been prepared to share. Now the scent of another man on his woman made his hackles rise.

Without thinking twice, he rose, still holding Rachel in his arms. Within seconds they stood naked in the shower beneath a torrent of scalding water.

Making love to her with Gazza had fucked with his head. The thought of Garreth touching his woman still made him so irate he could do his friend serious injury. Yes, sharing a woman with his friend was erotic beyond his wildest imagination, and sharing Rachel with Garreth... Christ. He was getting hard again just thinking about it.

But if Garreth ever came near his woman in a sexual way again, his housemate would not live to see another day. Their era of threesomes was over. Tonight had been the last hurrah. Tonight they'd crossed a line. They'd slept with the woman Jackson loved, and as hugely arousing as it had been, it had also disturbed Jackson no end.

"The water's too hot," Rachel complained.

He set his face in a stubborn frown. "It has to be this hot. It has to burn away every last trace of Garreth from your skin, from your memory."

Rachel squared her shoulders as water sluiced around them. "Don't you dare take your frustration out on Garreth." She scowled up at him. "He isn't the issue. He's not what's keeping us apart."

Jackson scowled right back at her. "He slept with you! You slept with him."

"Is that the problem?" Rachel demanded. "Me sleeping with your housemate? Seriously? It's just about sex?"

"What the fuck else could my problem be?" Jackson shot back. "Every time I close my eyes I see him fucking you. Fucking the woman I love."

"Garreth did this for us." Her voice grew louder as she became more agitated. "He did it for you and me, so we could be together. He said you'd come after me if you felt threatened enough by the idea of him and me in bed together."

Jackson had to give his housemate credit. "The little bastard knows me too well."

"He's not a bastard." She glared at him. "He's your friend. And he's a damn good friend if you ask me."

"Maybe so. Doesn't mean I didn't fucking hate watching him touch you."

"Why?"

"Because you're mine, damn it." It was his turn to raise his voice. "You are mine. Not his."

Rachel shrank back, moved away from him, as far away as the shower stall would allow. "No, I'm not."

"What the—"

"I'm not yours, Jackson." Her voice was calmer now, as was her face. "I never have been. Not in all the twelve years I've loved you."

A muscle worked in his jaw as Jackson tried furiously to think of a reply. Nothing came to mind. She was right. Didn't matter how much she loved him or he loved her, not once had she ever truly been his.

Reality had demanded she never would be.

If Jackson were honest with himself, one hundred percent honest, he'd acknowledge that the anger he'd targeted at Garreth had in fact stemmed from the situation that kept him and Rachel apart. It was their forced separation that infuriated him. It wasn't Garreth.

Rachel reached behind him and turned the tap, switching off the water. Silence and steam filled the bathroom.

Drops of water slid from his body, landing with tiny splashes on the floor.

"I love you, Jackson," Rachel said quietly. "I always will. But Jenna might as well be standing between us, right now, pushing us apart. I can never be yours, because neither of you would ever let that happen."

A sense of powerlessness suffused him. "She's my sister. I have to protect her." At least Rachel understood that much. Agreed with him on that.

"Protect her from me?"

Jackson froze.

"That's what it all boils down to with us," Rachel told him. Her hands began to tremble. "You're protecting her from me.

From her best friend. Because if you're with me, then Jenna stands a chance of being hurt again."

She placed her hands over her chest. The tremor was no longer restricted to her hands. Her whole body began to shake. "I've become the girl with the power to spread the rumors in high school. The one capable of ruining Jenna's life. You won't be with me because I might hurt Jenna."

Her eyes filled with tears. "I love Jenna. She's my best friend. She'll always be my best friend. I could never hurt her. No matter what happened between you and me."

Rachel's words struck him with the impact of a bullet.

Holy fuck. How could he have never seen it in this light before?

By refusing to be with Rachel, Jackson wasn't protecting Jenna from all the evils out there in the world, he was protecting her from *her own best friend.* A very real best friend, not a teenager with an infantile and selfish view of the world.

Rachel wasn't the selfish bitch who'd ruined Jenna's life. She was the woman who'd drawn his sister out of her shell and helped her find herself again. The woman who'd dried Jenna's tears every time she'd cried, who'd lifted her back up every time she'd stumbled. The woman who'd given up her life to move to another city, just so she wouldn't be tempted by Jenna's brother.

Christ, Gazza had called it the minute he'd met her. He'd seen what Jackson hadn't been able to. That in trying to protect Jenna from an old hurt, he'd turned Rachel into a possible threat.

Rachel wasn't a threat. She never had been. She never would be. She was the person who'd made his sister's life richer, and if he'd just give her the chance, she could be the person who'd make his life whole.

Jackson stared at her, stunned all the way down to his bones. She was the only one who could make his life whole. Fuck knew he'd tried to find someone else when she'd left, and that had been a dismal failure. He'd tried to bury himself in emotionless sex, because the physical relief and release had helped to hide the psychological emptiness. But his life was as hollow now as the day she'd left Brisbane.

"I think you need to leave my chalet," Rachel said quietly. She'd wrapped her arms around herself and stood shivering, naked and wet in the shower stall with him. "I can't do this anymore. I can't pretend I don't love you when I do, and I can't pretend to be the bad guy when I'm not. I'll pack my bags as soon as you're gone. I'll get out of your hair and Jenna's." She bit her lip and stood a little straighter. "And next time you have a birthday celebration, I promise not to come. I promise not to put you under this kind of strain again. It's not fair to any of us." She pushed open the glass door and stepped into the bathroom. "Happy birthday, by the way."

Shock rendered him speechless. He couldn't move.

Christ, it was officially his birthday. He was thirty.

Thirty and alone.

The thought of her leaving him, of her walking away again, powered him into action.

"No!"

He went after her, streaking out the shower and through the bathroom, leaving a trail of water in his wake. She was beside the bed when he finally caught up to her. He grabbed her arm and hauled her against him, slamming her body into his. "Damn it, Rachel. You're not walking away from me again. From us. I let you go the last time, thinking it was the right thing to do. This time I won't. I'll never let you go again."

"Jack—"

"You're right, Rach. About everything. I've been a fucking idiot. Blind to my actions. Without ever meaning to, I've made you into a potential threat. I've imbued you with all these evil powers you'd never use. God knows you're incapable of ever hurting Jenna. I know it. Jenna knows. I just never realized that we all subconsciously thought it."

"I'm not a threat, Jackson. I never have been. But Jenna's still my best friend, and you're still her brother. The restrictions are still there. We can't be together, even if we want to." Tears shimmered in her eyes.

"Yes, we can."

She shook her head. "Jenna—"

"Jenna will have to come to terms with it. I've spent my

entire adult life living alone because I didn't want Jenna getting hurt again. In the process I've hurt you, the woman I love. The woman I want to spend my life with. By protecting her I've overlooked you. And me. It's our turn, Rach. It's time for us to be happy. Twelve years is long enough to pay for a crime I didn't commit." No, he hadn't been able to protect Jenna when they were kids. Yes, he'd blamed himself. But when all was said and done, he hadn't done anything wrong.

Jenna had been caught in the revenge attack of a malicious teenager. She'd suffered for it. So had he. But it didn't mean he had to continue suffering for the rest of his life. And it sure as hell didn't mean Rachel had to suffer along with them.

He'd done his penance. They all had.

It was time to move on. It was time to be happy again. To live again, and the only way that could happen for him was to be with Rachel.

"We need to be together, Rach."

Her mouth dropped open.

"Enough secrets. Enough hiding. We love each other. Let's tell the world. Let everyone know. Let's give a relationship, a real relationship between us, a chance."

She shook her head. "I can't. I couldn't do that to Jenna."

"You and Jenna are close enough to be sisters. If I can see that you'll never hurt her, she'll be able to see that too."

She looked at him, incredulous, her mouth opening and closing like a fish. "I want to, Jackson. So much it scares me. But I've moved on, moved away from you. My life's in Sydney. My business is in Sydney. I can't just up and leave it."

She was worried about work? About geography? No fucking way. There'd been enough bullshit keeping them apart. Trivialities like cities and jobs would not come between them. "I'll move to Sydney. I'll apply for a job at one of the newspapers there."

She blinked. "You'd do that? For me?"

"For us, Rach. I'd do anything for us. We've earned it. We deserve it. It's our turn now."

A single tear slid down her cheek. "You're not kidding, are you?"

"I've never been more serious about anything in my life."

"Jenna—"

"Jenna will give us her blessing. Once I've explained everything to her, once she knows how much we love each other, she'd never stand in our way. She'd never be able to see you as a threat to her peace of mind. You've proven to her too often that you're her friend, not her enemy." It wouldn't be easy, and it wouldn't happen quickly, but eventually Jenna would warm to the idea. She'd have to.

"Wh-what about Garreth?"

"I'll thank him. For everything he's done to help us reach this point. For helping me see what a fucking idiot I've been." Christ, it stunned him how easy it was to see Garreth in that light now. Not ten minutes ago he was ready to tear the man's head off. Now he understood Garreth's only intention in sleeping with Rachel was to make Jackson good and jealous. Damn, the man had succeeded, in one big fucking way.

"What about you," she asked. "Are you sure?"

"More sure than I've ever been about anything. I want to be with you, Rach. I can't live apart from you anymore. I spent twelve years trying, and refuse to do it for one more day."

"I..." She frowned, as though searching for another reason to say no.

"Listen to you. You're so used to denying our love, you're looking for ways to deny it now. Looking for reasons we shouldn't be together. There aren't any. Not anymore. We don't need to pretend anymore. I don't want to pretend. I just want to be with you. I just want to give us a chance."

"I...uh... Okay."

His heart lurched. "Okay what?"

Her face broke into a smile. "Okay, let's do this. Let's give us a chance." The smile widened, blinding him in its brilliance. "I've fantasized about you and I being together my entire adult life. I'm not about to give up on the possibility now that you're dangling it in front of my eyes. Come and live with me in Sydney. Please."

It was all he needed to hear.

Their lips met in a kiss as inevitable as their next breath. It continued forever, a kiss born of love and desire. Born of twelve years of wanting each other. A kiss that told him this was it. They'd finally accepted each other. They could finally be together.

When at last they pulled apart, it was with a lightness he'd never felt before. A contentment that came with knowing he could kiss her whenever he wanted. Once Jenna knew about them, their love need never be a secret again.

"Remind me to thank Gazza when I see him." He nuzzled Rachel's neck. Garreth was responsible for him and Rachel being together now. If not for his housemate, Jackson would never have climbed into her bed again. He'd have continued to live the shadow of a life he'd been leading for twelve years, terrified to love in case Jenna got hurt. "He brought us together."

Rachel laughed with delight. "That's because your friend is an alchemist."

"Pardon?"

"Garreth created gold here tonight. He created us."

Jackson shook his head. "No, baby, we created us. Garreth just made sure we found each other again." And then he kissed Rachel again and pulled her onto the bed. It was way past time they created their own alchemy together. Just the two of them.

About the Author

To learn more about Jess Dee please visit her website at: www.jessdee.com. Or you can drop by her blog: http://jessdee.wordpress.com.

Jess loves to hear from her readers. You can contact her any time at: jess@jessdee.com.

Look for these titles by
Jess Dee

Now Available:

Ask Adam
Photo Opportunity
A Question of Trust
A Question of Love

Circle of Friends series
Only Tyler
Steve's Story

Three Of A Kind series
Going All In
Raising The Stakes
Full House

Bandicoot Cove series
Exotic Indulgence (with Vivian Arend & Lexxie Couper)
Island Idyll

Speed series
See You in My Dreams

Print Anthologies
Three's Company
Risking It All

Triple Dare

Lexxie Couper

Dedication

For Jess Dee, even though she can't stand vegemite sandwiches.

And Heidi, who dared me to do it.

Chapter One

Joseph Hudson tossed his snowboard aside, threw his goggles over his shoulder and swung a fist at his best mate.

His knuckles, covered as they were by tri-layer insulated gloves, weren't anywhere near as hard as they would have been if he'd been having this fight back home in Australia. They were, however, still hard enough to produce a satisfying crunch when they hit Robert I-dare-you Thorton's jaw.

"You right bloody wanker," Joseph stormed, watching his life-long friend, business partner and travelling companion stagger backward over the firmly compacted snow. "You told me the helicopter was going to pick us up before sunset."

Robert let out a snorting chuckle, rubbing at his jaw even as he struggled to stay on his feet. That his snowboard was still attached to his left boot wasn't making the job easier. "Yeah, yeah." He laughed, his wide grin almost hidden by his own gloved hand. "Sunset *tomorrow*, Hudo."

Joseph took a step toward him, the urge to kill him was stronger than it had ever been. Stronger than the time Rob had dared him to hijack the principal's mini back in their senior year of high school and leave it atop the barbeque pit at the top of the local lookout point. Stronger than the time Rob had dared him to run buck-naked across the cricket pitch during the regional grand final game with the word "Howzat?" scrawled in bright red lipstick on his backside. How was he to know Mrs. Woodcomb's mini was a rare collectors car on the verge of being bought by a museum for a very, *very* generous price? How was he to know the national manager of the camping-and-outdoor equipment store Joseph worked at was the umpire of the cricket match that day?

Thanks to Robert bloody Thorton, over the twenty-six years spanning their friendship Joseph had been suspended, sacked, jailed, robbed, handcuffed to a stripper pretending to be a cop, handcuffed to a cop who sure as hell *wasn't* a stripper, left stranded on a public beach without a stitch of clothing and almost married to a Russian buy-a-bride at the ripe old age of sixteen. None of those incidents however, could have resulted in Joseph's untimely demise like this one could.

He ground his teeth, removed his bright orange helmet and dragged his fingers through his hair as he did so. "Fuck a duck, Rob," he muttered, shaking his head. "We could die up here tonight. Do you have any idea how bloody cold the Rockies get at night? In the winter? We don't even have a bloody tent!"

"I saw you pitching a tent over that hot little number back in the lodge this morning, Hudo. The same one who caught your eye last night." Rob grinned wide enough to flash the dimple in his right cheek, an action guaranteed to make any woman forgive him anything. Joseph however, was not a woman. Not even close.

He yanked his gloves from his hands, storming towards his best mate. "Right," he growled, "that's it. I'm gonna kill you."

Rob burst out laughing, holding his still-gloved hands up, palms outward—the closest Joseph would get to an apology. "Uncle, uncle."

Joseph rolled his eyes and raked his fingers, already starting to tingle from the bitter chill on the winter air, through his hair again. As frustratingly annoying as the tall, lanky professional nuisance could be, Rob knew when he'd pushed too far. Now was one of those times. He'd always been this way. Since day one of kindergarten, Rob had been the instigator, the provoker, challenging Joseph to push himself beyond the boring safety of his conservative, politically correct, cotton-wool, upper-class upbringing. All Rob needed to do was utter the words, "I dare you" and Joseph was a cooked goose. Trouble always followed those words. Trouble and a world of fun.

If it wasn't for "I dare you", Joseph never would have started Hudo's Outdoor Equipment Online at the bright-eyed and bushytailed age of twenty.

If it wasn't for "I dare you", he'd never have taken his small online store to the next street-front level.

If it wasn't for Rob and his "I dare you", Joseph would probably still be sitting in Hudo's Outdoor Equipment's office beside the fridge in his kitchen, wondering where most of his ambition had gone.

"I dare you" had seen them both fly out of Australia to the US to take on the Rockies' ski slopes without any preparation at all except to pack their snowboards and equipment—and, in Rob's case, practically a whole backpack of condoms. By the time they'd landed in Colorado, Rob's blog had received over one hundred comments from women in the US offering to show them the best places to have fun on the snow. Something about those comments told Joseph snowboarding wasn't exactly the fun they had in mind.

"I dare you" had seem him singing Men At Work's "Down Under", the unofficial Australian national anthem, last night in the bar after just two hours in the country, standing atop a not-so-stable table with his Aussie-flag boxers on full and prominent display.

So here you are, Joseph, CEO of Hudo's Outdoor Equipment, Time Australia's *Businessman of the Year, stuck on the side of a mountain in the Rockies with Hudo's Marketing Director and all round professional partier and no one back in Australia knows where either of you are. Excellent.*

That thought, sarcastic as it was, made Joseph snort. He let out a sigh and looked around for his discarded gloves. "Okay, Thorton," he threw over his shoulder. "I know you're not a complete moron. What's your plan? Where are we staying tonight?"

Rob's dimple flashed again. "In the hut, Hudo. In the hut."

Joseph raised his eyebrows. The pristine snow surrounding them, barely marred by tree or rock let alone fellow snowboarders or skiers, didn't lead him to feel any more relieved. He turned back to Rob. "Hut?"

"Hut."

"Okay, I'll give. Where the bloody hell is this hut?"

Rob didn't try to hide his grin as he dropped his gaze to the slim compass embedded in the nose of his snowboard—a new device he was trialing for Hudo's Outdoor Equipment. Joseph may be pissed at him, but he'd stopped at one punch. By Rob's reckoning, that meant Joe had already forgiven him and was about to throw himself into the challenge, albeit begrudgingly, but along for the ride all the same.

Rob studied the small compass, noting the direction it told him was true north. Lifting his head, he gave Joe a wide smirk. "The hut is about forty minutes that way." He pointed northwest. "As long as you stop belly-aching, we should be settled in and knocking back the first beer before sunset."

Joseph cocked an eyebrow. "Belly-aching? Hey, I've got a right to complain. You may enjoy sleeping starkers in the middle of the Rockies, but I left my favorite boxers back at the lodge. And for the record, I still can't believe you're carrying a six-pack in your backpack."

Rob laughed. Joe's favorite boxers—a silk pair with an image of the Incredible Hulk printed on the backside—were tucked safely in amongst Rob's own long johns. "Yeah, yeah," he reached down and released the mechanism on his snowboard's binding harness. "You think I'm going to look at your bony arse?"

"No," Joe shot back. "I'm just worried you're going to go into a steep spiral of depression when you realize my nuts are bigger than yours."

Rob threw back his head and laughed. The sound bounced off the pristine white snow-covered hills around them. "I've seen 'em, remember, mate." He patted the front of his padded ski trousers. "*These* are bigger *and* made of brass." He snatched his snowboard from the ground and hoisted it up onto his shoulder. "C'mon. I'm thirsty and the beer is getting warm."

Joseph snorted. "Of course it is. The fact we're tromping through a bloody fridge doesn't mean anything to you, does it?"

Rob flashed his teeth at his best friend. "You know I like my beer cold."

He set off, the crunch of the untouched snow beneath his feet like music from heaven. Growing up in Australia meant two things to Rob. Surf and snow. He and Joseph had spent their childhood either on the waves or the ski slopes. The trouble was, with the planet increasingly getting hotter every year, the Australian snow fields were fast dwindling to snow patches. He pulled at the backpack slung over his shoulder. There wasn't anything like going on an adventure with his best mate, especially not at the moment.

When the call of the snow had hit him in the belly in the middle of a sweltering Aussie summer day while he and Joseph were in the most boring meeting Rob had ever had the misfortune to be in, he'd dared Joe to jump a 747. Six hours later they were settled into their first-class seats, beers in hand, watching Sydney become a tiny grey smudge thirty-thousand feet below them. Thirty-two hours after that and here they were. In Colorado. On the slopes.

Away from it all.

The hut—a rescuers cabin nestled in the trees at the lowest point of Knife Ridge in Wolf Creek Ski Resort, was the perfect place to force Joe to unwind. And to give him the bad news.

Don't think about that yet, Robbo. Get a few beers into him and then *think about it.*

Pulling an icy breath, he shot his best mate a quick look. The man was born for this. Not sitting behind a desk, no matter how expensive the desk was. What was going to happen to him when Rob was gone? Who was going to tear his ass from the chair and make him live his life?

Stop it. Not now.

"You sound out of breath, Hudo," he said, raising his eyebrows. "Too many days and nights power networking?"

"Ha ha." Joseph rolled his eyes. "I hear you puffing just as much as me. Too many nights partying, mate?"

Rob grinned at him again. "Yeah, that'd be it. And once again, I draw attention to the sexy thing back at the lodge. She was in the bar last night, sitting all alone after you left. She watched you leave, y'know. You could've been partying as well, if you hadn't needed to send off that email."

"Hey, I didn't break the rule." Joseph adjusted his snowboard under his arm, giving Rob an affronted look. Rob's "rule"—that no one was supposed to know where they were—existed for one reason only—to keep Joseph from working when he should be having fun. "I didn't mention where we were. I did however, approve your latest marketing push for the Chinese market, so shut up or I'll cut your expenses."

"Whoa, hit a man where it hurts, why don't you?"

Joseph shook his head, the corners of his mouth curling. "Where it hurts with you mate, is in your pants."

Rob puffed up his chest. "Can't argue with the truth."

Joseph shook his head again. "Idiot."

"Yep."

They continued farther, Rob checking the compass every few minutes. The undulating hills around them began to grow a little more unpredictable, dropping suddenly here, rising abruptly there. More trees—limbs stooped low under the weight of heavy snow—jutted up from the blinding whiteness, breaking what was otherwise a perfect blanket. He frowned, turning his head a little so Joseph wouldn't see. Okay, at this point he should be able to see the hut—at least the top of the hut's roof—somewhere before him.

But he couldn't. There was nothing. Just trees, snow, rocks and more snow.

"Did I tell you the Japanese consortium made another offer before we left?" Joseph said suddenly, and Rob started before forcing his face into a relaxed smile.

"No. How much this time?"

Joseph let out a sigh. "A stupid amount. Enough to make me think I'm an idiot for saying no."

Rob paused, giving his best mate a serious look. "Why *are* you saying no? How many blokes our age get the chance to say, hey, I don't have to work another day in my life?"

Joseph shook his head, an unreadable tension forming at the edges of his brown eyes. "If I sell up, who is going to keep you under control? Or living the unleashed life you've grown accustom to?"

A sharp stab of something very close to pain sank into Rob's chest, and he turned away and began the trek to the so-far unseen hut. "I'll be right. I'm super hot, super smart, I have a degree from Sydney Uni—with honors—and every marketing idea I come up with makes the company more money than God. Who's going to try and control *that* brilliance?"

"You forgot to add super humble to that list," Joseph pointed out behind him.

"And super thirsty," Rob shouted, trudging faster through the snow. Where the bloody hell was this bloody hut?

The crunching of snow under boots told Rob his friend had started walking again. "Hmm. Well, it's a mute point anyway," Joe said, his voice carrying over the still silence of the mountain. "I'm not selling and you're not going anywhere."

Rob squeezed his eyes shut for a quick second, his fists bunching tight. *God, I wish you were right, mate.*

The dark thought slithered through his head like a snake and he quickened his pace, searching the never-ending whiteness before him for signs of the rescue cabin.

"Where the bloody hell is this hut of yours, Thorton?" Joseph muttered. "Even I'd kill for a beer right now if it didn't mean freezing my nuts off out here."

"Wait your hurry," Rob shot over his shoulder, a knot of unease beginning to form in his gut. "I know you're just impatient to get your gear off."

Something icy cold and rather hard smacked into the back of his head and he turned to see Joseph swipe his snow-dusted hands against the back of his thighs.

"A snowball?" He raised his eyebrows. "Really? I thought I was meant to be the immature one?"

Joseph shrugged, a smirk playing with his lips. "Wasn't me."

With a laugh, Rob turned back to the hutless bloody hills and began walking again, doing his best to ignore the knot of unease twisting tighter in his gut.

Twenty minutes later, he clenched his fists and bit back a curse. Fuck it. He had to do the unthinkable.

He stopped walking, stabbed the nose of his snowboard into the snow beside his boot and gave Joseph a level look. "I think we're lost."

Joseph stared at him, his expression not even flinching. "I coulda told you that fifteen minutes ago."

"Funny bastard." Rob scanned the snow, squinting at the sun and its way-too-fast decline behind the hill to the west. "I'm serious. I think the compass on the snowboard is faulty."

"Guess we better not stock it then."

Joseph's casual reply made Rob bite back another curse. He'd expected another punch. What this laidback attitude from Joseph meant was his best mate was going to make his life a living hell later. When he'd calmed down. "It shouldn't be far," he offered, scanning the area around them again and pointing a little to the left. "Unless the compass is totally fucked up, it should be somewhere in this direction."

"Or it could be on the other side of the ridge."

He gave Joe a sheepish sideward glance. "That would suck, wouldn't it?"

"C'mon." Joseph started walking again, his footfalls like gunshots in the icy air. "There's no way the gods of lunatics would let you perish on a mountain in the US. Who'd they worship if that happened?"

"Ha ha. You really missed your true calling, Hudo. You shoulda been a comedian."

Rob picked up his board and hurried to catch up with his best mate, casting the sinking sun a less-than-impressed look. Night would be on them soon. When that happened, the temperature would plummet. There were other less-appealing ways to die, but being turned into an icicle on the side of a bloody mountain was right up there with the worst. How the hell had he gotten this so wrong?

"Remind me to send an email to the manufacturers of that compass when we get back home," he said to Joseph's back.

The words tasted odd on Rob's tongue. Like chalk dust and stagnant air.

Back home.

You're not planning on going back home, are you?

"Y'know," Joseph called over his shoulder, "I think I might write one as well."

Rob couldn't help himself. He laughed. Joseph may be the kid who needed a push to experience life, but when it came to business, he didn't mess around. An email from Joseph Hudson pretty much spelt the end of any outdoor equipment supplier foolish enough to promote a product not ready for the market.

Just like that.

"If it helps, you can have my beer."

"Won't say no."

Rob laughed again. If they survived the night, he'd buy Joe a whole bloody brewery.

Chapter Two

Anna McCarthy lowered her binoculars and shook her head. Australians. What were they thinking?

She returned the glasses to her backpack, adjusted the straps on her stocks and pushed herself forward. The sun would be completely behind the horizon in less than fifteen minutes, which gave her less than ten to get to the two men wandering aimlessly at the base of Knife Ridge Chutes and get them into Wolf Creek rescue cabin number four.

After that, she'd spend a good fifteen minutes giving them a damn good lecture on mountain safety before charging them with reckless endangerment and presenting them with a hefty fine. Tourists, she'd learnt from experience, only learnt their lesson when their hip pockets were injured. And by the look of the equipment these two men were decked out in, the latest and greatest and very most expensive, their hip pockets could afford the pain.

Gliding through the terrain, she kept her stare locked on their dark shapes, each one a tall black streak of stupidity against the stark white snow.

The wind bit at her face, even through her protective gear, and she growled low in her throat. Australians. Thought they knew everything.

She'd noticed them at the bar last night, their accents drawing more than just *her* attention. By the time the tallest one with the sandy-blond hair and hawkish nose had finished his off-key rendition of that song from Kangaroo Jack and left, just about every woman in the bar had been gathered around their table.

Dodging a low-hanging branch, she stabbed her stocks into the snow, hurrying her speed. As far as she could tell, none of the fawning women had gotten lucky, much to their chagrin. The tall one, Joseph, she thought she'd heard his friend call him, hadn't come back to the bar, and his friend had followed only a few hours—and beers and dances with said fawning women—later. Alone.

So is that why you've followed them for most of the day? They didn't pick up anyone last night?

She grunted at the ridiculous notion, swerving a cluster of jagged boulders as she forced herself faster over the snow. No, she'd followed them most of the day because she'd heard the friend—Rob? Bob?—mention to one of his many admirers they were going to heli-jump onto Knife Ridge Chutes and planned to stay overnight in the unused Wolf Creek rescue cabin.

The trouble was he hadn't informed her. And as the local ranger in charge of controlling Wolf Creek's slopes and ski runs, anyone planning on spending the night on the side of Knife Ridge, no matter how gorgeous and well-equipped and obviously daring-do, had to tell her of those plans.

And something about them had told her they were going to get themselves into trouble.

Maybe it was the devilish glint in Rob/Bob's way-too-sexy blue eyes? Or the dimple in his cheek? Or the way Joseph moved his hips on the table dancing to that annoyingly catchy song? Or the way your pussy fluttered and squeezed and got all warm and prickly when Joseph looked at you this morning in the lodge. Or the way you woke up covered in sweat after dreaming about them both undressing you with their teeth while their hands—

She cut the embarrassing thought dead before her face could get any hotter. She hadn't had a wet dream since she was a teenager, and she sure as hell didn't have one last night. She didn't. And no, none of those reasons were why she now followed the Australian men. She'd followed them because her gut had told her they'd need her, and she always listened to her gut. Not her pussy.

Yeah, right.

"Oh, shut up," she muttered with a savage thrust of her stocks. The push flung her past the last of the blanketed trees and, with another quick dig, she propelled herself closer to the two men. Close enough to hear them singing—singing of all things—some weird version of AC/DC's "It's a Long Way to the Top" with the word "top" replaced by "hut".

She ground her teeth and slid to a halt behind them, showering them both in snow, not even remotely interested in hiding her anger. "What the hell do you two morons think you're doing?"

They spun to stare at her, their faces—flushed by the icy chill on the air—registered their shock.

Before they could say anything, she poked a finger at them, her stock dangling from her wrist to bang against her right knee. "Do you have any idea how dangerous what you are doing is? How stupid?"

The tall one—Joseph—gaped at her, his eyes locked on her face. "Err..."

"What my mate means to say—" Rob/Bob began, that evil dimple she'd seen last night flashing into existence on his right cheek.

"Is he's a moron?" Anna snapped, cutting him off. The dimple was doing all sorts of unnerving things to her anger. And all sorts of unnerving things to her sex, damn it.

"Actually, I'm really very smart."

The statement, falling from Joseph's lips in a hurried jumble of accented words, seemed to surprise him. He blinked. And his friend burst out laughing. "Bloody hell, Hudo." Rob/Bob smacked a fist into his friend's shoulder, blue eyes twinkling. "It's a good thing you're loaded."

Anna frowned at them both. She had no idea what Rob/Bob had just said—loaded? Surely Joseph wasn't drunk on the mountain?—but whatever it was, it made Joseph glare at him. "Put a sock in it, Thorton," he growled.

Hudo? Thorton? Singing when they should be scared stiff they were going to freeze to death? Laughing in the face of her anger? Who were these people?

Still chuckling, Rob/Bob turned back to her and fixed her with a direct blue stare. "We kinda fucked up, thanks to a wonky compass. You wouldn't happen to know where the number four hut is, would you?"

Keeping a tight grip on her anger, Anna fixed him back with her own level glare. "I do. And if you promise not to sing anymore, I'll take you there."

Much to her dismay, Joseph started laughing. Much to her horror, her pussy started to flutter. Really quickly. And insistently.

Oh, Anna, don't go getting turned on by two Australian idiots.

"Any chance we can persuade you to stay overnight with us?" Rob/Bob grinned, dimple still there. "I promise Hudo here won't sing again."

"Shut the hell up, Rob," Joseph growled. "You sing worse than me."

Anna felt like she was watching a game of tennis. She couldn't stop moving her stare from one to the other. They couldn't be for real. She was dreaming this. She'd fallen asleep thinking about how they'd need saving and this is the scenario her psyche had come up with: two gorgeous, sexy-assed Australians asking her to stay overnight in the deserted, unused rescue cabin with them. All three of them locked up together, with nothing to do all night except—

"Shouldn't we be getting a move on?" Rob's deep voice, complete with that sinful Australian accent that made her pulse quicken, jerked her out of her confused trance.

She blinked, giving them both another hard stare, hoping like hell her cheeks weren't as red as she thought they were. "Follow me," she snarled, snatching at the grips of her stocks and pushing herself away from them. "And try not to get lost."

For an answer, Rob laughed.

"You're a fine one to laugh, Thorton," she heard Joseph say, his accent just as sinful as Rob's, "you're the one that got us in this predicament to begin with."

"And you can thank me later, mate," Rob replied.

For reasons Anna couldn't understand, her pulse kicked up a notch. And her sex grew damp.

Oh, Anna. You know where this is leading, don't you?

She pushed her way through the snow and trees, leading the two men to the rescue cabin on the northwest side of the valley. she had to admit their snowboarding skills were quite impressive. Better than their navigational skills, that was for certain. Much better than their singing skills, even if their accents were sexy as hell. The pit of her belly knotted and she scowled, doing her upmost not to think about staying overnight with them. She didn't have to stay. None of them did. If she got to the cabin quickly enough, she could contact Base and tell them to send up a chopper. They'd be back in the lodge, no doubt singing on tables again, before midnight.

And that's what you're going to do, isn't it? That is, because that's the right thing to do. The sane thing. Not *calling the chopper,* not *going back down the mountain, that's the wrong thing to do. Staying overnight in the hut with them, that's just plain...*

"Silly," she muttered, rounding a grove of pine. *The* grove of pine. The grove beside which sat—

"The hut!" Rob cried, his enthusiastic cheer making Anna's nipples pinch into hard little points. "See, Hudo? I wasn't that far off."

Joseph chuckled. "Yeah, you're a regular Saint Bernard."

The warm, happy sound made Anna's nipples pinch harder, and she bit back an exasperated groan. God help her, she wasn't just getting turned on by their accents, she was almost coming thanks to their foolhardy attitude to getting lost.

She titled her hips, preparing to swing around to face them, when Rob swooshed past, his tall, lean body looking deliciously confident on his snowboard. He cut to a halt at the door of the rescue cabin and flashed his dimple at her again. "So," he said, blue eyes shrouded in shadows cast by the almost sleeping sun, "you going to join us inside?"

Anna narrowed her eyes at him, refusing to acknowledge the eager throb between her thighs. "Do you have any idea how much trouble you two are in? How much this rescue is going to cost you? I can lay charges. I could—"

"Have the best night of your life," Rob finished with a grin.

Behind her, she heard Joseph moan. Low and almost inaudible, but a moan all the same. One filled with...hope?

She turned her head and looked at him over her shoulder, the memory of her dream flooding through her. No, it wasn't just her dream making her body thrum with an inexplicable, hungry urgency. It was the way Joseph had looked singing on the table—like all the happiness in life, all the joy and fun, had somehow been poured into this one man. It was the memory of how her lips had curled into a smile watching him. It was the disappointment she'd felt when he'd left the bar before she could get the chance to muster up the courage to introduce herself. Not to mention the relief she'd experienced when he'd left the bar alone.

His eyes moved to her, their cookie-brown depths asking a question her body knew the answer to, even if her head didn't.

Oh, Anna.

"I dare you." The three words passed Rob's lips with silken devilment, and her pussy contracted in eager want. She stared at him, her heart racing, thumping in her throat with such force she could barely draw breath. Two men, two Australians. Both somehow the embodiment of every fantasy she'd never known. Both dangerously gorgeous, both sinfully sexy. Both capable of making her almost orgasm just by speaking, let alone what they could do with their hands. Two men. One mountain. One momentous dare.

Without saying a thing, she bent down and unlatched her boots, disconnecting them from her skis.

Her blood roaring in her ears, she crossed to the cabin's door and searched for the key to its lock in the top pocket of her jacket. Her fingers brushed her breast through the thermal material of the garment and she hitched in a gasp, the jolts of pleasure darting through her body at the completely un-sensual contact making her head spin.

She withdrew her hand, her fingers gripping the key tightly, her breath stuck in her throat.

You're really doing this, Anna? Really really?

She slipped the key into the lock and, closing her eyes for a split second, pushed the door open.

Joseph watched the woman from the lodge step through the doorway into the hut. He stood frozen, not from the sinking temperature of the winter air, but from sheer, dumbstruck cowardice.

A threesome.

He'd never had one before. Rob had. More than once Rob had ended up in a bed that wasn't his own with two women. Tonight wasn't two women though. Tonight was him, Rob and a woman he'd been attracted to the second he'd seen her in the lodge last night.

He couldn't do it.

He slid his stare to his best mate. Rob leant one shoulder against the doorjamb, studying him. He knew there'd be no contact between them both. Without saying it, there wasn't any doubt about that. They were both strictly hetero, even if they did love each other as only mates could. And he'd been starkers around Rob too many times to be hung up about what his friend thought of him standing so near without any clothes on. But this...

Is it really Rob you're worried about, Hudson?

No, it wasn't. He'd never been one for one-night stands. Sex was too...too—fuck—too personal. It was a connection of more than just body. What if he couldn't...what if it didn't...

A jerking spasm in his pants made him snort out a quick laugh. Okay, that answered that question. He was as hard as ever. His dick strained against the lining of his snow pants with such insistent force he was surprised it didn't tear the material. He'd sported an erection almost as hard this morning in the cafeteria just *watching* the woman now inside the hut. The thought he might actually touch her, hold her, make love to...

He drew in another breath, his lungs burning as icy air streamed into his body. His balls rose high and he knew they were firm and swollen. Ready.

Bloody hell, he wished he was back in Australia. Listening to the company's insurance director drone on again.

No, you don't.

He stared at his best mate, mouth dry.

Rob cocked an eyebrow. "Do I need to say it, Hudo?"

He shook his head. "Don't."

For a moment, he could almost see the words "I dare you" forming on his friend's lips. And then a strange stillness passed over Rob's face, an unreadable light flickered in his eyes and he nodded. A single, simple nod. “Okay. But don’t do this for me, Joseph,” he said, his voice uncharacteristically serious. “Do it for you.”

Joseph frowned, the words puzzling him. Since when had Robert Thorton ever backed away from laying down a dare? What was going on here? What was going on with Rob?

Before he could say anything, Rob gave him one of his patented grins, dimple creasing into existence on his cheek, and swiveled on his shoulder until he disappeared into the hut.

Joseph studied the doorway, dragging his hands over his face and through his hair. He pulled in a deep, slow breath. “Fuck it,” he muttered. “It’s getting cold out here anyway.”

Two steps into the cabin and he realized something wasn’t going the way he suspected.

“Shit, shit, shit.” The woman—damn, he really needed to get her name—was stamping her foot beside the tall and ancient heater in the centre of the surprisingly large cabin. She swung her foot, the toe of her boot connecting with the steel heater with a solid *thunk*.

He shot Rob a quick look, raising an eyebrow in a silent question.

Rob laughed, obviously enjoying himself. But then again, when *didn’t* Rob enjoy himself. The bloke was a walking advertisement for being high on life. “It seems we can’t get the heat on.” He paused. “Well, not *this* way anyway.”

The woman stopped her baleful glare of the uncooperative heater and turned it on Rob. “I’m about two seconds from radioing Wolf Creek command and having you taken away in cuffs, you know that, don’t you?”

Rob laughed again, zipped up his jacket and tugged his beanie from his pocket. “How ’bout I go get some wood.”

Joseph snorted before he could stop himself, the expression on Rob’s face telling him the wood his mate most eagerly sought had nothing to do with trees.

Bloody hell, Hudson. You got the mind of a teenager at the moment.

He watched his friend leave, the bang of the door closing a sudden and daunting reminder he was alone in the cabin with a woman who made his dick harder than...well, harder than wood. He shuffled his feet, feeling ridiculously stupid. "Err..."

"The emergency gas reserves seem to have evaporated," she said, flicking her eyes at the heater beside him. "Which means the pilot light won't ignite."

He nodded, wishing to hell he could think of something intelligent to say. For Pete's sake, he owned Australia's most successful camping and outdoor equipment and supply business. He should be able to talk about pilot lights and gas heaters until the cows came home.

"Tell me, when *did* you two decide it would be a good idea to come to America to go snowboarding?"

He smiled at the abrupt and almost caustic question. Leaning his board against the wall, he slid his sleeve up his arm and looked at his watch. "About thirty-eight hours ago."

She laughed, the first real joyful sound he'd heard from her since she'd arrived out of nowhere and led them to safety. "Thirty-eight hours."

"Yep. We touched down and checked in last night."

She shook her head, tugged her gloves from her hands and stuffed them into her jacket pocket. "Which tells me one or both of you has lots and lots of money. More money than sense, I'd guess."

Joseph gave her a puzzled frown. "Why do you say that?"

"It's peak ski season. Every room in every accommodation from here to Utah is booked out. Unless you've got serious dollars, there's no way you're getting a room with just thirty-eight hours notice."

"Is it a problem one or both of us is loaded?"

A dawning smile stretched her lips, and his cock, still rigid in the confines of his snow pants, gave a little spasm. Damn, that was a gorgeous smile. The corners of her mouth curled first, creasing the sides of her lips just a little, before her teeth—perfectly white and even—came into view, followed by a tiny little crease just between her eyes. Eyes, he hadn't failed to notice, a very piercing, very sexy shade of grey.

"Ahh," she said, nodding as she moved away from the cold heater toward a bench under the shuttered window on the far wall. "That explains what loaded means." She leant her butt against the bench and folded her arms over her breasts. Joseph felt his cock jerk again. Such a simple action, but it made him horny as a bloody dog. What would it feel like to place his hands on her breasts and cup them? Squeeze them gently?

"So, you're the one with the money."

Her question, delivered in the form of a statement, sent a rush of warmth to his face. He hated talking about his money. True, he had a lot of it, a bloody lot of it, but it didn't define him.

"And Rob is the one without the sense," she finished, the smile on her lips curling wider. She titled her head to the side, crossing her ankles in front of her. "Yeah, I can see that."

Despite himself, Joseph grinned. His cock lurched again in his trousers, enjoying their tête-à-tête almost as much as he was. He liked her dry wit. And her accent. A drawling caress of vowels and consonants that made him wish she'd say his name.

"I guess I should ask your name," he said, removing his own gloves and shoving them into his back pocket. "I should at least know who to address the thank you card to."

She laughed again, and Joseph decided there and then he could seriously become addicted to the soft, throaty sound. "Anna McCarthy. Your local saver of lost Australian lunatics, yeah, that's me."

He cocked an eyebrow. "All Australian lunatics? Do you get many here?"

Her direct grey gaze leveled on his face, a small smile playing with her lips. Lips he wanted to kiss. Soon. Real soon. "No, you're my first. But depending how it goes tonight, I might have to find some more to save."

A low growl rumbled in Joseph's chest at the idea of Anna McCarthy saving any other Australians but himself. "Hmm," he said, "I think you'll find saving Aussies is an exhausting, sweaty business."

She cocked her own eyebrow, the finely arched line of dark blonde hair moving up her forehead with smooth ease. "Is it now? Then perhaps I should take it slow to start with? Saving too hard and too quickly at this altitude could be hazardous to my health, is that what you're saying?"

Pulse pounding in his ear, dick so hard he thought it was about to explode, he held her gaze with his own. "Too hard and too fast definitely not the way to begin. Slowly, steadily. An exploration of the terrain, followed by a well-executed penetration of the area, that's the way to begin when saving an Aussie."

Her lips parted and Joseph could see the ragged way she drew breath into her body. "Then after the beginning it gets hard?"

He unzipped his jacket and shucked it off, placing it on the seat beside him as he took a step closer to her. "It's already hard. Very hard."

She swallowed. "Hard is good. I'm always up for a challenge. It's why I like saving Aussies so much."

"Glad to hear that," Rob said, stepping into the cabin and swinging the door shut behind him. He looked at them both over the armful of broken branches and twigs he held against his chest. "Wait. We're talking about sex, aren't we?"

Chapter Three

Anna held her breath, trying—in vain, she realized—to slow her heart rate down to something close to normal. Her pussy throbbed and pulsed and generally carried on in the most disturbing of ways, telling her in no uncertain terms she was horny. Damn horny.

She swallowed again, her mouth dry, her throat thick. The sexual tension mounting between her and Joseph Hudson hadn't abated a bit with Rob's unexpected arrival. No, to the contrary, the moment he'd entered the cabin and made his presence known, she'd almost come there and then.

She studied both of them, knowing one of them was going to make the first move.

Joseph.

Her gaze slid to the taller man, her pulse quickening when she looked at him. Damn, he was stunning. He made Brad Pitt look ugly. Not just tall and lean, but broad shouldered and slightly scruffy, the bristles on his jaw and chin adding to the overall charm, the messy tumble of sandy-blond hair falling over his forehead heightening that charm until the crotch of her panties were sodden.

Oh boy, Anna. You got it bad already.

The loud thud of branches hitting the floor made her start, and she blinked, her gaze snapping to Rob just in time to see him remove his gloves and step over the pile of dead wood at his feet to close the distance between them. "Let me begin to show our appreciation for saving us," he said, his fingers skimming her cheek as he cupped her jaw in his hand.

A flutter of disappointment danced in her belly for a brief moment, like a hundred butterflies had suddenly taken flight, but she forgot it as soon as Rob's lips brushed hers.

The kiss was gentle and yet, at the same time electric. His breath mingled with hers, the tip of his tongue touching the inner edge of her bottom lip, a slow caress charting a path deeper into her mouth.

She parted her lips, meeting his tongue with hers, her nipples growing hard, her pulse racing away from her.

Oh...

She'd been kissed before. Many times, in fact. As far as looks go, she knew she'd been generously smiled upon. But there was something about the Australian's kiss...a delicate passion she hadn't expected. Almost sad.

The notion made her heart quicken. She moaned, the sound vibrating softly in her throat only to be swallowed by Rob's kiss.

He slid his hands up into her hair, his fingers tangling in the strands, her ponytail preventing him from doing anything more than hold her head. It didn't matter. At this point, the feel of his lips on hers, his tongue on hers, was enough to make her pussy weep.

"Ah, fuck."

The growled curse scraped at the heated desire rolling through her. She pulled away from Rob's kiss, her gaze moving to Joseph where he still stood at the chair. He stared at them both, his nostrils flaring, his jaw clenched tight.

"Think we need to get some heat happening quickly," Rob murmured, his hands slipping from her face as he turned back to his friend.

Anna nodded, unable to find anything to say. Her body ached for more, set alight by Rob's simple, tender kiss. And yet, it was Joseph's hands she hungered. Joseph's lips she wanted to taste next.

God, woman. You're a—

The sound of Rob unzipping his jacket squashed the unsettling thought and she turned away from both of them, sucking in a long, shaking breath. Resting her hands on the bench, she stared hard at the old maps of Wolf Creek pinned to the wall before her. *Be sure you know where this is going, Anna. Be certain before you commit.*

"Why Wolf Creek?" she asked, needing to hear something apart from the rustling sounds of the two men behind her moving about. She didn't know if they were undressing, rearranging the cabin's meager furniture or preparing to reenact the Battle of Gettysburg, although seeing as they were Australians, that was unlikely. The battle of...of...damn, did Australia even have any battles?

You're babbling in your head. Do you know that?

"There's a Wolf Creek in Australia," Rob answered, his voice calm, relaxed. "Well, a Wolf Creek Crater. Thought we'd see the reverse of ours over here."

"The snowboarding's better here though," Joseph continued, his voice almost a facsimile of Rob's. Almost. "Not as rocky. Or dusty."

Rob laughed. "Or hot."

Hot. Anna touched her hand to her throat at the word, her skin flushed beneath her fingers. Was it hot in here? Or was it just the surreal situation she'd found herself in?

"That oughta do it."

A dull clunk followed Rob's statement and she turned around, surprised to find them both standing beside the heater, stripped of their jackets and holding out their palms to the heater's flue.

She gazed at them, or rather, the lean muscled strength of their torsos revealed by the snug tautness of their thermal T-shirts. Her mouth went dry and it took her a while to realize the air in the cabin was no longer icy cold.

"You got the heater working?"

Joe gave her a lopsided smile, rubbing his palms together in such a way his shoulder and arm muscles rippled. "Yeah. The pilot light just needed a little encouragement."

She licked her lips, the room's rising temperature making her skin prickle. Or was that the layers of clothing she wore? Or the sight of Joseph and Rob with less clothing than her?

Damn, they were good looking.

And complete strangers. So why did she feel so safe with them?

Why was she just about to do the unthinkable with them?

Her gaze slipped to Joseph again, knowing he held the answer even if she couldn't decipher it yet.

"How 'bout we help you with your clothing?"

Rob's murmur tickled her ear and she started, more than a little stunned to discover he'd somehow moved to stand behind her without her even noticing.

Too busy staring at Joseph?

Warm hands smoothed up her back, over her shoulders. His fingers slid up the sensitive column of her neck, brushing at her nape before skimming back down to the neckline of her jacket. There was a slight tug, and before she knew it, her jacket slipped from her body, falling to her feet in a crumpled heap of fluro-magenta.

She watched Joseph watching her, his nostrils flaring again, the muscles in his jaw bunched.

I want him to kiss me.

Rob's hands travelled her shoulders, barely touching her. The slight caress of his palms on her arms through the thin material of her thermal sent a shiver up her spine. She pulled in a shaky breath, her nipples once again hard. Oh, God.

"C'mon, Joe," Rob spoke against her neck, his lips warm on her flushed skin. "Don't make me say it."

Say what? Anna wanted to ask, but she couldn't. The way Rob's hands moved over her shoulders, her arms, down to her palms and back up to her shoulders again seemed to have stolen her words. It was a gentle caress that somehow still spoke of urgency.

Joseph swallowed once, twice, his Adam's apple working up and down his throat. And then he was standing right in front of her, so close she could feel his body heat seep into her. "You don't have to, mate," he said, holding her gaze with his cookie-brown eyes. "Not at all."

Joseph lowered his head and brushed his lips over hers. The kiss sang of such sweet hesitation her heart stopped for a still moment, only to burst into fevered flight when he snaked his arms around her waist and yanked her against his body with a growl.

His mouth crushed hers. His tongue plunged past her lips, mating with hers, battling it with possessive hunger.

So, there is an Australian battle after all. And I'm a part of it.

The surreal, absurd thought wafted through Anna's head, and she whimpered, curling her arms around Joseph's neck to press her hips to his. His cock rammed against the flat plane of her belly, a rigid, stiff pole not even remotely hidden by the bulk of his snow pants. Its size and width made her head swim, or perhaps that was the feel of Rob's hands working their way down her waist to the band of her own trousers.

"You have a fucking hot body," Rob told her, his fingers working their way between her and Joseph until they dipped below the elastic band of her pants. "I saw it last night in the bar. Couldn't miss it thanks to the tight jeans you wore." He slipped his fingers closer to the mound of her sex, his other hand holding her hip as he pressed his groin to her ass. "The tighter T-shirt."

Rob pushed his hips forward, his erection—as long and as impressive as Joseph's—nudging the crevice of her ass cheeks through her snow pants. "Still," he whispered against her ear, lips nipping her earlobe as he did so, "I think I'd like to see more of it."

With a gentle but insistent tug, he pulled her back to his hips as his fingers moved to her waistband. He inched it down over her hips. Her thighs.

Joseph broke the kiss and stepped away from her a step to stare at what his friend had revealed. "Jesus Christ," he said, the words choked. "I knew you would look like this."

She stood between them, her torso covered in a thin, shell-pink thermal top, her legs bared to their hungry inspection. Rob stroked the back of her thigh, his thumb tracing a languid line over the curves of her butt cheeks. Her panties—skimpy and black—offered little protection from the slow contact, and she let out a ragged breath, feeling her crotch grow damp.

Joseph's nostrils flared again. "I can smell your desire, Anna." His stare roamed her body, the thin space-age material of her top was so stretched against her nipples it felt like a caress. "I can see it." He raised his hands and took her breasts in each, rolling the pad of his thumbs over her puckered nipples. The contact caused her bra—a silky little thing that was highly unsuitable for skiing and matched her panties perfectly—to scrape against each one. She hitched in another breath and gazed up at him.

"And I want to taste it," Rob said behind her.

Joseph's lips curled into a lopsided grin. "Me too."

He pushed her backward, her surprised shout turning into laughter as Rob scooped her off her feet, carried her over to the old cot in the far corner and dumped her there unceremoniously. "Now don't think you're staying there, Anna." He grinned, dimple flashing. "This is just so I can take your boots off."

With a flourish, he dropped into a crouch. His hands snared her right ankle to lift her leg up, gravity fighting him as it pulled on the awkward weight of her ski boot. Her pulse slammed in her neck as he flipped open the straps, one by one, each sudden release of pressure on her ankle an undeniable announcement of what was about to happen.

Her first ménage.

With two men from Australia, no less.

Well, you do believe in taking life by the balls and living the fuck out of it, don't you?

Her breath shuddered from her in a trembling laugh, the sound becoming a soft groan when Rob at last slipped her boot from her foot. "One down," he muttered, his thumbs kneading the arch of her foot for an agonizingly exquisite second.

"One to go," Joseph murmured from his place beside the heater.

She slid her gaze to his face, the sight of him still standing in the exact spot he'd kissed her was for some reason the sexiest thing she'd seen. He watched her, his arms loosely crossed over his broad chest, his legs splayed slightly. Everything about him spoke of extreme confidence, almost ruthless poise, except his eyes. His eyes spoke of another Joseph. One burning up with want, and yet still tempered by hesitation. Whatever he did to be "loaded", she didn't doubt he did it well. His body language radiated utter control. But his eyes... If it was possible, the uncertainty in his eyes made his composed *sang-froid* so much more desirable. So much more goddamn sexy.

The sensation of her left foot being elevated turned her attention back to Rob, and she held her breath as he released the fasteners on her remaining boot and slid it from her foot. He pressed his thumbs into her arch before smoothing his hands up her now exposed ankles. He smiled at her as he hooked his fingers over the tops of her thick, woolen socks. "I will give you a foot massage later. One so good it'll make you come, but for now..."

He yanked her sock from her foot, the abrupt action dislodging her semi-seated position on the cot.

She dropped backward, the cabin's toasty air kissing her newly bare toes a microsecond before Rob touched his lips to them. For an insane moment, all Anna could think about was how sweaty her feet would be after skiing for so long. And then even that thought was lost as the man snared the waistline of her trousers and removed them as efficiently as he'd removed her left sock.

"Oh, Jesus Christ, you look so good."

It was Joseph who moaned the proclamation. Still from his place by the heater. The raw hunger in his voice flooded her pussy with fresh moisture, turned her clit to a nub of throbbing flesh.

"That she does," Rob agreed, straightening from his crouch enough to kneel between her legs. His hands found her inner thighs and he inched them farther apart, the tips of his fingers teasing her folds through the sodden crotch of her panties. "And she is so very wet for us."

Anna's breath turned shallow. Choppy.

This was a kind of torture. She'd never wanted to come as badly as she did now, and all they'd done—all *Rob* had done—was remove her boots and trousers. For Pete's sake, she was still wearing her underpants. How could she be so close to coming while still wearing her underpants? While still being essentially untouched by either of them?

"Please," she whimpered, the word surprising her.

Rob chuckled, dimple flashing. "Please what, Anna

McCarthy?"

She closed her eyes and arched her back, just enough to draw her crotch closer to his fingers. "Please..."

"I think she wants me to lick her out, Hudo." Rob's breath fanned her inner left thigh, just above her knee. A heartbeat later, his lips brushed the skin a little higher. "What do you think?"

"Fuck," Anna heard Joseph groan. "I think you're right."

"Is that what you want, Anna?" Rob's breath tickled the curve of flesh where her thigh dipped into her groin. His hands pressed gently on her knees, holding her still. "Do you want me to fuck your pussy with my tongue?"

She let out another ragged breath and nodded.

"Say it aloud."

Joseph's raw command made her already rapid heart thump faster. "I want Rob to tongue-fuck me," she said, trying to lift her ass off the cot. "Now."

Before the single syllable fell from her lips, Rob's tongue stoked over her clit through the cotton of her panties.

She cried out, ribbons of pleasure unfurling through her core. Her back arched, and this time Rob let it, his hands taking advantage of her upward thrust to slide beneath her butt and cup her ass cheeks. He stabbed at her shielded clit again, working the little point of flesh through her underpants. The friction of material on her flesh, drenched from her own juices and Rob's tongue, sent new ribbons of pleasure chasing the first, twisting and binding around them until ropes of tension knotted in the pit of her belly. Driving her so quickly toward an orgasm her lips tingled.

"Oh, God," she panted, burying her hands in the Australian's thick black hair, holding his head for fear he'd do something foolish like try and remove his mouth from her pussy.

She heard Joseph moan from his position by the heater, a rustling noise joining the strangled sound. She wanted to look at him, she wanted to see if the noise was what she suspected, she wanted to see the aching want she knew would be blazing in his eyes, but she couldn't. The pleasure of Rob's tongue rolling over and over her still-cotton-covered clit overwhelmed her, and all she could do was lie on the cot and let it consume her. "Oh, God, yes."

And still Rob's tongue worked her sex. No penetration, no skin-to-skin contact, just his tongue stroking her clit through the sodden material of her underpants. Just his hands pressed to her knees, holding her legs spread. Two simple things, and she was going to come. Now.

The first detonation ripped through her sex, her inner muscles clamping down on a cock that wasn't there. She cried out, aching to be filled even as her pussy gushed with cream and her clit throbbed with pleasure.

The second detonation hit her harder, spiking wet electricity into her sex and through her body. She grabbed at the cot's course blanket beneath her, fists bunching the wool until her knuckles popped. "Fuck, yes!" she called, rolling her head from side to side. Rob's assault on her protected clit was a rhythmic echo of each constricting pulse shuddering through her.

The third, the fourth, the fifth detonation crashed over her, followed by too many to count. It swept her away, pummeling her until all she could do was whimper and beg for him to stop, beg for mercy, beg for more.

With one sudden yank on her sopping underpants, Rob stripped her lower body naked.

Chapter Four

Joseph stood and watched Rob plunge his tongue into Anna's spread sex. Her moans and gasping breaths sank into his ears, driving him almost insane. His cock ached in his pants. No, not just ached. The bloody thing was an agonizing rod of rigid lust. He'd never been so hard, so fucking ready to erupt. He'd never thought watching his best mate give head to a woman could be so arousing, but holy shit, watching Rob go down on Anna...

He shifted his feet, trying to find a better position to take the pressure off his dick.

You know the only thing that will do that is either Anna or your own hand, don't you?

He bit back a low groan at the thought. He'd never wanted to sink his cock into anyone as badly as he wanted to sink it into Anna McCarthy, but at this point, he couldn't move.

Not just because he didn't know how to approach the two people so thoroughly enjoying each other, but because he didn't want to stop watching Rob fuck Anna with his mouth.

Jesus, Hudson, is this what you've been missing all this time?

The twisting knot in his gut and the hot tension in his balls told him the answer was no. He didn't doubt watching Rob in a three-way would turn him on. But watching Rob fuck just anyone? No. It was Anna McCarthy that made his prick so goddamn hard. She'd done so this morning in the lodge, and all he'd done was watch her walk from the cafeteria. Watching her lie stretched on her back, her bare legs spread, her breasts thrusting upward, her nipples stabbing at the material of her thermal...watching his best mate devour her cunt... Christ, there was something in that sight he couldn't turn away from.

Anna.

She was perfect. Slim, athletic. Tiny in a pocket-rocket kind of way. He knew she was a park ranger, but it wasn't her authority that got him off. No, it was the soft kindness in her eyes, the crinkles on her nose when she laughed. The way she moved...

Hell, man, you've only known her for all of about an hour. Probably not even that.

But it didn't matter. He knew the second he saw her in the lodge that he wanted her. Wanted to get to know her. As corny as it was, she spoke to him without uttering a word. And now here he was, watching Rob bury his head between her thighs.

It should have made Joseph angry. It should have made him jealous.

It didn't. It made him fucking hard. And his breath so fucking shallow.

He shifted his feet again, his cock straining at his boxers. He'd removed his trousers, the thick snow pants too restrictive. He'd let them fall to the floor and kicked them aside. He wanted to curl his fingers around his dick and pump it until he came, but he controlled himself. He waited. For what, he didn't know—hell, this was all so new, so unfamiliar to him. He waited until the moment he would know it was time to move. In the same way he did at work, knowing when to make the deal, when to sit back and watch his staff, or his competitors.

Rob was neither. Sure, he worked for him, but he'd never been his staff. And as for now, he wasn't his competitor, even if his mouth was thrusting and lapping at the pussy of the woman Joseph had instantly desired.

Joseph shifted again, his stare moving from Rob's face pressed to Anna's pussy to Anna's face. Her eyes were closed, her lips parted. She grabbed at the blanket beneath her, holding it in two tight fists. The tip of her tongue slipped over her bottom lip, making it glisten in the cabin's low light. He sucked in a breath. It was a powerful sight and he wanted to see it closer.

He needed to see it closer.

Not just see it. He wanted to feel it. Wanted to feel the moisture from her tongue on her lip. Wanted to feel it on his own.

Oh, yes.

He moved, and in two long strides he was standing at the side of the cot.

"She's beautiful, isn't she, mate?"

Rob's low murmur jerked his stare from Anna's lips, and he studied his best mate for a short second.

"Show her how beautiful you think she is."

He didn't need to hear the rest. He didn't even know if Rob was going to say it. He didn't need to be dared. Not at all.

He dropped to his knees and his thick, stiff cock banged on the side of the cot. It should have hurt. It didn't. Nothing hurt except the overwhelming need to kiss Anna's lips.

A soft moan slipped from her and her back arched a little as Rob did something she liked. The move tilted her chin a fraction higher, turning her neck into a smooth, elegant curve, and it was too much. He lowered his head to hers and took possession of her lips.

They were soft, as soft as her moan, and warm. So very warm. She gasped, his presence no doubt surprising her, and her hands came up to his chest, his shoulder. She snaked her arms around his neck and pulled him closer to her, her tongue coming out to meet his before he could penetrate her mouth.

Hot tension shot into his balls. She was kissing him. With far more aggression than he'd imagined. Far more demanding urgency. He liked it. Hell, did he like it.

Her tongue mated with his, fierce and wild. She nipped at his bottom lip, each bite harder than the last. Shards of sharp pain sliced down through his body and he couldn't stop his own moan vibrating low in his chest.

"Bloody hell, Hudo," Rob growled from his left. "I never thought the sight of you kissing a woman would turn me on so much."

Joseph tore his mouth from Anna's lips and shot his friend a quick look. "And I never thought I'd get off watching you tongue-fuck a woman either." He turned back to Anna, gazing down at her. "Especially this one."

"What's so special about this one?" she whispered, her direct grey eyes holding him prisoner. She skimmed her hand down his chest, over his belly, until her fingers brushed the engorged length of his erection trapped by his boxers.

Joseph sucked in a swift breath, black swirls of pleasure blossoming in his vision as fresh blood surged to his cock.

Rob laughed. "You, my fine little American, caught my mate's eye. That never happens. Old Hudo here has always been too busy with work, to controlled and reserved to fall head over heels in lust before."

Anna brushed her fingers over Joseph's cock again and he ground his teeth, fighting the dire urge to grab her hand and make her hold its length in a punishing grip.

"Is that true?"

He nodded, unable to deny it. Hell, he was a workaholic. The only fun he ever had was with Rob. Usually after the words, "I dare you." Until now...

"I wanted you the second I saw you," he said, pushing his hips forward into Anna's teasing fingers.

"The feeling's entirely mutual."

Her whispered confession stabbed into him. At the exact moment she stopped teasing his dick and took his erection in her hand. Raw pleasure washed through his whole body. He shuddered, his balls swelling, his sphincter contracting.

"Fuck a duck, Anna," he ground out. "If you squeeze that too hard, I'm going to come."

She grinned at him, the sides of her mouth curling. "Do you have something else planned?"

He grinned back. "Yes, actually."

Without preamble, he snared the hemline of her thermal shirt and yanked it up over her head.

"Oh, Hudo," Rob laughed behind him, "I knew you'd be good at this."

He let his gaze roam over Anna's newly exposed torso, both infuriated and aroused by the silky sheen of her black bra concealing her breasts. He reached out his hand and traced one fingertip along the ribbon-edged cup of her left breast. "I've always been one to rise to the challenge."

Anna moaned slightly, her skin rippling at the barely there touch of his finger. She stared up at him through half-lidded eyes, her hands resting in loose fists beside her head.

"That you have been, my friend," Rob agreed. "And one for making bad puns. Now, if you'll excuse me, I have a sweet, hot, tight and very wet pussy to eat."

Joseph's ass tightened again on Rob's dirty proclamation. He hooked his fingers under the edge of Anna's bra and held her gaze with his. "*Bon appétit.*"

He saw Rob move from the corner of his eye, knowing by Anna's sudden intake of breath exactly when his friend's tongue touched her folds.

"Oh." The single word fell from her on a shaky breath and she arched her back, her knees bending as she placed her feet on Rob's shoulders. "Yes."

Joseph swallowed, his heart thumping. Hot lust surged through him and he tugged on the edge of her bra, working the soft cup to the side. He pulled it from her breast until her nipple popped free.

It was perfect. A beautiful dusky pink, round and pebbled and just waiting to be sucked. By him. He lowered his head, taking the puckered tip in his mouth.

"Oh, yes," Anna moaned again, louder this time, her hands finding their way to Joseph's hair. She tangled her fingers in the cool strands, holding him hard to her breast.

Pleasure threaded through her. Twin ribbons of exquisite pleasure. One unfurling from between her legs where Rob's tongue darted in and out of her sex and rolled over and over her clit, the other from her breasts, where Joseph's lips and tongue fondled her nipple, circling it in gentle laps and nipping it in playful bites.

Two ribbons flowing through her body to meet in the very center of her core. They threaded and twisted and knotted together until each ribbon became indefinable, indistinguishable.

"Oh, fuck." The expletive fell from her lips in a ragged whisper. She rarely used such language, not because it offended her sensibilities, but because she'd never felt a need. But what the two Australians were doing to her now, the absolute...ecstasy they wrought on her body...

"Oh, fuck me."

She arched her back, knotting her fingers in Joseph's hair and shoving her pussy harder to Rob's tongue. The man between her legs chuckled, sending wicked vibrations into her sex. She fisted her hands harder in Joseph's hair as the thrumming in her center mounted quickly.

Joseph's tongue flicked at her nipple and she whimpered, the sensations from such a simple caress almost undoing her. God, what would she do when he actually *sucked* her nipple? What would she do when he stopped teasing her and truly began to—

Joseph sucked on her nipple. Hard.

"Oh, oh, fuck!"

She cried out, her breast swelling with indescribable warmth.

Joseph suckled on her breast, his right hand cupping it towards his mouth, his left hand kneading the other. He pinched her nipple, rolling it between his finger tips, his actions echoing those of his mouth.

As if he knew exactly the rhythm his friend set, Rob lapped at her pussy and clit the same way, delving into her folds only to withdraw and lick at her inner thighs.

She rolled her head, holding Joseph to her breast even as she wished them both to stop. She couldn't take this much pleasure. She couldn't. Her body wasn't made for this. Made to be consumed, worshiped, reveled and—

Before the delirious thought could finish, Rob's fingers curled over her hips as he lifted them a little higher and stroked his tongue over the tight hole of her anus.

"Oh, oh!" She bucked, concentrated, forbidden rapture spearing into her.

Joseph lifted his head and smiled down at her through heavily lidded eyes. She almost expected him to say something—anything that would save her from being taken away by the onslaught of sensations his friend's tongue was creating, but he didn't. Instead, he took her mouth with his in a crushing kiss before returning his attention to her breast, the left one this time. He closed his lips over its pebbled nipple and bit at it. Shards of delicious pain detonated in her chest, blossoms of constricting pleasure in her pussy.

"Oh, God," she moaned, her breath so shallow, so rapid her head swam, "please, I can't..."

She couldn't finish. Not when Joseph suckled so greedily on her breast. Not when Rob lapped so hungrily at her ass.

She thrust her hips higher, the ribbons of pleasure knotting in her center. Growing tight. Impossible to unravel. Her orgasm was coming. She couldn't stop it. And still, the two men sucked and licked and bit.

Rob's fingers dug harder into her hips, his tongue not just lapping at her anus, but pushing on it. Pressing at its opening. She bucked, the unexpected shockwaves of sensations stealing her breath.

And scaring her.

She'd never been touched there. Not by finger, tongue or cock.

"No," she panted, shaking her head. Rob paused, his fingers relaxing—a little—on her hips, the tip of his tongue resting on her sphincter. She tugged at Joseph's hair, wanting to look into his face. His eyes. Needing to see his warmth.

He lifted his head and gazed at her again, his nostrils flaring, his eyes ablaze. "Do you want us to stop?"

His question, spoken with such gentle concern, made her heart hammer. She shook her head, combing her fingers through his tousled hair. "No."

"But you need us to slow down?"

The fluttering in Anna's belly intensified. How did he know? How was he so in tune with her already? She closed her eyes for a second and released a shaking sigh. "It's just...I've never..." She faltered over the confession, looking back up at Joseph. God, how did she say this without sounding so naïve? So...so...virginal?

"And we've never rushed anyone," Rob spoke from between her legs, saving her from doing so. His hands smoothed up her waist, over her stomach and back down to her hips once again, Anna couldn't believe how quickly the two men knew her. It was intense.

"We've never made them do something they don't want," he continued. "Well, *I* haven't. Hudo here has been known to rush a customer or two into signing a contract. And he makes plenty of people do things they don't want to do. Bloody pushy business mogul that he is."

Joseph laughed. "Up yours, Thorton. Mr. I Dare You."

The unexpected moment took Anna by surprise. The apprehension twisting into her core dissipated and she gazed up at Joseph. "I'm sorry."

He shook his head, tracing small circles around the nipple of her left breast with his fingertips. "Don't be." The sides of his mouth curled. "Trust me, I know all about being caught up in Rob's enthusiasm."

"And I'm entirely enthusiastic about making Anna come," Rob stated, and Anna couldn't stop her small giggle bubbling up the back of her throat. "And I'm going to do it by totally and thoroughly exploring this gorgeous pussy right—" he blew a fine stream of breath on her labia, "—here."

He dipped his tongue into her folds, and she gasped, the ribbons of pleasure unfurling through her once more.

She tightened her fists in Joseph's hair, holding him to her. Something told her he was about to move away and she didn't want him to. Not at all. She looked into his eyes, the pit of her belly flip-flopping at the urgent hunger she saw in their light-brown depths. "Kiss me?"

He grinned, a boyish, roguish grin. "I can do that."

He took her lips with his, his tongue delving into her mouth as he smoothed one hand over her body. His fingers explored her throat, her shoulder, followed the strap of her bra until they reached its cup. He flicked at her nipple through the straining satin, chuckling against her lips as the nub of flesh instantly puckered into a rock-hard point. She chuckled back, the sound lost in her gasp as Rob sucked her clit into his mouth.

Raw pleasure threaded through her and she pulled Joseph

deeper into the kiss, parting her lips to him completely.

Oh, God. Here we go again.

The incredulous thought whispered through her mind. She didn't think her orgasm would come back to her so quickly after stopping the two men, but it had. And tenfold. She curled her toes, planting her feet harder on Rob's shoulders.

Here we go...

Rob sucked on her clit, nibbled it, sucked again.

Joseph sucked on her tongue, pinched her nipple and squeezed her breast.

Here we...

Here we...

An orgasm detonated in Anna's core. Wild and hard and fast. She thrust her hips upward, tearing her lips from Joseph's, unable to hold back her cries. "Yes, yes!"

She writhed on the cot, holding Joseph as if he was her life support, refusing to let him go as Rob milked her pussy of its cream.

Chapter Five

"I want to come so fucking much I think my dick's about to burst."

Joseph's choked voice stirred something tight in Rob's balls. He lapped one last slow, languid stroke of his tongue along Anna's swollen pussy-lips and then lifted his head and cast his best friend a steady inspection.

Joseph knelt beside Anna's head, his jaw bunched tight, his chest heaving. There was a protective air about him, as if he'd taken upon himself to guard the woman stretched out on the cot between them. It was typical Hudo behaviour—he may be *Time Australia*'s Businessman of the Year, he may be a ridiculously wealthy, ruthless CEO, but Joseph Hudson was always, *always*, a guardian. Fuck, he'd taken care of Rob so many times, Rob had lost count. And yet, he couldn't contain the need Anna McCarthy had awakened in him. Rob could see that. Try as hard as he might, Joseph couldn't be the gentleman here. He wanted Anna too damn bad.

"I can understand that," Rob said, leaning back from Anna's most perfectly delicious pussy. He slid his fingertip along the velvet edge of one of her folds, his prick twitching at the sight of her ass constricting at his touch. "I'm pretty bloody hard myself."

He was. Fucking hard. His cock felt like it was about to burst a seam.

But he knew he had to let Joseph and Anna call the next shot. The urge to flip Anna onto her stomach, shove her legs apart and sink his dick into her sodden sex scorched through him with such potent force he could feel his balls rise up in anticipation. But he held back. Controlled himself. He was always the aggressor in sex, but tonight he needed Joe to take the lead.

He needed to know his best mate could leap at life when he was gone.

Jesus, that's a morose thought, Thorton.

It was, and he shoved it aside, sliding his hands over the tops of Anna's thighs and rising to his knees.

"I think I can do something about that," she said. She shifted on the cot, and Rob's nuts rose up higher as the smooth, toned length of her inner thighs slid over his shoulders. He watched her as she moved on the cot, her body—no doubt the result of hours and hours of skiing—the stuff of a hot-blooded man's fantasy. Everything was where it was meant to be, and it was where it was meant to be with bloody sublime perfection.

"Christ," Hudo groaned as Anna settled herself on her knees before Rob, presenting her most gorgeous derrière to Joseph. Rob grinned, unable to miss the way the tented front of his friend's boxers danced.

"You have the sexiest arse..." Joseph murmured.

Anna looked at Joseph over her shoulder and shuffled a little closer to him. "I love how you say ass."

Joseph snorted. "If I say it again, will you let me bite yours? Arse. Arse. Arse."

Anna laughed and the soft, relaxed sound sent tendrils of tension into Rob's gut and groin. He liked the sound. A lot.

"I've often wondered," she said, turning back to Rob. "What it would be like to make two men come at the same time."

Before Rob could think of something witty to say—a first for him, really—she placed her palm against his stomach, just below his navel. "Take your shirt off, Rob. And your trousers."

Her order, spoken with such authoritarian weight, made his mouth water. He did as she commanded, stumbling sideways as he tugged first his snowboarding boots and then his socks from his feet. She laughed again. Hudo groaned, though whether it was from the sight of Rob's uncharacteristic clumsiness or the pain in his massive erection, Rob couldn't tell.

Finally stripped bare, he stood before Anna and held out his arms. His cock poked straight up, long and much thicker and stiffer than it'd ever been. "What happens now, Ranger McCarthy?"

"I'll tell you," Joseph suddenly growled, and Rob blinked as his friend crawled onto the cot behind Anna and hauled her back against his body. "I make her come again with my cock, while she makes us both come."

Anna whimpered, her lips parting and her pupils dilating as Joseph closed his hands over her breasts. She straightened, leaning her back against him as she snaked her arms up around his neck and turned her face to his.

He kissed her, squeezing and cupping her breasts as he did so, lifting and pushing them together.

"Fucking oath," Rob murmured, closing the distance between him and the cot. "I like that plan." He ran his hands over Anna's torso, loving the taut feel of her skin. He lowered his head and placed a kiss first on the subtle line that ran down the middle of her belly, moving down to the dip of her naval and lower. Her trimmed pubic hair tickled his chin, and for a brief moment he contemplated slipping his tongue into her folds again. She tasted so bloody good his mouth filled with saliva at the possibility. Instead, he slid his lips back up her stomach and over her ribcage until they found her breast. Joseph's hands cupped them together, his friend torturing her nipples with the pad of his thumbs as he continued to kiss her.

"Let me suck her, Hudo," Rob said, and Joseph removed his thumbs straight away and held her breasts still for him.

Rob took one of her nipples in his mouth, sucking on it hard.

"Oh, God," Anna burst out, her words muffled by Joseph's lips. "Wasn't this meant to be me pleasuring you two?"

"You are, babe," Rob heard Joseph growl. "Can't you feel how bloody hard I am for you?"

Rob's dick jerked and he wrapped one hand around it. He'd been as stiff as a pole now for what felt like a lifetime. If he didn't come soon...

A fresh wave of respect surged through him for his best

mate. Hudo had been harder for longer. He'd been hard for this woman last night, and Rob didn't doubt he'd been hard since she'd arrived on the slope, right royally pissed at both of them.

Rob dragged his mouth to Anna's other nipple and sucked on it. Joseph's thumbs dug into his cheek and he started, surprised at how turned on the innocent contact made him. He'd shared everything with Joe. His Tonka trucks, his skateboard, his lunch, his terror over his first wet dream. When it came to Joseph, Rob didn't mind sharing. And now, they were sharing a woman, a beautiful, feisty, sweet woman.

There was nothing more he could share.

Nothing more he wanted to.

He pumped his cock, feeling his balls flood hard. He couldn't hold out much longer. Anna's breasts were too perfect, her nipples too divine. The way Joe cupped and squeezed them was perfect, an offering of the most delectable meal from the gods.

With a guttural moan, he closed his free hand over Joseph's right and pushed Anna's breasts even closer together, flicking one nipple and then the other over and over again.

"Oh...oh..." Her breath left her in stripped gasps. She writhed in Joseph's arms, the air heavy with her musk. "Oh, God."

"Fuck, Rob," Joe ground out, "I'm going to blow soon. Watching you suck her tits like that..."

Rob tore his mouth from Anna's nipples and stared up at them both. "If you don't want to be showered in come, sweetheart," he growled, "I suggest we think about a change of position. Or some raincoats."

She laughed. "Raincoats. And a change of position."

She shoved at Rob's chest, and before he knew what she was doing, she'd slipped from Joseph's hands and wrapped her fingers around Rob's erection, trapping his hand against his own cock. "Position change," she said with a wiggle of her backside as she dragged his hand down his length and back up again. "Now tell me you were talking about condoms when you said raincoats."

Rob's head swam, something very akin to raw rapture rushing through his veins. He was an adrenaline junkie. He'd base jumped from "El Capitan" in Yosemite. He'd swum with the sharks in the Tasmanian Bite. Fuck, he'd friggin' run with the bulls in Pamplona. But holy shit, nothing compared to this. He was about to get a blowjob from a woman while she was being fucked by his best mate.

He shot Joe a quick look. "Grab my backpack, Hudo."

Nostrils flaring, Joseph climbed from the cot and crossed the floor, out of Rob's line of sight. He heard his friend unzip the pack he'd thrown on the floor after first entering the cabin, followed by the rustling of its contents.

"Hurry up, mate," he ground out through clenched teeth. That Anna was continuing to make him pump his own dick didn't help his tenuous state. "Don't want to embarrass myself here."

The woman sending him mad with pleasure increased the pressure of his grip, squeezing his erection more firmly. "There's nothing embarrassing about *this*, Mr. Thorton."

"Jesus, Rob," Joseph laughed behind him and Rob ground his teeth together harder. "How'd you get Vegemite sandwiches through customs?"

"I didn't, you moron," Rob burst out, his balls so swollen he could barely think. If Anna pumped his cock one more time... "I made them this morning in the lodge's kitchen. While you were jerking off in the shower. Now hurry the fuck up!"

Joseph laughed again, and then he was standing at Anna's side once more, a small gold foil square in his hand.

"Raincoat?" she asked, looking up at him.

He smiled and nodded. "Raincoat."

Anna's own lips curled into a slow smile. "Care to put it on? I've got my hands full."

"And she really means full," Rob rasped. "This fucker's bigger and harder than it's ever been. So if the pair of you could just hurry along?"

Joseph laughed, and even in his pleasure-tortured state, Rob recognized it. Joseph was in love. Just like that.

A momentary shard of pain shot into Rob's chest—loss for something he didn't want to analyze at this moment in time—and he gave his best friend a long, level stare. Christ, he loved him. And if it was at all possible where he was going, he was gonna miss the shit out of him.

"Ready, Mr. Thorton?" Anna's low, husky question jerked his stare back to her face, just in time to watch her part her lips and slide them over the purple head of his cock.

"Oh, *fuck*!"

His groaned roar bounced around the room. If he was a gambling man, he'd put money on it being heard on the top of Knife Ridge peak as well.

Anna's mouth enveloped his length and she sucked, drawing him deeper. Deeper.

Jesus, he was going to come soon.

He let his head lull back, incapable of finding the strength to hold it up, and gazed blankly at the cabin's ceiling, the wooden support beams doing nothing to draw his attention away from the concentrated pleasure of Anna's mouth and teeth and tongue on his dick. She sucked him harder, sliding farther down in length until the dome of his cock pressed the back of her throat.

"Christ, that is so goddamn hot to watch."

Joseph's mutter scraped at Rob's flaying control and he rolled his head to find his friend stripped naked. His body, leaner and far more muscled than a CEO of any business should have, glistened with sweat in the cabin's muted light. His cock jutted up from between his thighs with stunning insistency.

"Bit horny, mate?" Rob asked on a ragged breath, watching Joseph roll the latex sheath over his erection with shaking hands.

Joseph's nostril flared, his attention flicking briefly to Anna's head, his Adam's apple jerking up and down in his throat as he watched her work Rob's cock. "You could say that."

Without further warning, he pressed his face to Anna's pussy.

She reacted quickly and wildly to the sudden contact, moaning around Rob's length with such fevered force he felt the vibrations all the way to the base of his spine. It was too much. If he didn't start drawing images in his head soon of his hairy

Aunt Beryl in a bikini, complete with mole and saggy appendix scar, he was going to come before Joe even entered Anna. And he didn't want that.

He wanted to go at the same time as his best mate. And he wanted them *both* to go just as Anna did.

"I know you're having fun back there, Hudo," he muttered, unable to stop the quickening of his thrusts in Anna's mouth—Christ, her mouth was talented—"But I need you to get with the game plan here, okay."

For a moment, Joe's head didn't leave its place between Anna's thighs, and by the way she was moaning and sucking harder on Rob's dick, something told him Joseph wasn't in any hurry to stop licking her out.

He squeezed his eyes shut, the beginnings of Aunt Beryl forming in his head. God, he didn't want to do *this* either. He didn't want Aunt Beryl in his head when he came. He didn't. It would mess him up for what remained of his life. He didn't want—

Anna's teeth dug into the length of his shaft with sharp pressure, her nails sinking into the backs of his thighs as another wild moan thrummed in the back of her throat. Loud enough to make Rob open his eyes. And see Joseph drive his cock deep into her pussy.

Oh, thank fuck!

Joseph had died and gone to heaven. He must have. How else could he explain the pure, concentrated pleasure searing through his body? He thrust his shaft, engorged beyond pain, into Anna's drenched pussy, the feel of her tight muscles gripping him, sliding over him, almost too much to bear.

The second he'd seen her in the lodge's bar last night he'd wanted to do this. The moment he saw her in the cafeteria this morning he knew he'd have to. Lust at first sight? He didn't know. Lust was too dirty, too temporary. This wasn't lust. With every penetrating stroke into her sex, he knew it. He didn't know what it was yet, but it wasn't lust. It was...more.

The thought made his head swim. He ground his teeth, sliding his hands over Anna's gorgeous backside until he gripped her hips with both hands. He lifted his head and watched her suck on Rob's cock.

Damn, he couldn't believe how turned on it made him. And yet, at the same time, how jealous.

He'd never felt like this. He'd had more than his fair share of lovers—not as many as Rob to be sure, and none as adventurous—but Anna fit him unlike any other.

He drove his length deeper into her sex, wanting to fill her completely. Wanting her to feel how fucking unbelievable they felt together.

She moaned and pushed back into his penetrations, spreading her thighs to take him deeper. The slight shift in position made her pussy clench his cock in a gripping pulse and he bit back a groan, digging his fingertips into her hips instead. It wouldn't take long—he'd shoot his load soon. There really wasn't any way to stop it. He'd been thinking of doing this very thing to Anna since he'd seen her in the lodge. He'd sported a semi-hard-on all day. He'd been hard while dropping out of the helicopter and barging down the side of Knife Ridge Chutes. Hell, even when he'd gone ass-over-tit and eaten snow for a good five hundred meters, his dick had never softened.

He leant forward, laying his stomach on Anna's back, her warm flesh branding his as he smoothed his hands around her side to cup her breasts. He held them loosely, their small but perfect shape slapping against his fingers with every thrust he punched into her. "Jesus, Anna." He swallowed, sliding one hand from her breast, over her belly to stroke his fingers through her trimmed pubic hair. "You feel so damn good. This feels so damn good."

"Ain't that the truth."

Rob's hoarse pant made Joseph smile. His friend was on the verge of losing it. Sweat beaded on Rob's forehead, his stomach jerked in a series of little hiccups and the muscles in his jaw were bunched.

Joseph returned his attention to Anna's face, entranced with the vision of Rob's cock pumping in and out of her mouth. Her lips glistened with moisture and a wave of giddy hunger crashed through him at the memory of those lips against his. Ah, Jesus, she had a beautiful mouth. And she moved it so well over Rob's dick. Just as her pussy moved so well over his.

The soles of his feet began to tingle and he tore his stare from the sight of his friend's cock disappearing into Anna's mouth and pressed his lips to the back of her neck. "Gonna come soon, babe. Can't hold on much longer."

"Me either, Anna." Rob's voice sounded strangled. "I'm about to erupt. If you don't want to take it in your mouth you better stop now."

Anna's body shifted under Joseph, and he lifted his head enough to watch her reach out with one hand and close it around Rob's balls, sliding her mouth deeper down his shaft as she did so.

Rob sucked in a swift breath, his belly quivering. "I take it that's a no for stopping?"

In response, Anna tugged on Rob's balls and wriggled her backside, her pussy muscles pulsing around Joseph's driving length. He groaned out a laugh, pinching her nipple in retaliation. "No fair."

Working his fingers over the hood of her sex, he parted her folds until he found her clit. "You're going to come before we do, babe." He rolled one fingertip over its swollen form and watched her closed eyes squeeze tighter. "We're close, but we're not coming first. Not until you do."

He pressed on her clit again, rubbed it with increasing speed as he pumped his cock harder, faster, deeper into her pussy.

She moaned around Rob's cock, her mounting pleasure not just evident in the sound but in the pulsing pressure of her sex on his dick. He stroked into her faster, rolled his finger over her clit harder. Harder.

"Fuck, Anna, your mouth is so fucking..."

Rob's raw growl got lost in a groan. Joseph saw his friend throw back his head, his nostrils flaring. He knew his best mate's pain. He was there with him—the pain of an orgasm about to explode, not just through his balls and cock, but through his entire body.

"Come for me, Anna," he ground out, rubbing her clit. Sinking his length into her sweet, tight pussy again and again and again. "Come for us now."

He pinched her clit, squeezed it once between thumb and

forefinger. She bucked beneath him, her hips thrashing into a wild, rhythmless spasm. Her orgasm claimed her, possessing her, making her sex constrict around his cock with such gripping force there was nothing he could do but erupt with her.

"Oh, Jesus, yes!" He slammed into her, head back, spine arched, teeth clenched. Wads of his semen spurt from him, pumping into the condom, coating his own dick as Anna's pussy contracted and squeezed. Milking him of his seed with each pulse.

And still he thrust into her, incapable of stopping, the far-off cries of Rob's climax, his best mate's shouts of "fuck, fuck, yes, oh, yes, of fucking yes" only feeding his pleasure. Pushing him higher, higher, higher until he lost cohesion, all solidity, and fractured into a million pinpricks of rapture.

Chapter Six

"Pass me a sandwich, Hudo."

Joseph turned his gaze from Anna where she sat at a rather antiquated communications radio in the far corner of the cabin and grinned at Rob. "You got hollow legs tonight, Thorton?"

Rob leant back in his chair—a wobbly wooden construction more suitable for fire tinder than a place to rest your backside. He crossed his ankles on the desk before him, taking, in Joseph's humble opinion, his life into his hands. "Hey, I'm allowed to be hungry." He wriggled his toes in his own thick fluorescent-green socks, took a mouthful of the beer he held in his hand and then grinned at Joseph. "I expended a lot of energy today."

Joseph gave him a snort before digging around in the backpack at his feet for one of the saran-wrapped sandwiches Rob had packed that morning. His fingers closed around a spongy square and he tossed it to his friend. "That's the last one. You may want to keep a hold of it."

"What?" Rob raised his eyebrows, the very notion of saving food obviously filling him with mock distaste. "Not eat it now?"

Joseph shook his head and laughed, settling himself more comfortably in his own chair next to Rob. He turned his attention back to Anna and watched her flick a couple of the switches on the radio and turn a dial or two. She'd spent the last fifteen minutes trying to make contact with the Wolf Creek base station, cursing the old radio more than once, even giving it a thump every now and again.

He chuckled silently. At some stage of the game, he'd offer her his satellite phone, or draw her attention to the two-way walkie-talkie he couldn't help but see poking out the top of her backpack by the door. But not yet. He suspected the fight with the old radio in the corner was a ruse to gather herself after what they'd just done. Some time to herself to think. That he could understand. What they'd just done was...

Awesome?

Amazing?

Profound?

Life-changing?

All four?

"You really like her, don't you?"

Rob's statement got him to swing his head back to his friend and give him a wry smile. "You could say that."

Rob laughed, placing his beer on the floor beside him before pulling the sandwich in his hand into two uneven pieces. "I could say that? Well, apart from the fact you haven't stopped looking at her for more than two seconds since we...finished...you offered to give her your vegemite sandwich *and* your beer. Gotta be serious when a bloke does that." He smiled at Joseph before taking a bite out of the meal in his right hand. "I know *I've* never given a woman my sandwich and beer before."

Joseph leant forward and snatched the half in Rob's left hand. "Which is why," he said with a wide grin, "you will die a lonely man."

The smile on Rob's face faltered—a split-second twitch Joseph would never have noticed if he didn't know his friend as well as he did. He frowned, a small knot forming in his gut, and gave Rob a level stare. "What's up, mate? Anything you want to tell me?"

A slight tension pulled at the edges of Rob's eyes, almost imperceptible, and then he nodded, leaning farther back in his chair, his snow pants rustling like dry parchment. "Yeah. You owe me half a vegemite sandwich."

"I don't know how you Australians can eat that stuff." Anna walked past the table and dropped into the seat beside Joseph, stopping him from demanding Rob tell him what the hell was up. She reached behind her head, pulled the band from her ponytail, and scruffed up her honey-blonde hair until it fell around her face in a golden mess. "It's vile."

Rob pulled an affronted expression, his eyebrows dipping in melodramatic, wounded pain. "Take it easy, love," he said. "You attack vegemite, you attack Australia."

Joseph studied his friend. For the first time since Anna had arrived on the mountainside not ninety-five percent focused on her. The uneasy knot in his gut rolled over on itself. Rob was hiding something. Rob never hid something. Not from him.

So, why's he doing it now? And what is *it he's hiding?*

"You don't happen to have any Tim Tams in that backpack, do you?" Anna gave the pack at Joseph's feet a hopeful look. "I've heard they're yummy. Especially if you suck hot coffee through them."

"The Tim-Tam Slam." Rob nodded sagely. "A uniquely Australian and truly life-changing experience."

Anna laughed, the relaxed sound easing the knot in Joseph's stomach. Whatever Rob was hiding, it wasn't stopping him being his usual flippant self. Flippant enough for them all to feel completely comfortable in each other's presence despite what they'd shared after such a short space of time. Well, *he* felt comfortable, and seeing as Anna hadn't gone running for her walkie-talkie the second Joseph withdrew his spent dick from her sweet wet sex to radio for help, he kind of figured she was comfortable too.

Actually, comfortable *was* the wrong word, at least to describe his current state. With every second he spent looking at her, he was growing distinctly *un*comfortable. His cock was growing thicker and longer far too quickly for public decency. His snow pants were far too chaffing to sit still and take it like a man.

He shifted on his chair, lurching a little to the side. "Bloody hell," he muttered.

A fine, warm hand pressed on his hip, searing his skin through his trousers, and he looked up from the floor to see Anna smiling at him. "Falling for me so quickly, Joe?"

The question, asked no doubt in jest, sent a shard of

tension straight to Joseph's suddenly very hard cock. He stared at her like a dumb-struck teenager, lost for words.

She gazed back at him, the smile on her lips—her full, totally kissable lips—fading.

"I think the answer to that is yes, Anna McCarthy," Rob offered. "Very much a yes."

She flicked a glance at Rob, but only a quick one, before her attention fixed on Joseph again.

The cabin fell silent, the only sound the night wind rising outside, streaming over the side of the mountain like an icy river. Joseph looked at Anna, his mouth dry. He wanted to say something, but couldn't. Jesus, why was he feeling so flustered? He never felt like this in corporate meetings, staring down bank managers and supply executives. Why couldn't he think of a thing to say now?

Because it's important now, Joseph. It means *something now. What you say next could change the rest of your life.*

He swallowed, a numb pressure growing in his chest, his eyes eating her up. How had this happened? How had he fallen so deeply so quickly?

Fallen where? In love?

Can't be. Not yet. He knew so little about her.

A wild gust of wind slammed against the cabin, shattering the tense silence within with a squealing protest of wood. The windows rattled and Joseph jumped. They *all* jumped. Anna blinked quickly as she jerked in her seat, as if coming out of a trance. Rob burst out into loud, if somewhat nervous laughter.

"So, Ranger McCarthy," Rob said, his socked feet hitting the floor with a dull thud, "we're obviously not heading back to Wolf Creek tonight. What do you suggest we do?"

Anna's cheeks turned pink, a delicate shade that made Joseph want to cup her face in his hands and place his lips on hers.

Deep, Joseph. So deep so damn fast.

She flicked him a quick look, her eyes reflecting something he couldn't decipher, and then turned to Rob. "Poker?"

Rob lifted an eyebrow. "Strip poker?"

Joseph's cock—rapidly growing harder than semi-hard—

pulsed in approval, and he bit back a low groan.

Anna gave Rob an enigmatic little smile. “Strip poker? Isn’t it too cold for strip poker?”

Rob leant forward in his seat, the wood creaking beneath him, a grin playing with the corners of his mouth as he ran a deliberately suggestive inspection over her upper body. “I’m game. Are you?”

She flicked Joseph another look, and he couldn’t miss the way her nipples pinched into rigid points. Nor the way her tongue flicked out to wet her bottom lip. “I’m good at poker.”

Joseph *wasn’t* good at poker. And he was wearing nothing more than a pair of snow pants, socks and his thermal. Which meant he’d be buck-naked in about three hands.

Or sooner if you throw the cards away and do exactly what you want to do instead.

His cock jerked in his pants, in total, eager agreement. What he wanted to do...

Well, do it, Hudo.

His ass clenched as thick desire poured through his groin.

Do it.

He snapped to his feet, his plastic seat jolting away from the back of his thighs to tumble over. In two strides, he rounded the table and stopped directly in front of Anna to give her a level stare. “I don’t want to play poker.” He leant forward a little, combed his fingers into the golden strands of her hair at her nape and held her head still. “I want to make love to you. I want to bury myself in your sweet wet pussy and fuck you until you scream my name.”

He lowered his face closer to hers. “And I want to do it while Rob fucks you at the same time.”

Anna’s eyes widened, her lips parting.

“Bloody hell, Hudo.” Rob shifted in his chair, his voice tight. “When you decide to go for it, you don’t hold back.”

Joseph raised his head a fraction, gave his best mate a direct look and then returned his gaze to Anna. “Come on,” he said on a low whisper. “I dare you.”

Anna’s pulse didn’t just pound in her neck, it hammered. *I dare you.* She licked her lips, her pussy already squeezing in damp anticipation.

I dare you.

There was so much in those three words: a challenge of sexual contact beyond any she'd experienced before. A challenge to release herself to the fantasy she'd harbored the moment she'd set eyes on the two Australians. A challenge to deny the apprehension of their earlier threesome. But there was more, so much more in his eyes. In his eyes, those cookie-brown eyes she'd been drawn to from the start, she saw his desire. Not just sexual, but emotional. It made no sense. They hardly knew each other, but this man, with his sexy-as-sin accent, his caring eyes and warm wit, made her just plain gooey inside in the most wonderful way imaginable.

Her heart leapt faster and her mouth went dry.

Love at first sight? Who would have thought you were a romantic, Ranger McCarthy?

She tilted her face up to Joseph's, letting a slow smile curl her lips. "I accept your dare, Joseph Hudson."

"God, you have no idea how much I wanted to hear you say that," Rob murmured, his breath warm on her neck. He ran his hands over her hips, up the flat plane of her belly, the curve of her ribcage, until his fingers found her breasts. Her sex pooled with liquid pleasure and she swayed toward Joseph, eager for him to join in.

"Anna?" A male voice crackled from Anna's backpack. *"This is Bartowski. What's your situation with the Australians? Over."*

"Fuck," Rob swore.

Anna's pulse rate tripled. "It's Wolf Creek base." She placed her palm on Joseph's chest and gave him an apologetic look, the moisture between her legs growing at the impatient gleam of hunger in his eyes. "I better let them know what's going on."

Rob laughed, sliding one hand down her stomach to delve his fingers into the junction of her thighs. "You think they might want to join?"

She twisted in his embrace and punched her fist against his shoulder in a soft rebuke. "You wish."

Disengaging herself, she hurried over to her backpack,

withdrew her handheld transceiver and rammed her thumb against the PTT button. "This is Anna. I've located the Australians and have escorted them to number four cabin. We'll be staying put tonight. Will report back at—" she shot her watch a quick glance, "—twenty-two hundred. Over."

She released the press-to-talk button, the feel of Joseph's and Rob's impatient, hungry gazes roaming over her back almost making her squirm.

"You sure?" Bartowski asked, his uncertainty scratched with static. *"If I send out the chopper now, Hal can get to you in under an hour. Over."*

"Negative," Anna almost snapped, aware her own voice sounded curt. "Too risky. The winds kicking the mountain's ass up here. I've got it under control anyway. The heater's fired up, the Australians are safe and they very thoughtfully packed sandwiches before getting their asses lost. Over."

"If you say so. Over." Bartowski sounded hesitant. What she was suggesting wasn't protocol, but she was also the boss. He knew better than to question her too much.

She flattened the press-to-talk button. "I do," she said into the microphone. "Don't worry about me. They're Australian city boys with more money than sense. I'm making them regret their stupidity, trust me. Over."

Rob burst out laughing behind her as she released the PTT button and swung about to fix him with a steady gaze. Her heart began to thump harder. "Now," she said, tossing her walkie-talkie onto the crumbled top of her backpack, "where were we?"

Joseph crossed the cabin floor in three strides and scooped her off her feet before she could utter a squeal of shocked delight. He held her against his chest, his arms under her knees and back, his nostrils flaring, his stare holding hers captive. "Right about here."

He kissed her. Hard. Brutal. His tongue lashing at her lips, her teeth, with a ravenous aggression she reveled in.

"And here," Rob stated as he fisted a hand in her hair and tore her lips from Joseph's, crushing her mouth with his.

His kiss was equally forceful but far more playful, and her head spun at the contradiction of one barely contained with power, the other almost teasing. Both however, made her pussy weep with moisture. She whimpered and curled her arms around Joseph's neck as his lips began to scorch a line up the column of her neck.

"You are so fucking beautiful," he ground out in her ear.

"Beautiful," Rob echoed, pulling his lips from hers to taste her chin, her jaw.

Joseph kissed her again, nipping at her bottom lip with a series of bites that grew harder and more uncontrolled with each one. He plunged his tongue into her mouth, exploring its well with increasing fever.

"There's no bed big enough for this," Rob spoke, skimming a hand down her back and over the curve of her ass. His fingers stopped at the folds of her pussy, exposed to his touch by her position in Joseph's arms, "and the floor's a might cold, so we're going to have to worship your body standing up."

His statement sent a shard of wanton excitement into Anna's sex and she felt her juices wet Rob's fingers. Fingers he slowly, deliberately slid into her folds. Two at once, wriggling them until he couldn't penetrate her any deeper.

She sucked in a breath through her nose, the scent of her pleasure filling her body, driving her faster to an unexpected orgasm.

Oh, God!

Her pussy clamped shut on Rob's fingers, constricting on them, squeezing them in fast, powerful pulses.

"Oh, yes," Rob scissored his fingers inside her sex, plunged them in and out and wriggled them some more, "that's my girl. Come for me. I want you so fucking wet I could drown in your cream."

Joseph growled against Anna's lips at his friend's words, hauling her closer to his chest as he sucked her tongue into his mouth.

"She's so wet for us, Hudo." Rob continued to fuck her pussy with his fingers. "So very, very wet."

Joseph broke the kiss and stared into her face. "I want her wetter."

Rob chuckled, a low, dirty laugh. "No worries, mate."

He slapped her ass. A swift, sharp slap that made her cry out in surprise.

Stinging heat branded her ass cheek, but before the pain could register in Anna's mind, Joseph pressed his lips to her temple. "Do you want him to kiss it better?"

She nodded, her breath hitching in her throat.

She sensed Rob move beside her, his hand sliding over her butt, caressing the spot he'd smacked until it wasn't his palm on her skin but his lips.

And then, his lips weren't on her ass cheek but on her folds, his tongue flicking at her clit, his fingers delving into her slit.

"Does that feel good?" Joseph whispered, his stare holding her still in his arms.

"Yes," she panted. "Yes."

"I want you so wet there'll be very little pain when Rob enters your arse."

Her heart slammed into her throat, her rock-hard nipples aching. She gazed into his eyes, knowing she should feel something other than absolute trust and blissful rapture. She didn't.

Rob's tongue rolled over her clit, already swollen from her last orgasm, and she hissed in a gasp.

"I can't hold on much longer, Anna." Raw tension wrought Joseph's statement into a strangled groan. "My dick is so hard and I want to sink it into your pussy so much."

"Then do it," she rasped. "Do it. Please."

He shook his head. "Not yet. Not until you are ready for both of us."

As if Rob knew exactly what Joseph wanted, he placed his hands on her ass cheeks and spread them apart, dragging his tongue from her pussy to her anus. Smearing her hole with his saliva and her cream.

She clung to Joseph, a distant part of her mind in awe of his physical strength—he'd held her for what must be a lifetime now—a more elemental part of her mind more aroused than ever by it. "Oh, Joseph."

It was the first time she'd called his name during their

sexual contact and he let out a shaking groan, his eyes clouding with desire. His arms tightened around her and he slanted his lips over her mouth.

Rob laved her anus with his salvia, dipping his thumb into her pussy as he did so. She thrust her hips upward, her inner muscles constricting, another climax mounting. Fast.

It hit her. An explosive tension shuddering through her body.

Bringing with it fresh moisture from her sodden sex.

"Hmmm," Rob hummed against her ass. "You taste so good. My face is so wet with your come."

He lapped at her ass, stabbed at it with the point of his tongue, fucking her pussy with his fingers. Smearing her juices to her anus.

"I think she's ready for us, Joe."

The statement uttered against her backside made Anna's ass squeeze tight with a wanton thrill she'd never experienced before. Her heart quickened faster still and she wrapped her arms around Joseph's neck with desperate need.

She was ready. More than ready.

Without a word, Joseph removed his arm from beneath her knees and her feet hit the floor with a soft thud.

Rob was there immediately. From the time it took to remove his mouth from her ass and straighten to his feet, he'd stripped himself of his snow pants and shirt. She heard a condom packet tear and then he pressed his naked body to her back, smoothing his hands under her thermal. She drew in a shallow breath, the feel of his warm skin on hers almost as wonderful as the feel of his rigid erection nudging the crevice of her ass. He skimmed his palms over her belly, her ribs and breasts, a taunting journey that made her knees wobble before he embraced her in a firm hold and tugged her backward.

The tips of her toes brushed the floorboards a split second before Joseph stepped in front of her—now gloriously, proudly naked, his thick erection stretching the condom he wore—and gathered up her legs, draping her knees over his bent arms. Hooking them in the inside of his elbows.

He met her gaze, a small smile on his lips. "To the hilt," he whispered.

He moved. Raising her knees higher and leaning into her body with fluid grace. His massive cock first pressed and then parted her folds, separating her sex until, with a groan and a clenching of his jaw, he sank his length into her very core.

"Oh, yes!" She threw back her head, the surreal sensation of being suspended on Joseph's arms while being impaled on his cock almost driving her mad. She'd never felt anything like it, like she was connected to the world even as she hung above it.

Joseph sucked in a sharp breath, and another, his hips thrusting up, driving him deeper inside her.

"Damn, Hudo," Rob growled, his lips against Anna's throat. For a dizzying moment she realized she'd forgotten he was there.

How could you forget? The man has made you come four times in the space of two hours.

"If I don't..." Rob didn't finish.

His lips on her neck turned hungry, each kiss growing more wild.

"Touch me, Anna."

She did as he asked, reaching down between their two bodies to close her fingers around his straining cock.

"That's it," he murmured. "Feel how hard I am for you. Feel how thick and long."

She gripped his length a little firmer, all the while drowning in the thrusting strokes of Joseph's dick in her pussy.

"I'm going to take you soon, Anna," Rob continued, sliding one hand down her body until he wrapped his fingers over hers. He held his cock with her hand, pumped it once, twice. "Here."

With a slight shift in the position of his hips, he aligned the domed head of his cock with her sodden, puckered anus. The beads of pre-come anointing his shaft's tip slicked over her hole, adding to the natural lubrication he'd so thoroughly painted her with.

In response, Anna's ass squeezed closed. A wicked thrill shot into the pit of her belly, and with it came the undeniable realization she didn't just *want* him to, she *needed* him to.

She lifted her free arm above her head and tangled her fingers in his hair. The musky aroma of her essence was potent on the air. "Now," she begged through clenched teeth. "Please."

He groaned, the guttural sound echoed by Joseph.

"This will hurt," Rob panted, each word as gentle and controlled as she knew he could be, "but only for a moment."

He pushed his hips upward. Slowly.

Anna's cry rose in her throat and she stiffened, fear lacing her ecstasy.

"Shhh," Rob hushed in her ear, just as Joseph leant into her body, his length burying deeper into her sex, and placed his lips on hers.

"Tell us to stop, Anna, and we will. If you need us to stop..."

She shook her head, the burning sting in her ass radiating through her lower body. It hurt, but underneath the pain, like a blazing sun behind dispersing thunderclouds, was unbelievable pleasure. Intense. Unfathomable.

Rob released his grip on her hand and his cock, smoothing it up over her stomach to cup her right breast. "Take a breath for me, sweetheart."

She did as he told her, and drew the undeniable scent of Joseph into her lungs.

"That's it," Rob's voice left him on a ragged breath. "I'm going deeper."

A wave of concentrated, delicious sensations rolled out from Anna's stretched ass and she tightened her fist in Rob's hair. "Oh...oh..."

"Fuck a duck, Thorton," Joseph groaned, stroking his cock in and out of Anna's sex. "Holy shit, this feel so good." The muscles in his arms quivered, and for a moment the steady rhythm of his penetrations turned erratic.

The awe-struck claim sent a spear of liquid electricity into Anna's core. She moaned, any lingering apprehension destroyed by the image of Rob and Joseph together. She drew her knees closer to her body, wanting Joseph to bury himself to the hilt just as he promised.

Wanting Rob to do the same.

"God, I want..." She couldn't finish the demand. She didn't

need to.

Without uttering a word, the two men drove their cocks into her body, simultaneously filling her, stretching her. Possessing her utterly and completely.

"More," she ground out the single request, awash in pure rapture.

Both Joseph and Rob obeyed, their thrusts alternating, their cocks rubbing against each other through the wall of her sex. "I'm not going to last much longer," Rob panted.

Anna fisted her hand tighter in his hair and stared into Joseph's eyes. She saw his own pleasure, as molten as hers, smoldering in their brown depths. "Harder, Joseph," she begged. "I'm almost there already."

He thrust into her, each stroke growing faster, each pushing her higher, higher. Closer to the edge.

Closer to exquisite release.

She gazed into his eyes and ground her pussy down onto his cock. "Harder. Fuck me harder. Please. Harder."

He did. Rob did. Their rhythm in perfect harmony with each other, their grunts and moans a chorus sweeter than a choir of angels.

"I'm going to come soon," Rob burst out. "Christ, I'm gonna..."

He closed his fingers around her breast just as Joseph leant forward and crushed her lips with his, plunging his tongue into her mouth, and it was all that was needed to push her over.

Her first contracting pulse rocked through her, a great shudder so forceful blossoms of blinding color filled her vision. The second pulse followed immediately after, more powerful.

She rode each constricting peak as she rode the two men's cocks, and just when she thought she couldn't take any more, when her orgasm had drained her, scoured her away, Rob let out a roar and came in her ass. It plunged her over another edge she didn't know she balanced on. As she fell, Joseph called out her name and slammed into her with one final thrust, his cock pumping inside her, and she came again, calling out his name in return.

She gripped him with her sex as her heart thumped into her throat, from her body.

Lost to her forever. The property of the Australian with the caring brown eyes. The one buried to the hilt inside her.

Chapter Seven

Joseph studied the snow-covered mountainside looming over him, the sun bouncing off it in blinding sheets of golden-white light. He rubbed at the crink in the back of his neck, his warm skin almost hot against his ungloved hand. They'd all three fallen asleep on the old cot last night, squished together on the narrow space only to wake a little while later and do the whole thing over again. This time lying on the blanket and clothes-covered floor admittedly, with Rob beneath Anna claiming her pussy and Joseph claiming her from behind, filling her tight ass. Joseph was strong, but he didn't think his arms and shoulders could take another standing-up session.

The pleasure of their coupling was just as explosive in that position, with Anna sandwiched between them. A far better, more delicious, more addictive culinary experience than vegemite sandwiches could ever hope to be.

He snorted a light chuckle and rubbed his neck again.

At some stage of the night, they'd fallen asleep again, after talking about favorite movies and food and pastimes into the wee hours of the morning, Anna's cheek pressed against Joseph's chest, her legs entangled with his, Rob holding her from behind, one long arm and leg draped over them all.

When Joseph had opened his eyes this morning to the pale winter sun streaming through the cabin's windows, he'd found Anna still asleep in his arms and Rob stretched out in the plastic folding chair, head back, mouth open, his snores almost soft.

Joseph laughed again, kneading his fingers into his neck. He had a sore neck, but he bet Rob was going to wake up with one just as sore.

He let his gaze roam over the steep mountainside towering to the heavens in front of him.

Knife Ridge Chutes, Wolf Creek. The place everything in his life changed.

Well, not everything. Rob was a constant.

And now he wanted Anna to be as well.

His stomach knotted at what he was planning to do next. Jesus, for a bloke who rarely took life by the balls unless dared to by his best mate, he was grabbing a handful right now.

He shoved his hands under his armpits, the chill in his fingers beginning to get nasty. Gloves. He really needed to pull on his gloves. Otherwise he'd have a hard time feeling Anna's beautiful body when he went back inside and woke her—

"So, big fella," Rob's hand—gloved, he couldn't help but notice—slammed down on Joseph's shoulder. "Another dare successfully accomplished. What's next? How 'bout base jumping off the—"

"Oh no." Joseph shook his head with a wide grin. "That's it for me for a while. I think you've pretty much reached your dare-me limit for a few months."

Rob laughed. "No such thing as dare-you limits, Hudo. Who else is going to drag you kicking and screaming into all the fun stuff?"

The question was typical Rob, and yet this time it made Joseph's chest constrict, not with nervous anticipation—the kind felt on a rollercoaster with suspicious-looking harnesses—but a warm feeling of...

Happiness?

"I think," he said slowly, the notion behind his words still far too new and daunting to rush, "I'm going to hang around here with Anna for a while." He shot Rob a sideward glance. "If that's okay with you?"

Rob cocked an eyebrow. "What? Here in the cabin? Won't you two freeze your nuts off? Well, won't you freeze *your* nuts off? Anna, as we both know doesn't have nuts." He pulled a contemplative face. "I guess she could freeze her—"

"Funny bastard, aren't you." Joseph gave him a shove,

rolling his eyes at him. "No, here in the US."

Rob raised both eyebrows at him this time. "Really? Mr Workaholic is thinking of staying put for a bit?"

Joseph shrugged, watching a bird—an eagle by the size of it—soar effortlessly through the sky above them. "It's that or ask her to come back to Australia with me."

"Just you?"

Joseph swung his stare onto his best friend. There was no challenge in Rob's blue eyes, nor aggression in his body language. Despite the explosive passion of the last twelve hours, Joseph bore no delusions Rob had designs on Anna. For his mate, the sex had been just that—sex. Mind-blowing, amazing, unbelievable sex. For Joseph however, mind-blowing, amazing and unbelievable didn't even cut it. "Yeah," he nodded. "Me. I like her a lot, Rob. A lot." He narrowed his eyes at his friend. "Besides, something tells me you've got your own agenda."

An unreadable expression flittered across Rob's face before he turned his attention to the mountain. "It's beautiful, isn't it. Dangerous and magnificent all at once." He studied it for a long moment and Joseph felt the knot in his gut—the one twisting there since last night when he'd laughingly told Rob he was going to die a lonely man—twist again. "We faced it together, my friend. Laughed at death in the face and came away with something wonderful." He let out a sigh and returned his gaze to Joseph's face. "Yeah," he said, "I've got my own agenda."

The knot in Joseph's gut rolled over on itself. "And what's that, mate?"

Rob dragged his hands over his face, and for some reason the whisper-quiet sound of neoprene acrylic scraping against his skin made Joseph's hair stand on end. Or was it the look in Rob's eyes. A look he'd never seen there before—regret? Sorrow? Grief?

"Fuck, I've rehearsed this speech I don't know how many times in the last week," Rob muttered, shaking his head, "and now I have to do it, I haven't got a bloody clue how."

Joseph's gut rolled again, churning into a heavy ball. "What's going on, mate?"

"I've got brain cancer, Hudo," Rob stated, the words even and hideously calm. "The doc diagnosed it last week, and the oncologist confirmed two days before I convinced you to fly out here."

Joseph stared at his best friend, the man he'd grown up with. The man who knew him better than he knew himself. "You've got fucking what?"

"Brain cancer. Specifically, anaplastic astrocytoma."

"Anaplastic astrowhat?" Joseph shook his head, the words making no sense. Especially not when attached to Rob.

"Anaplastic astrocytoma. It's inoperable and advanced."

Inoperable. Advanced. Joseph blinked, a weight beginning to form on his chest. Jesus, Rob said those words like he was talking about a bit of a head cold. "No," he said. "No, you don't." The weight on his chest grew heavy, so heavy he could barely draw a breath. He couldn't believe what Rob was saying. He couldn't. Rob and cancer didn't go together. They didn't. "Stop being a dickhead and tell me what's really going on."

Rob smiled, a wry grin that made Joseph's chest ache. "I wish I could, mate. But this is it. I suspected something was up for a while. Remember the headaches I've been having the last few months? You said they were from too many nights partying. I said they were from too many days working. Well, turns out they were from too many cells in my head doing both."

Joseph shook his head again.

Rob couldn't die. No way. Rob personified life. Death and Rob did not, just did not connect. They couldn't. Because if they did it would mean Rob was going to die. Rob wouldn't be around.

Joseph blinked again, a numb sensation tearing through him, making his heart cold. If Rob and death connected, it meant Rob wouldn't be part of his life anymore. He shook his head. Not fucking possible. "No, Rob," he snarled. "They're wrong. The doctors are wrong."

"They're not, mate. It's all good though. Think of it this way, you won't have to clean up any of my messes with the insurance manager or human resources again."

Rob's jest sent a shard of anger into Joseph's gut. "This is not the time to joke, Rob."

Rob looked at him. "Yeah, it is, Joe. What better time?

We've just had the best night of our lives. You're on the verge of starting the next phase of yours. What better time to laugh at the unavoidable?" He smiled again, placing his hand back on Joseph's shoulder. "It's okay, Joseph. It really is. I've come to terms with it. Honest."

"Well I haven't fucking come to terms with it." Joseph glared at him, his blood roaring in his ears, making him feel like he was about to scream. He wanted to scream. He stood motionless, driving his nails into his palms. Sucking in breath after icy breath through his nose.

Anaplastic astrocytoma. Inoperable. Advanced.

He shook his head, grinding his teeth and giving his friend a flat stare. He'd never felt more angry. Never felt more like punching the shit out of his best friend and telling him to grow up. "How can you stand here in the snow on the other side of the bloody world and tell me you've got cancer with a smile on your face." He pushed at Rob's chest, shoving him back a step. "Is this another sick dare? 'C'mon, Hudo, I dare you to die before I do'? Jesus, Thorton, you've pulled some low stunts but this..." He trailed off, the sickened rage in his gut stealing his words.

Rob waited, not saying a thing. Joseph wanted to smash his fist against his jaw.

How dare he do this?

Who else would, Joseph?

"What about surgery?" he asked. "Chemo? Shit, I've got more money than I'll ever know what to do with. We'll call the best specialists, the best doctors. For Christ sake, we're in the States, I'll call the freaking Surgeon General. There's got to be something you can do, we can do—"

Rob shook his head, his grin growing lopsided. "It's inoperable, Hudo. That means they found it too late. Besides, do you seriously think I'm going to let some bloke who probably drives around in a Porsche and drinks lattes cut into my head? And I look atrocious bald. Remember the time we both shaved our heads the day before senior photos?" He laughed. "Damn, my girlfriend—what was her name? Alice? Ally? Amy?"

"Andy," Joseph murmured, the world buzzing. Cancer. Jesus, cancer.

"Andy!" Rob slapped him on the chest, grin stretching wide again. "Damn, she gave good head. Andy wouldn't speak to me for a week."

Joseph felt the knot in his stomach clench, even as the memory of Andy Tellerman's incensed fury at Rob's new do drew a shaking laugh from his shocked disbelief. She'd ranted and raved and carried on as if Rob had cut off *her* hair, growing more enraged when Rob wouldn't say sorry. Or wear a hat until his hair grew back.

Joseph frowned at his friend, refusing to let the warm memory temper his stunned anger. Not yet. It was still too raw to let Rob fool him into laughing.

He's never going to fool you into laughing again, Joseph. Not anymore.

The devastating thought sank into his anger.

Never again.

His eyes stung with prickling heat and he blinked, turning his head away from the sight of his best friend.

He didn't want to talk to him.

"Hudo?"

Joseph squeezed his eyes shut, denying the stinging pressure behind them. He swallowed, the thick lump in his throat almost suffocating him.

Rob remained silent for a long moment, letting the reality of his news sink it.

Joseph didn't want it to sink it, damn it. He drove his nails harder into his palms, waiting for the pain of his nails in his flesh to register in his brain. It didn't. All he felt was the pain in his heart. He sucked in a shuddering breath, his chest not just aching but burning.

Oh, fuck, Rob. No...

A sob escaped him, ripped from the center of his soul and he scrunched up his face. He'd only cried once in his adult life—when the Sydney Swans beat the West Coast Eagles in the 2005 AFL Grand Final—and he sure as shit wasn't going to cry now over Rob's revelation. He wasn't.

Yeah, sure. That's what you're doing now, isn't it? Not crying. That wet stuff on your cheeks is you not crying.

"It's okay, Joe," Rob placed his hand high on Joseph's back and Joseph swiped at his face, his stomach churning at the hot moisture scalding his skin. "And it'll be okay. Honest."

"How will it be okay?" he muttered.

"It just will be." Rob's answer, spoken with such acceptance, ripped another sob from Joseph's chest. "It's gotta be, right?"

"Why didn't you tell me before now?"

Rob chuckled. "Because I knew this is how you'd react, trying to fix something that can't be fixed." He shook his head. "No. I wanted my last few days spent doing what I've always wanted to do, what I've always loved doing."

"Snowboarding down a bloody mountain?" Joseph knew he was being irrational, but he didn't care. Cancer. Fucking brain cancer. It wasn't right. It wasn't fair.

Rob laughed, the sound rising above them, its undeniable happiness clear in the pristine air. "No," he said, giving Joseph's shoulder a thump with his fist. "Pushing you to live."

Joseph glared at him. "I live."

"Yeah, when I dare you to. Otherwise you'd spend every day in that office of yours. Remember what my dad used to always say? We should work to live, not live to work? If I'd let you, you'd have lived to work my friend. But I've lived more with you than I ever would have by myself." Rob grinned at him. "You know that, don't you? And now it's time for me to finish off that life."

Joseph shook his head. "No, it's not."

"Ah, Hudo." Rob squeezed his shoulder, the cheeky grin on his face belayed by the sadness in his eyes. "This is why I love you, mate. You're a bloody stubborn pain in the arse." He paused, his smile faltering for a second before returning wider and far more...Robbish...than ever. "I'm going to live more in my last few weeks than anyone else could live in a lifetime." He flicked the cabin a sideward glance. "Well, anyone apart from you. Something tells me Ranger McCarthy's going to help you live your life the way it was meant to be lived. Keep giving you those kicks up the backside you usually get from me."

Joseph felt—of all things at this stupidly dark, surreal nightmarish point in time—his heart fill with a wholly unexpected heat at the thought of Anna.

Rob laughed as if he could see into Joseph's soul and the burgeoning happiness there. He slapped his biceps with his hands and blew out a breath. "Now, let's get inside. It's fucking freezing out here and I'm sure Anna's awake by now. Probably radioing Wolf Creek base as we speak, telling them the moron Australians are lost again."

Before Joseph could say otherwise, Rob turned and shuffled back to the cabin, his snowboard boots crunching the new snow, his black hair dancing in the mountainside's icy breeze.

Joseph stood and watched him disappear into the hut, numb. Not from the cold, but from...

He swallowed, a lump the size of the mountain before him suddenly making itself at home in his throat. Cancer.

He tried to imagine a life without Rob. Tried to see his future without his best friend. He couldn't. He just couldn't. It was impossible.

Cancer.

His eyes stung. Jesus, he didn't want to cry. At least not now. It would hurt too much. *At least let me get back home to Sydney. Then the waterworks can—*

"You okay?"

Joseph started. The soft sound of Anna's voice, plus the gentle feel of her hands smoothing around his waist made him blink.

He turned his head to her and lifted his arm a fraction. She ducked under it and pressed her body to his in a loose hug.

"Yeah." He frowned, wrapping his arms around her back. He rested his chin on the top of her head for a moment, staring at the mountainside. "No."

His stomach—no, his soul ached. An agonizing emptiness he doubted he'd ever truly lose. He pressed his lips to her hair, the cool silk not a balm to his grief, but an affirmation that some things happened for a reason. He knew why Rob had told him he was dying this morning. Rob knew—as only Rob could—what was going on in Joseph's heart.

Did Rob plan this? Getting lost up here? Did he do this for you, Joseph?

He closed his eyes, staying the tears threatening to undo him. It was the kind of thing Rob Thorton would do. Piss you off so much you didn't realize how alive he made you feel until after the anger—the grief—had passed.

Anna pulled away from him a little and he tightened his arms around her, needing to feel her warmth and softness against him.

"Can I help?" she asked, her voice kind, her eyes searching his. That she didn't ask what the problem was only made him love her even more.

How is that possible? To have your heart ripped out and find it all in one morning?

He didn't know. But if he had to blame someone, it would be Rob. Bloody bastard was always messing with his life.

He chuckled, the sound very close to a sob, and shook his head. He lowered his head to brush his lips over Anna's in a kiss as gentle as the desire he saw in her clear, direct eyes.

She smoothed her hands up his back to his shoulders and tugged him closer still. "I'm here if you need me."

He let his lips move over hers again, tasting her. Knowing he wanted to do so forever.

Take life by the balls, Hudo. He heard Rob laugh in his head, as roguish and irrepressible as ever. Go on. I dare you.

With a steadying breath, he raised his head and gazed down into her eyes. "Come back to Australia with me?"

She stared at him, not saying anything. Not moving. Not even blinking.

And then a small smile curled the corners of her mouth and she pressed her body closer to his. "Okay," she said. "As long as you don't make me vegemite sandwiches every day for lunch."

Joseph laughed, resting his forehead on hers. "Never for lunch." He snatched a quick kiss. "But maybe on toast for breakfast..."

She pushed at him, laughing, her eyes twinkling, and he kissed her again, this one not so quick.

Her tongue moved against his, promising a life of wicked

fantasies realized, of romantic dreams fulfilled. She kissed him back and soothed his pain.

"C'mon," he murmured against her lips, sliding his arm down her back and tucking her into his side. "Be buggered if I'm going to let Rob get the jump on us. He'll be back in the lodge scoffing all the beer if we hang around here too long."

Anna tilted her head at an angle and gave him a searing look. "Or we could stay just a little bit longer. Y'know...see what comes up?"

Her hand smoothed down his back, under the waistline of his snow pants, until her fingers skimmed the cheeks of his ass. "C'mon," she nudged his hip with hers, "I dare you."

Epilogue

Eight months later.

Joseph closed his eyes, the hammering rhythm of his heart stealing any capacity to think. Jesus, how had he gotten himself into this predicament?

How had he let her—

Warm hands slid up his stomach, fingers charting a path over the quivering muscles of his abs and up to his chest. His nipples, already twin points of aching need, puckered harder. He swallowed a groan, knowing he'd lose if he made a sound.

If he lost, Anna had control for the rest of the day. When Anna had control, they could easily end up in Peru for a dirty weekend. Not that he had a problem with spending a dirty weekend in Peru with Anna, but he had other things planned. Like a dirty weekend in Paris. They hadn't done Paris yet. They hadn't—

"If I suck on your nipple will you moan for me?"

Anna's lips brushed Joseph's right nipple, the tip of her tongue flicking over its distended shape in a teasing little caress that almost sent him mad.

"Just a little moan?"

Fuck a duck, with the scent of her juices still lingering on his face and her tight, wet sex gripping and sliding over his shaft as she rode it with slow, steady movements, how the hell wasn't he going to make a sound?

He opened his eyes to gaze up at her and bit back a curse, wishing he hadn't. The sight of her tousled blonde hair, heavy-lidded eyes and parted lips—swollen from the crushing kiss he'd delivered not a few minutes earlier—was almost too much. That she was gloriously naked and her breasts dangled but an inch from his chest didn't help.

Jesus, why had he agreed to this challenge? If she could make him utter a sound before either of them came she got to decide the rest of the day's events. He should have known he'd lose. As soon as Anna touched him he was one big, turned-on six-foot bag of man groans. When they made love...

The incredulous realization he had no one else to blame but himself for his situation ran through Joseph's pleasure-fogged mind, just as Anna dipped her head closer to his chest.

She traced the puckered circle of his areola with her tongue and Joseph ground his teeth, his ass clenching, his cock jerking inside her at the wicked sensations the action set off in his body. Damn her, she wasn't playing fair.

When did she ever?

"Just a little moan," she whispered, squeezing her pussy muscles around his dick in a series of quick, mind-blowing pulses and then taking his nipple between her teeth and giving it a soft bite. "A little one."

Liquid heat flooded his balls and his heart pounded faster. Right, that was it. He wasn't going to let her win. He wanted to go to bloody Paris this weekend.

With abrupt force, he flipped Anna onto her back and drove his cock deeper into her sex. He snatched at her wrists, capturing them in a fierce grip as he captured her delighted squeal with his mouth.

He plunged his tongue into her mouth, kissing her with brutal hunger, dominating her mouth. Fucking it with his tongue just the way he knew she liked it. Taking his pleasure from her whimpers.

He thrust harder, faster into her pussy, slamming the root of his shaft against her clit over and over again, mirroring his penetrations of her sex with his tongue.

She arched beneath him, her legs coming up and wrapping around his hips, locking him to her as she rode his pounding rhythm. Until she tore her mouth from his and cried out, every muscle in her body quivering, her sex constricting around his cock, her climax detonating his own.

"I win," he moaned, after what felt like rivers of come spurted from his dick and hours of exquisite, scalding pleasure throbbed through his body.

"Yeah," Anna laughed, the sound breathless and ragged. "You win. I so lost that challenge."

He chuckled at her quip and slumped onto her for a moment before rolling to her side. His cock slid from her pussy, the sensation making his head giddy. Damn, he'd never get sick of making love to her. Eight months of rarely stepping foot outside his apartment, of doing little except getting to know each other in every way imaginable...

As it did every time Joseph marveled at his new life—retired at the age of thirty-one with more money than the Prime Minister, free to do pretty much whatever he wanted with the woman he loved more than life—he heard his best friend's voice in his head.

Something tells me Ranger McCarthy's going to help you live your life the way it was meant to be lived.

He let out a sigh, his lips curling into a slow smile. Ranger McCarthy was two interviews and a ceremony outside the Sydney Opera House away from becoming Nationalized Australian McCarthy. All thanks to Rob and a faulty compass.

Joseph snorted. He never did send the manufacturers that email. Come to think of it, he wondered if Rob had forgotten as well.

Doesn't matter now, does it, Hudo?

The soft chime of the doorbell floating from the front of his apartment made him scowl. Who the hell was that?

"I'll get it." Anna bounced off their bed, snatching up his polo shirt discarded earlier in a jumble of arms and legs.

Joseph threaded his fingers behind his head and stared up at the bone-white ceiling of their bedroom. Eight months. Who would have thought eight months without a single doubt or regret.

Eight months—

"You got a parcel." Anna jumped onto the bed and squirmed about until she settled into a relaxed position beside him, legs crossed, a wide grin on her face.

He rolled onto his side and leant on one elbow as he watched her rip into the large rectangle package. Its wrapping was beaten and worse for wear, the outside covered in more colored stickers and customs labels than he'd ever seen. Which meant it probably came from…

The pit of his stomach tightened.

With one final flourish, Anna freed the parcel within of its confines. She burst out laughing and held up the most hideous powder-blue tuxedo jacket ever created.

A small square of paper slipped from the jacket's collar and Joseph caught it before it could come to rest on Anna's bare, bent knee.

"'Guess who'll be coming home for your wedding, guys?'," he read aloud, the familiar scrawl of Rob's handwriting on the paper note making his stomach flutter. "'Yep. Your best man's in remission, boys and girls. Gotta love the doctors here at the Centro de Medicinas Alternativas. When you lay down a challenge they really know how to pick it up and run with it. Particularly one doctor. She really knows how to handle a challenge. And I mean really really.

"'Oh, and Joe, the suit's for you. I've already got mine packed and ready to go. I dare you to wear it on your wedding day. Go on. I dare you."

About the Author

Lexxie's not a deviant. She just has a deviant's imagination and a desire to entertain readers with her words. Add the two together and you get darkly erotic romances with a twist of horror, sci-fi and the paranormal.

When she's not submerged in the worlds she creates, Lexxie's life revolves around her family, a husband who thinks she's insane, a cat determined to rule the house, two yabbies hell-bent on destroying their tank and her daughters, who both utterly captured her heart and changed her life forever.

Contact Lexxie at lexxie@lexxiecouper.com, follow her on Twitter http://twitter.com/lexxie_couper or visit her at www.lexxiecouper.com where she occasionally makes a fool of herself on her blog.

Look for these titles by

Lexxie Couper

Now Available:

Death, The Vamp and His Brother
The Sun Sword

Savage Australia series
Savage Retribution
Savage Transformation

Bandicoot Cove series
Exotic Indulgence (with Vivian Arend & Jess Dee)
Tropical Sin

Party Games series
Suck and Blow

True Heart

Delilah Devlin

Dedication

Thanks to my wonderful editor, Lindsey, for her faith in me, and to Heidi for presenting me a new challenge...

Chapter One

True Wyatt prided himself on control—control over the multitude of responsibilities that came with riding herd over a successful ranch; control over his brother, who thought life should be enjoyed rather than conquered; and control over the desires he'd kept in rein since the demise of his marriage. And yet, the sight that greeted him this cold winter day told him he'd only been fooling himself.

From his perch high atop the ridge overlooking the lonely cabin, True Wyatt watched the shapely brunette as she made another trip to her car to pull boxes and suitcases from her backseat, one after the other. Grumpily, he wondered how she'd managed to stuff so much inside a Corolla. The trunk had held a similar assortment of printer-paper-sized boxes, which she'd manhandled into the house, her face growing rosy with exertion.

Despite the biting wind, she'd dispensed with her down coat and wore only a sweater with a crew neck, the sleeves pushed off her wrists. The dark blue knit hugged her upper torso, defining a lovely bosom and narrow waist. Every time she bent to pull out another box her designer jeans hugged her small rounded bottom, and his loins tightened.

Which annoyed the hell out of him. Fact was, he wished he could turn his horse away and pretend he hadn't noticed trouble had arrived on his mountain. He knew exactly who to blame. His anger smoldered like hot coals ready to erupt into a full blaze. The clop of hooves approaching behind him carried just the fuel to add to the fire.

"Did you know?" True barked without glancing back.

"Know what?" his brother asked, humor underlying his slow drawl as he pulled up alongside him.

"That our tenant is a woman."

"Sure did. I'm surprised that you're surprised since I gave you a copy of her book. Picture's right there on the back cover."

The book in question sat on the credenza in True's office. Exactly where his brother had left it two days ago. The fact he hadn't bothered turning it over made True's cheeks heat. *Dammit.*

Lonny had asked him just last night if he'd read the story. The wicked gleam in his eyes when he'd said it should have clued True in that his little brother was enjoying a joke at his expense.

"You do know this is gonna complicate things. If we weren't busy enough after letting go of the seasonal hands, now we have to babysit—"

"She's not looking for anyone to babysit her, True. Said she wants the privacy to finish up a book."

True speared him with a glare. "We can't leave her alone. What the hell does she know about surviving a winter in high country?"

"Probably not any more than the male author you thought you were gettin'."

True gritted his teeth as Lonny's mouth stretched into a gleeful smile.

"Tell the truth. You planned on having to check up on *Mr.* H.A. Cahill. You don't trust tenderfoots."

"But I wouldn't be as worried. If a man's stupid enough to get himself into trouble out here, it's a damn shame, but not something I'd lose sleep over. But she's..." He waved his hand toward the woman hopping down the steps for another load.

Her breasts bounced enticingly, distracting him from what had to be said.

At Lonny's chuckle, he swung back with a narrowed gaze. "It's not safe. Does she know she could be shut in for a month? That bears and wolves pretty much think a cabin is a drive-through?"

"The bears are hibernating. She'll be gone before they stir.

And you know wolves are shy of humans."

"Does she know how to shoot a gun? Dammit, does she even own one?"

Lonny shrugged. "I asked if she needed me to leave one. She gave me a funny look."

True cursed. "You show her how to light that cantankerous stove?"

"Showed her twice."

The woman bent, reaching deep to the back floorboard of her car. Her sweater rode up, exposing a set of deep dimples right above her sweetly curved ass.

"Electricity's bound to go out," True muttered.

"There's plenty of gas in the shed for the generator. 'Sides, she said candlelight gets her in the mood."

True's gaze swiveled back.

Lonny raised the hand not holding his reins. "For writing her stories. Although gotta wonder myself if she wasn't talking about more. Her book was damn hot."

"You thinking to give her inspiration?" True growled, his voice rising.

"Well, she did invite me down for a meal..." At True's deepening scowl, he flashed a grin. "Out of gratitude. Said when Leroy's hunting cabin went up in that brushfire her plans for a retreat were all shot to hell. She's forever in my debt." He waggled his eyebrows at the last statement.

True looked away, hoping to keep from saying something really nasty, because for whatever reason, the thought of his brother with the curvy woman below made him feel even meaner.

When he glanced back down the hill, his gut clenched. H.A. Cahill had stacked two boxes and was walking slowly toward the porch. The height of her burden was taller than the top of her head.

"Dammit," he cussed and nudged his horse forward. She was gonna break her neck—and on his property. Sooner he helped her get inside, the sooner he could move on to more important things, like moving the last of the cattle to the box canyon where they'd stay to weather the worst of the winter.

As his horse picked its way down the slope, he kept sending darting glares her way, willing her silently to stay put. The brief thaw they'd experienced the past week had ended. Snow clung to patches of shaded earth, but had melted away everywhere else, leaving mud and slicks of slush. However, today's cold snap was re-freezing the ground, the roads—the damn steps.

She slowed as she approached the steps, kicking out one booted toe to find them. Then tentatively, she stepped up. His worst fear was realized when she took another step and her foot slid out from under her. She toppled backward to the ground, giving a startled yelp as her boxes opened and the wind carried away pages of paper.

He kicked his horse's sides, hurrying him down, ignoring the pounding of his brother's horse behind him.

Before his own palomino came to a full halt beside the woman struggling to sit, he was out of his saddle and glaring down.

Ready to tear into her for her carelessness, he opened his mouth—but a strange thing happened. One look into her cornflower blue eyes, and his breath hitched. The caustic complaint he was about to voice stuck in his throat.

"You must be the brother," she said breathlessly, her voice impossibly chipper for a woman who looked as though she'd gotten the wind knocked right out of her. "True, right? Your parents...got really creative with...your names," she gasped. "I like that. Don't be surprised...if they turn up in a book somewhere." And then she grinned.

True's dick hardened in one blazing instant, and he knew with a fatalistic certainty just what kind of books she wrote.

Honey had never seen a man look so angry and flummoxed at the same time. And that shouldn't have been the case since she managed to ruffle men's feathers faster than a hurricane. It was a talent.

She came up on her elbows in the mud and glanced at the papers cartwheeling across the yard. If you could call it a yard. The space around the cabin was more of a rough-cut clearing.

Nothing fancy, Lonny had warned her. He hadn't overrepresented the small two-room cabin with an efficiency kitchen and tiny bathroom.

And yet the rugged utility of the place appealed. The cabin smelled of pine sap and wood smoke, and when she'd stood on the porch the view of the mountains around her took her breath away.

The view from the ground right this second wasn't that bad either.

"I'll get those," Lone Wyatt said. He gave her a quick glance, raised an eyebrow at his brother, then dismounted in a fluid, graceful move that had her envious of every flex of muscle that delivered him to the ground. Could any two brothers be more alike and conversely so different at the same time?

True Wyatt moved with rugged force. She couldn't help wondering how that economy of motion and deliberation translated to how he moved in a bed. True wore "Cowboy" like some men wore Armani.

Her gaze crept upward from his scarred boots, past legs encased in sturdy, mud-stained denim, to a dark, dirt-streaked coat that fell to his knees. He looked like he'd stepped out of an old western movie. Even the cowboy hat, broad-rimmed and shadowing his deep-set eyes, emphasized his individualistic, rugged appeal.

Her glance flew back to Lonny, who chased the newspaper clippings and her own dog-eared notes across the clearing.

Lonny was a sweetheart. A flirty man with wicked intentions in his dark green eyes. She'd already decided she wouldn't turn down an invitation to go to bed with the man. But that was before she'd clapped eyes on the brother.

She came back to True to find his gaze narrowed on her face. All brooding darkness and hard-edged features. Same dark green eyes, weathered skin and dark brown hair as the brother, but his expression set him apart. Made him seem even older than the thirty-six years Lonny had volunteered.

Lonny was in his late twenties, still footloose and straining against obligation. Facts she'd gleaned easily the first time they'd met. After all, she was a writer and a master at pulling information from a person without him realizing just how she did it.

Something told her big brother wouldn't be nearly as easy to pump for information. "Pump" stuck in her mind, and her brain again leapt to sexier pursuits.

She'd gathered a lot of information during her brief encounter with little brother at the diner in town. She'd arranged to meet her original landlord to pick up the keys to the hunting cabin she'd rented for a writing retreat. Lonny had been hovering over the counter, sweet-talking a waitress, when he'd overheard her dilemma. After accepting his invitation to coffee, where she'd winnowed out his life story, she'd also managed to acquire an invitation to stay in the Wyatts' hunting cabin, situated in a "lonesome high meadow". She'd smiled at his attempt at waxing poetic, amused that he was trying to impress her after hearing she was an author.

Likely, he'd hoped that she'd use some of her pain-staking research into human sexuality and desire to show him how truly grateful she was for his last-minute save. Not that she felt under pressure to provide a little sexy quid pro quo.

Lonny was easy on the eyes and built like a brick house. Very like his brother in that respect. Although she was pretty sure by the way his gaze burned over her that True didn't need the benefit of her expertise.

Pulled between two forces of nature, her attention was drawn once again to the tall brooding man who stood over her, his thickly muscled legs braced apart, the impressive bulge at the apex holding her attention longer than was polite.

Since he hadn't offered to help her up, she cleared her throat, pushed a half-filled box off her lap, and struggled to sit.

A hand dangled in front of her face. A large hand with thick callused fingers.

Her heart hit a speed bump before hammering faster inside her chest. She accepted his firm grip and came up more quickly than she'd expected. She swayed against his chest before she got her feet underneath her. Then she had the whimsical thought that if he leaned forward just an inch, her mouth would graze the canvas material of his duster coat just over his heart. True was a big man.

"Thanks," she said breathlessly.

Slowly, he eased his hand from hers then took a step back,

his glance going back to her car. "We'll finish the unpacking. Those boots of yours aren't made for walkin'."

"Really?" she said, glancing down at the pretty cowboy boots she'd bought for her retreat that now had a thick layer of mud crusted around the bottom.

"Why do you think you fell on your ass?" He cleared his throat then stomped away.

Honey didn't know whether to take his comment as an insult or not, but she liked the sound of his deep growl. It rasped along her nerves, stirring long-dormant desires she'd sublimated in order to write the kind of surly, dominant men her readers seemed to love. Fictional men were easier to say goodbye to.

She stepped forward to help him, unwilling to just stand by and watch him do her work. However, a twinge of pain pulled across the muscles of her lower back, and she grimaced, reaching back to rub the spot only to discover her backside was covered in mud. Her grimace deepened.

"Did you hurt yourself?" Lonny asked, striding toward her with his hands clutching her papers. His gaze trailed down her body to where her hand rubbed.

"Just a twinge," she said. "What with the heavy lifting—"

True snorted and stepped past her, his arms filled with three boxes stacked high.

Her gaze followed him, wondering whether she should call him on his rudeness or let it pass. Something made her want to challenge him.

"He's always like that," Lonny said, smiling. "Don't take any offense."

"I didn't. Much," she murmured. She aimed a tight smile his way. "Would you two care for a hot cup of coffee when you're through?"

"We don't have time to chit-chat," True said, stomping right back out the door and down the steps.

She stepped into his path, forcing him to halt or slam right into her. "Did I say something that offended you?"

True's hands came up, gripped her waist and picked her up to set her aside.

Her jaw dropped. Heat filled her cheeks. When he walked away, she glared at Lonny. "He always does that too?"

Lonny's eyebrows were high, a little smile curving one corner of his mouth. "That's not something I've ever seen him do. Whatever you said to him—"

"I didn't say a thing."

He shook his head. "Something sure as hell set him off. I better go give him a hand before he tries to walk right through me without the courtesy of moving me first." He handed her the papers he'd rescued and followed his brother to her car.

Feeling off-balance because she didn't understand what had angered the gruff cowboy, or whether he'd simply taken an instant dislike, she wandered up the steps and into the cabin, scuffing off the mud on the doormat before striding inside. The boxes were stacked near the kitchen table where she'd decided to set up her office. The rectangular surface already held her laptop and portable printer.

She wondered what they thought of her array of boxes. There were reams of paper, a couple filled with research, but she'd shoved clothes and camera equipment into the rest because she'd been in a hurry to escape the telephone when she'd left her snowbird house on South Padre Island.

True stomped in again and set three more boxes beside her. "These are the last and kinda light," he muttered.

Probably held her underwear. The thought tugged a grin from her mouth.

His gaze dropped to her lips for just a second, and then it swept her body—so quickly she might have mistaken the once-over for a blink. When he'd finished, he tipped his hat and stomped out of the house.

Maybe he always stomped. Might not have a thing to do with her.

Lonny hovered in the doorway. "If you don't mind, I'll come by later to check in and see if you need anything."

Did she need anything? A hug? A smile to assure her she hadn't grown a second head or a wart on her nose. "I'd like that."

Lonny flashed a grin then hurried down the steps. Big

brother was already riding back up the ridge, his broad shoulders stiff.

Still, the sight of him, his sturdy body outlined in the snowfall that had begun sometime in the last few minutes, made her chest hurt. He wore loneliness like he did his long, dark duster.

She closed the door, shutting out the cold and the view. A shiver reminded her she'd better check the wood-burning furnace again. It was time to get to work anyway.

She hadn't come all the way to the Colorado mountains in the middle of winter to pine over a man she didn't even know and probably wouldn't like if she did.

Honey bent and tugged off box tops until she found the ones holding her favorite knit scarf, another pair of clean jeans and a gray sweater. She shucked off her boots and muddied clothes, dressed in the clean ones and wound the sky-blue angora around her neck. Then she hunted for the bottle of scotch she'd packed, knowing she'd need it to get to sleep as the anniversary approached.

She poured herself a finger of amber anesthesia into a coffee cup she found in the small cupboard over the sink and settled down in front of her computer.

Her glance strayed one last time out the window beside the door. Snow had begun to fall steadily in fat flakes. Not that she minded. She'd wanted solitude.

Looked like she'd get it too—other than the occasional visit from one sexy young cowboy.

Chapter Two

Lonny glanced up at the gray sky—what he could see of it anyway between the fast-falling snow. What had started as soft flakes had hardened to icy flecks that stung his cheeks. "You check the forecast?"

"Course I did. It said we'd get snow."

Lonny grinned at True's terse reply. The woman had really gotten to him. He'd barely spoken a word all afternoon. "How much snow?" he asked, goading him.

True stuck his pitchfork into the hay they were scattering for the cattle crowding closer to the flatbed where they both stood. "About three feet tonight. You might want to hold off visiting your girlfriend until tomorrow. It'll be deep enough for the snowmobile by then."

"I told her I'd stop by tonight. And she's not my girlfriend. Yet."

True stuck the fork in harder and tossed hay over the side where Lonny stood. "You hoping to get snowed in?"

Lonny brushed off hay and picked bits from his hair. "Dammit, True, you've been cross as a hungry bear all afternoon. Why don't you just spit it out?"

"She's trouble."

That hadn't taken much coaxing. Lonny eyed his brother, amused he'd let the woman get under his skin. "She's a big girl. Smart too, if you'd taken a couple of minutes to get to know her."

"Why bother? She'll be gone in a couple of months."

"Well, so will I come spring." He darted a glance at True,

but his brother's set expression didn't betray a thing about what he thought. "You know I'm heading back out on the circuit."

"Didn't ask you to stay."

No, he hadn't, but he'd certainly made his disapproval known in a hundred other ways. "You know what your problem is?"

True blew out a deep breath and leaned on the handle of the pitchfork. "No, but I'm sure you're gonna tell me."

"You need a woman, True. A wife. Someone to warm your bed and cook your meals. Someone you'll have to talk to."

"Tried that. Didn't work out so well, remember?"

Lonny grimaced. "You were both young. Don't you think it's time to try again?"

True's lips twisted. "Just who do you think I ought to marry?"

Lonny thought for a minute then shrugged. Fact was, he didn't know of any woman strong enough to stand up to his brother's hard-headedness. Becky had wilted beneath the long brooding silences.

A picture of Honey Cahill stepping into his brother's path flashed through his mind, and he smiled.

"I didn't think it was a joke."

Lonny pressed his lips together to kill the smile. "It wasn't. I was just thinking of Honey and the way she stood up to you."

"*Honey.*" True grunted and picked up the fork, thrusting it deep into the round bale. "Maybe we shouldn't talk about her."

"Why? Don't you like her?"

"I don't *dis*like her."

"She's a pretty little thing."

"Little being the biggest problem."

"Why's that?"

"She's not cut out to be here."

"Becky wasn't little and she—"

"We're not goin' there. Think I'm in a bad mood now..." He dropped the fork to the floor of the flatbed. "Ms. Cahill's *your* problem. You invited her. You can look after her."

"That won't be a chore." Lonny watched the way his

brother's jaw clenched and thought he might know what the real issue was. "True, you interested in her?"

"What?"

"Honey. Do you want her?"

True picked up his coat and thrust his arms through the sleeves, his always dark expression looking like a thundercloud. "I'll drive the truck back. Can't leave it here another night. You'll have to lead my horse." That was all he said before he leapt over the side of the trailer and stalked toward the cab of the truck.

Lonny felt undecided for a minute. Unsure whether he ought to cut his brother out of the chase by making the first move. But the thought of Honey's warm humor and womanly curves going to waste when his brother would never approach her out of sheer stubborn pride made the decision easier.

Maybe that didn't make him the best brother. He understood what drove True, but couldn't do a thing to make him budge. He'd been there when True's marriage ended. By all outward appearances it was an amicable split, but Lonny had seen the true devastation later in the darkness that settled over True. All happiness was crowded out of his life. He led a solitary existence that was unbroken by any urge for him to stir from their mountain.

Lonny leapt over the side of the trailer into a foot of soft-packed snow. He crammed his hat onto his head, gathered up the reins to his brother's horse and mounted his own. He turned toward the valley on the other side of the ridge where a plume of smoke promised warmth and feminine company.

If he felt a twinge of guilt, he quickly tamped it down. Honey was just too much temptation for a man to ignore.

Footsteps scuffing across the porch pulled Honey from her story. She glanced to the clock at the corner of her screen, surprised to discover hours had passed since the brothers had left.

The air inside the cabin was chilly, and she realized she'd let the fire go out. She rose, wincing at the dull ache in her lower back, then strode toward the furnace in the corner of the open room. She pulled the lever to close the flue and opened the door, careful to stand to the side as Lonny had shown her in case flame billowed out at the sudden influx of oxygen.

A knock sounded at the door.

"It's unlocked," she shouted, reaching for a log. "Come on in."

The door swung open. "Let me help you with that," Lonny said, stepping inside.

Grateful, she straightened, easing her muscles with a quick rub.

Lonny's brows lowered. He took off his hat and brushed the snow off the brim and his shoulders while he stood on the mat. He tugged off his gloves with his teeth, hung his hat on a peg beside the door then strode toward her. "You forget the fire?"

She wrinkled her nose. "I started working and forgot the time."

"That's a good thing, right? For your story?"

"Yeah, means I was in so deep everything else disappeared."

They stood studying each other's faces. His expression was watchful, but open. Friendly. And if the quick glance he gave her body before he bent and threw more logs inside the furnace was any indication—he was also interested.

"Did you eat dinner?" she asked, trying to remember how one of her heroines would ask a man to make love to her, but she was out of practice. Dinner was just a stalling tactic.

"Not yet," he said, closing and latching the door of the furnace. "Wanted to stop by before it got too late."

Maybe she'd been too subtle. "Do you have time to have a meal with me?"

Lonny's gaze locked with hers. "The way that snow's comin' down, if I stay longer than half an hour, I may as well wait until morning to leave."

There wasn't any pressure in the way he said it, but she understood what he was asking. Lonny wanted to spend the night with her.

Just what she'd been fishing for.

Her body, chilled only a moment ago, reacted with a surge of warmth that spread from her breasts up her neck to flood her cheeks. Embarrassed to be blushing like a virgin, she shifted her feet and winced when her lower back throbbed.

He sighed, pulling her attention back. The corners of his eyes wrinkled with good humor. "Tonight's not a good time for *dinner*. I better get on down the road. But first, I have something for you to try. Let's move over toward the light," he said, aiming his chin at the kitchen table.

They moved toward it. Then he fished in his pocket for a tin, which he unscrewed and held up for her to sniff.

The scent of camphor and something not quite as minty opened her sinuses in an instant. "What's that for?"

"For your back. It's a liniment I use on my horse when he's limping."

Her eyebrows shot up. "And you want me to do what with that?"

Lonny smiled his wicked, flirty smile and lifted a hand, finger pointed toward the floor. He twirled it.

Honey groaned. "You want to do this standing up?"

"I might get ideas if you insist I do it when you're stretched out on a bed. 'Sides, my horse never complains when I do it this way."

Honey laughed then slowly turned to give him her back.

Lonny cleared his throat. "Um...you'll have to push down your pants a little and lift your shirt."

"Lord, who turned up the heat in here?" she murmured.

His husky laughter stirred her hair, which told her he stood only inches from her. Standing this close, she caught a whiff of barnyard and mint. She wondered if he'd popped a Tic-Tac before coming inside. She decided she liked his earthy-sweet smells and relaxed.

She unbuckled her belt, undid her jeans and shoved them just past her hips. Then she took a deep breath and pulled up her sweater to bare her midriff.

"Nice dimples." Then his fingers stroked salve over her lower back, the camphor heating her skin. He set the tin aside. "I'm going to brace your front. Promise I won't take advantage."

"Sure," she whispered.

He placed his large hand over her lower belly. Her breath

hitched when his little finger entered the vee of her open pants. But her next breath was a sigh when he pushed the heel of his hand hard against her back, soothing muscles and making her sway. After a few moments, the hand pressed against her front was the only thing holding her up.

He glided and smoothed, working the liniment into abused muscle. Then he gently dug his knuckles into her, which caused her to rise on her toes and her head to dip toward her chest.

"Gettin' it?" he whispered.

"Mmm-hmm." Was he ever *gettin'* it. Getting her hot, getting her horny.

His hand slowed on her back.

She held her breath, listening to his deepening breaths that fanned against her neck.

The hand in front slipped beneath her open waistband, and then stilled. The warmth of his palm against her vulnerable belly was one of the sexiest sensations she'd felt in a long, long time. She knew he waited to let her make up her mind. She inched apart her feet.

His fingers sank deeper, touching the hair covering her mound. "Bend over. Grab the edge of the table."

The way he said it, his voice thick and raspy, sent a quiver of lust through her. She bent, gripped the edge while her heart pounded hard against her chest.

The first gentle scrape of callus over her hooded clit made her groan. She bit her lip to hold back more sounds.

"It's okay to make some noise, you know," he said, stroking deeper between her folds.

"It's been so damn long, I'll sound like a porn queen."

His chuckle sounded strained. His long fingers swept over her lips, gathering her moisture. One digit thrust into her entrance and swirled. The hand at her back resumed the massage, heel grinding into bruised muscle.

Aroused and soothed, all at once, her body began to quiver.

Honey wished she had the nerve to shove her pants off her bottom, to lift herself higher and beg for his cock, but that would have required her prying her fingers from the table. She gave an agonized groan and lowered her head, resting it on cool wood.

Two fingers stroked inside and she clamped her thighs together, holding him there.

He held still, but then she rocked her hips to fuck them. So wet now, his hand was sliding in slippery honey and he moved easily in and out, his thumb caressing her clit.

"Lone..." she moaned, turning her head, ready to beg him to fuck her.

"This is all you get tonight, sweetheart. Take it. Fly with it."

An apt description of just what she felt. Her body undulated in sublime heat. The flick of his thumb and thrust of those digits burrowing deeper, sliding faster, had her arousal building, surging...and then she came, shattering happily, her cries broken and aching.

"Sweet," he whispered, a kiss landing on her cheek as he leaned over her.

She gave a shaky laugh and pushed away from the table. He straightened behind her, pulling his fingers from her pussy. They made a slick trail up her belly.

"I'll let myself out," he said softly.

His footsteps moved away, and she zipped her jeans, leaving the ends of her belt dangling as she followed him to the door.

Honey was tempted to ask him to stay. *Really* tempted, but then she thought about that bottle of scotch and the fact she really didn't know Lonny all that well. Not yet anyway. "Guess you better go," she said softly. "But thanks. For...everything."

Standing next to the door, hat in hand, he turned. "If the power goes out, you won't have a phone."

She nodded. "I know." When he hesitated again, she laughed softly. "I do want that kiss you're thinking about."

Lonny's slow grin was filled with devilment. "Was I that obvious?"

Laughing softly, she stepped closer and tilted back her head. "I haven't felt this awkward since high school when Donny Mathis walked me to the door, then hemmed and hawed for ten minutes before working up the nerve."

"Should I be nervous?" he said, moving in, his hands landing on her hips to pull her against him.

When their bellies rubbed, she forgot all about why she shouldn't want this. The heat in his gaze soothed away her doubts.

His kiss was hot, not so much tongue that she felt like a snake wiggled in her mouth—nice. Very nice. His tongue withdrew, his lips suctioned hers. Then he lifted his head. "Be safe. And don't forget that stove again. I don't want you sick."

She warmed to his concern. "I won't forget."

He bent and gave her cheek a quick peck then ducked out the door.

She shut it behind him and leaned against the cold wood, her body still humming from the delicious thrill of their encounter. More than ever, she knew she'd done the right thing getting away from familiar surroundings. Not once while he'd been with her had she felt a twinge of sadness. Maybe she really was ready to move on.

True heard the clomp of Lonny's boots as he strode down the hallway. His office door swung open, and Lonny stuck his head inside.

His mouth stretched as he looked down to see what rested in True's lap. "Finally reading it, I see."

True set aside the book and dropped his feet from the ottoman he'd rested them on. "How's she doing?"

Lonny stepped inside the door, but came no farther. "Settling in."

"Didn't expect you back."

"Are you fishing to know whether we had sex?"

"Not any of my business."

"That's too bad," Lonny said, his face hardening. "She's mighty pretty. Took some of Mustang Joe's liniment over there to rub on her sore back."

True's body tightened. "She let you?"

"Didn't need much coaxing. Must have been hurting bad."

"That the only reason you didn't stay?"

"Nope." Lonny stepped deeper into True's inner sanctum.

He rubbed the back of his neck, and then aimed a pointed glance his way. "Things haven't gone so far I wouldn't take a step back."

True narrowed his glance then grunted. "Why are you so worried about my sex life?"

"Because you don't have one," he drawled. "And I'm not selfish. I have fuck buddies I can call on whenever I have urges."

"That's what you plan to make her? A fuck buddy?" He hated even repeating the phrase, especially in reference to Honey Cahill.

"Maybe I do."

True's gaze fell to the book.

"She's not like that. It's just what she writes."

True tightened again at the thought of the things he'd read. "Did you ask her what she had in all those boxes?"

"Think she's got slings and toys packed inside? Maybe a leather corset?" Lonny waggled his eyebrows. "I'd like to see her in one of those."

So would True. Which made him angry at himself. That wasn't him. To him sex wasn't a game. Wasn't something you had to dress up for. And he didn't have it in him to leave a mark on a woman. The images she'd painted of a woman so enthralled with a man she'd let him tie her up and whip her made him feel a little queasy—not to mention inadequate.

"Just say the word, bro," Lonny said softly.

"I don't need you to make any hookups for me. I'm not interested."

"Then why bother with the book?"

"Just wanted to know what kind of person we'd let onto our property." Damn, he was getting good at lying.

"She's nice, True. Sweet."

"You talking her personality or her flavor?"

Lonny shook his head then turned toward the door. "I'm gonna grab a bite. Later."

The door slammed shut, leaving True alone. The book lay face down, Honey Cahill's smiling face turned toward him. The picture wasn't her. It looked airbrushed. Her hair was darker in the black-and-white photo, and her smile looked forced.

He picked it up again, settled deeper in his chair and fought the erection burgeoning between his thighs as he read on. Did Honey like the *kiss of leather branding her ass*?

He remembered that sweet ass, those two dimples peeking from under her sweater. It was round and firm. Her skin was pale cream. He imagined his hand spread over a cheek, imagined lifting it to strike her soft skin. He'd leave thick rows of pink.

Would her pussy melt? Would she moan, *her breathy cries rising into a crescendo*?

If he had a mind to, could he even give her what she needed to be happy?

Foolish thoughts given the fact she'd be gone as soon the season changed. Still, the thought of spending a few nights in her bed, spending his frustrations and disappointments while he stroked her to satisfaction, tantalized.

He wondered about that massage Lonny had hinted at. How far out of hand had it gotten? Not that the thought of taking her, even if his brother had already been there, should really matter.

It wasn't like he wanted her in his life forever. The memory of her gaze landing on his cock for those long seconds while she'd lain sprawled at his feet teased him. Maybe he should stop by to see her.

He wouldn't be the one to make the first move. He'd let her actions, her expressions, tell him whether she wanted him. But then what? True cussed softly and picked up the book, looking for clues for how to please a worldly woman like Honey Cahill.

Chapter Three

The next day, Honey sat at the kitchen table, her fingers flying over the keys. Ever since she'd awoken that morning, she'd been filled with so much energy and ideas her fingers couldn't type fast enough to keep up. *And good Lord, the images...*

The story she'd begun had taken a decided turn. A delicious one. Sure, she'd explored the BDSM lifestyle, visited dungeons, interviewed Doms and subs, but this story wasn't about "what" the characters were doing. It was all about who they were.

This story felt natural, real...maybe because the heroine was every bit as conflicted emotionally as she was. Her own stirrings were seeping into the pages...a woman torn between her attraction for two men and bittersweet memories of the past. And since this was her book, her imagination, she released the reins and let it happen...on the page.

She wondered what Lonny would think when he read her book a couple of years from now. Would he recognize himself and his brother? She imagined he'd be thrilled and amused. But how would True feel?

The whine of an engine sounded from outside. She blinked away the haze she'd existed in since she'd started working, pulling free of the eroticism that had kept her body warm and her pulse thrumming.

She hurried to the coffee pot, listening as the engine quieted, and quickly refilled the pot with water, the basket with grounds. When it began to drip, she headed toward the door just as the heavy tread of footsteps approached it.

She swung the door open, and then stepped back, surprised because it was True. He held his hat between his hands. He'd cleaned up since yesterday. His clothes were tidy, his scent was fresh.

Inside, she melted just a little because she knew he'd gone to some effort, interrupted his routine to make an impression. It had worked. Her mouth dried in an instant as she looked him over. He was every bit as dark, as brooding as he had been yesterday, but today there was a hint of something else in his watchful gaze.

She stepped aside and waved him in without a word.

He stepped over the threshold and cleared his throat.

Was he nervous? Should she be? She felt only a stirring of happiness inside.

"I read your book." He blurted it—like the words were poison he had to rid himself of or choke.

Happiness was certainly fleeting. Her back stiffened. "Not to your taste, I take it?"

"It wasn't like anything I'd ever read," he said, his tone as surly as ever.

She crossed her arms over her chest, her face heating with embarrassment. Her stories were a reflection of her own yearnings, even when exaggerated as that particular book's had been. Anger slowly burned, because he'd managed to put her on the defensive, and she didn't think she deserved it. She worked damn hard to make a living at writing. She wouldn't apologize for the fact she'd found a way to keep food on the table.

"I take it you don't approve."

"That's not what I meant."

"Then why are you here?"

His eyebrows drew together in a fierce frown. "Because I wanted to know if you'd like to go out with me."

Surprise made her lift her chin. "Because what you read excited you? Do you want to tie me up? Spank me, maybe?"

His face turned crimson. "I want a lot of things, but those aren't top on my list."

She narrowed her gaze. "I'm not sure I like you."

"You don't know me," he growled.

"And you think you know me because of what you read?"

A ripple of tension tightened his jaw. "I read it because I wanted to know what it is you do—so we'd have something to talk about."

"You want to talk about dungeons and titty clamps?" God, had she really said that? She swallowed hard, feeling heat creep across her own cheeks.

His head canted, his gaze swept her face. "Are you always this uptight?"

She realized she was equally at fault for the fact this wasn't going well. The last thing she wanted was for him to stomp out the door in anger. They hadn't made the best start yesterday. Today's fiasco could spell doom for the rest of the winter.

She dropped her arms and strove for a less militant expression. "Would you like a cup of coffee?"

His nod was crisp. His mouth crimped. She wondered if he didn't speak because he was afraid he'd stick another boot inside his mouth, and that thought made her smile.

His frown deepened, his gaze dropping briefly to her mouth. Then he looked away—at the ceiling. Was he counting to ten?

"I promise I'm not that scary," she said softly.

His gaze slid back. "I apologize for jumping down your throat yesterday. I was angry."

"Because of me?" she drawled, beginning to enjoy the fact that his gruffness was apparently due to his uneasiness around her. Maybe he didn't get out much.

"Yeah," he said, then shook his head. "No. Because you're a woman."

"You wanted me to be a man?"

"Yes," he bit out, and then snorted. "No. *Dammit.*"

She couldn't help it, she laughed. His glower deepened even further. "True, I'm sorry too. But there's something about you that brings out the ornery in me."

His expression lost a little tension. "I guess I'm out of practice," he said, more slowly this time, as though trying to pick his words carefully.

"Out of practice with what?"

"Talking to women."

"Let me guess. You stay holed up on this ranch most of the time, with only men, right?"

He nodded, seemingly relieved he didn't have to explain himself.

Honey stepped closer. "Let's make a deal. I promise not to take offense the next time you bark at me, and you'll try not to." She held out her hand.

He eyed it for a moment then raised his. "Dammit." He tugged off his glove and took her hand, holding it gently inside his. His gaze rose to meet hers again, this time not as hard.

Her pulse leapt at that light touch. *How intriguing.* "I promise I'm not fragile."

He squeezed a little and pumped it up and down.

She laughed again.

This time the corners of his mouth twitched. "You always this forward with men?"

"You've read me. There's not a lot that shocks me."

He cleared his throat. "I'd be much obliged for that cup of coffee now."

She eased her hand from his, immediately missing the warmth. To hide the feelings swamping her, she turned to walk to the kitchenette and busied herself with cups and pouring coffee.

"I like mine black," he said from right behind her. He set his hat on the countertop.

"Good thing," she said evenly although her heart was tripping faster. "Because I didn't bring any creamer or sugar with me."

With the coffee poured, they stood beside the counter, both leaning their hips against it, as they quietly sipped from steaming mugs.

"What are you working on?" True asked. "Lonny said you were here to finish a book."

She sighed. "I was having trouble with my original idea. It felt forced. So I decided I needed a change of scenery. A friend of mine put me in touch with Leroy, but you know where that led."

"Too bad about the fire."

She let a little smile curve her lips. "I'm thinking it wasn't such a bad turn of events. For me, anyway."

"Really?"

"The story..." She shrugged. "It's coming now. It's not the same one I started, but I like how it's changed."

"What's it about?"

She blushed.

He studied her expression. "I'd ask, but I don't quite know how to."

"Without making us both blush, you mean?" She laughed. "Guess I can tell you. You're in it. Or at least someone like you is in it."

He snorted, but one side of his mouth quirked. "Should I be worried?"

"Only if the thought of a threesome makes you cringe."

His cup halted just in front of his mouth and he blinked. "A threesome?" he asked, his tone casual. However the glint in his eye was anything but.

She turned away, walking toward the table and her laptop, nervously closing the lid and searching for a way to explain without letting him know just how much she'd been thinking about it. "I usually write about a couple exploring their sexuality—breaking taboos to find out what they need from their intimate lives. This time, I have a heroine, Helen, who's attracted to two men. Brothers." She glanced up to see how her words had affected him.

His eyes narrowed. "Can I assume Lonny and I are the inspiration?" At her nod, he frowned. However, it wasn't an angry look. He looked as though he was trying to find the right words to ask another question.

"Okay," she blurted. "I'm attracted. To both of you. You're both so different—personality-wise. But alike in the way you look. It got me thinking—doing the what-if game—because I was stuck for an idea. I hope you aren't offended."

"Why should I be?"

"Because I patterned the characters after you and Lonny."

"It's not like it's ever gonna happen. It's just a story."

Disappointment, sharp and bitter, flooded her—which surprised her, because she hadn't thought far enough ahead to really wonder about the possibility—but now that particular door was closed. Firmly too, if his expression was anything to go by.

She cleared her throat. "I'm glad...that you aren't offended."

He set aside his coffee cup. "What about my question?"

"About us going out?" At his nod, she stalled. Making up her mind to have casual sex with Lonny hadn't made her this unsure. "Can we? I thought the roads are closed."

"I came to invite you to the ranch house. To have dinner at my place. I'll cook."

"You cook?"

"I do a lot of things that might please you."

That was his first blatant come-on, and he managed not to garble it. She suspected that he'd been thinking about saying that line, maybe even practiced it.

Inside, she felt that melting heat flicker into flame again. "I'd like that."

"About Lonny..."

She stiffened, remembering she had a problem. "What about him?"

"Are you going to tell him?"

"Tell him what?"

"That you're taken."

She blinked. "Taken? You mean claimed like a prize?"

"I don't want to step on his toes, but he did offer you to me. I don't think he'll mind."

"He offered me?" Her eyebrows shot up.

"Don't get your back up," True said, impatience in his tone. "That's not how it was. And remember, we had a deal."

"I said I wouldn't take offense if you barked, but you expect me not to take offense when you and your brother talked about me? Divvied me up like a piece of property?"

He sighed. "Look, you're mad. I better leave. I'll be back later to pick you up."

"And you think I'll still want to come?"

"Don't you?" He stepped closer, crowding her against the counter. "Don't you want to be with me?" His hands cupped her hips, not a tentative grip at all. He pulled her against him and then bent his head.

She leaned away, her gaze searching his expression. "You take a lot for granted," she gritted out.

"I saw the way you looked at me yesterday. *Where* you looked. You're interested."

"And you're crude, True Wyatt."

"Only bein' honest. I think we'd be good together and it's gonna be a long winter."

His mouth came down, and she stopped trying to defy him. Pride wasn't going to get her what she wanted. And he was right. She wanted him.

She reached up, smoothed her hands over his shoulders and sank her fingers in his hair and tugged it, bringing him closer.

When their lips met, she felt another fundamental difference between True and his brother. Lonny's kiss had been hot, enticing. True's made her tremble, head to toe. He pulled her lust from her core, as ruthlessly efficient at kissing as everything else.

His firm mouth glided over hers, rubbing twice before he opened and tugged her bottom lip between his. He bit.

She gasped—and he swooped inside, growling, the sound vibrating through her. Their torsos slammed together, her soft breasts crushed against a wall of muscle. Her nipples prickled, tightening instantly, and she moaned into his mouth.

His hands slid down to cup her ass, and he lifted her. She opened her legs, wrapping them around his waist, riding his long, hard ridge.

He leaned her against the counter as he rutted, driving his denim-covered cock between her legs, burning her sex with friction until she writhed wildly, rubbing her breasts and pussy against him, doing everything he'd allow while locked inside his embrace.

He turned his head, breaking the kiss. He dragged in deep breaths while she did the same.

"Be ready," he whispered.

Then he pushed her legs to the floor and stepped back. Palming his groin, he adjusted himself while his dark expression roamed her face and body.

She gripped the counter behind her, hoping the trembling would stop so she wouldn't sink to the floor because he was already turning away. Leaving her. When she'd been that close...

"Bastard," she whispered.

He didn't look back. "Been called that before. But I'm guessin' that's what you need."

She blinked, and then a lop-sided smile tugged up one corner of her mouth.

He reached the door, slammed his hat on his head and turned for one last glance. When he saw her smile, a rueful grin stretched his own mouth. He shut the door quietly on the way out.

Honey walked on air to the table, flipped up her screen then sighed. She could hardly wait to begin the next chapter.

Lonny heard a strange sound coming from the far side of the paddock where True had said he'd be working to repair rails that had loosened. Someone was whistling.

And since they were the only people on this side of the mountain, he knew it had to be his brother. Bemused, he rounded the corner of the barn to find True lifting a new board into a slot.

"Someone sounds happy."

The whistling stopped. True aimed a glare over his shoulder.

Okay, that was the brother he recognized. "Need help?"

"Got it handled," True said, reaching into a pocket of his coat and coming out with nails. He hammered the first into the wood, his motion sure—but his expression was thoughtful.

"You finish that book?" Lonny asked, pretending only idle curiosity.

"Didn't need to."

"Have her all figured out already?"

True grunted.

Suspicious, Lonny looked off to the ridge that divided the ranch for the high meadow. “I was thinkin’ about paying her a visit.”

“No need to.”

“And you know that because you’ve already seen her?”

“As a matter of fact, yeah.” True turned to face him.

By his expression, Lonny surmised he had something to say. “You did more than check on her, didn’t you?”

“I don’t kiss and tell.”

Lonny grinned. “But you did kiss her. Tastes sweet, doesn’t she?”

True’s expression hardened. “Find some other fuck buddy to mess around with.”

Didn’t take him long to figure out just the right words. “Took my advice, I see.”

True hammered in another long nail between his fingers and lifted the hammer. “She’s coming over for dinner.”

“Want me to make myself scarce?”

“Would you if I asked?”

“Not a chance. This I have to see.”

True grabbed the top of the board and pushed to test the strength of his repair, then moved along to the next board.

Lonny picked up an end and fit it into the groove on the next post.

“You don’t mind me cuttin’ in?” True asked too casual for it to be real.

“Sure I do. But I’m not near as interested in her as you are.”

“She said something today. Wondered if she’d mentioned it to you.”

“About what?”

Three taps and he stood back from the fence, meeting Lonny’s gaze. “About her story. The one she’s working on now.”

“She hasn’t said anything about what’s in this one. Hasn’t been time. Something bothering you about it?”

“She’s writing about us. Or at least two brothers like us. And a girl.”

Lonny waggled his eyebrows. "She writing a ménage?"

True's jaw tightened. "I don't want you gettin' any ideas."

Lonny couldn't help teasing him. True took everything too darn serious. "Think I'd be into it?"

"Wouldn't you?"

"Hell yeah. But I'm guessing you're not comfortable with the idea."

"Sex isn't a game."

"Can be. Can be a helluva lot of fun." He laughed. "I wish I could have seen your face when she said it."

True snorted and reached for the gloves he'd lain over a post. "Wasn't pretty."

"You let her down easy?"

"Not hardly. Fact is, hearing her say it made me pretty mad. I took it out on her. Not that she couldn't handle it."

"You make love to her?"

"Not yet."

"Thinking it will happen tonight?"

True nodded.

"Well, then I guess it would be in my own best interests if I left you two alone. A happy True isn't one who's gonna bust my ass all winter." Lonny clapped his brother on the shoulder then swung his arm over it, giving him a man-hug. "I'm proud of you."

True shrugged him off and pushed him away, but he wore a little smile as he headed back to the barn with the hammer and the boards he hadn't needed.

Lonny walked away, picking up the tune True had been whistling. He wondered how he could convince two stubborn people that this wasn't just hormones following their natural course.

He'd never seen a couple more suited.

As for himself, the road off the mountain was closed. He wouldn't be going to town until the snowplows made it this far. He'd be stuck listening to the sounds of someone else getting busy for once.

The thought of his brother hugging that sweet, dimpled ass made him sigh with envy, but he knew True needed this. He'd be a good brother and do his best to make sure the two of them had all the privacy they needed to get to know each other.

Chapter Four

Honey hugged True's waist and snuggled up as close to his back as she could while he expertly steered the snowmobile through the snow. They followed a wide indention in the thick white blanket that she figured was the road. Sure it was cold, but she loved any excuse to touch him. Even under the cold-weather gear she could feel the tensile strength in his hard, muscled frame.

He'd come for her at dusk, warning her to pack for the night in case the weather turned and he couldn't bring her back.

She appreciated that he didn't say outright, "Plan to stay the night with me", because she already blushed every time his gaze landed on her.

When she'd opened the door, he'd eaten her up with his forest green gaze. Dressed casually in layers to ward off the nip in the air, she knew her curves were muted, but that didn't stop him looking, like he was imagining her naked. She'd chosen a soft blue sweater, dark blue jeans and those boots he disapproved of.

He'd waited patiently while she'd tugged snow pants over her legs and then held her coat while she bundled into it. She'd wound her scarf around her neck and tucked her hair into the hood of her coat, all while he'd waited—and watched.

She'd watched him too, liking the breadth of his shoulder under his clean insulated jacket, the length and thickness of his thighs below. Lord, she couldn't be casual, couldn't pretend to be cool, knowing she'd see every part of his body before the night was through.

The snow had stopped around mid-day and even through the darkness the white drifts reflected moonlight. He didn't really need the headlight on the vehicle to find his way. Fifteen minutes later, he pulled up beside the porch of a large log home, as rugged and immutable as its owners. He cut the engine and waited while she climbed off, then swung his leg over, took her arm and led her up the stairs.

She grinned because his touch was firm. No way was he going to let her fall on his steps. She imagined he had plans for her ass other than nursing bruises.

The door swung open before they reached the top step. Lonny's wide smile eased her embarrassment over the fact she was arriving with his brother. The wicked glint in his eyes when he shook her hand told he was thinking about where his hand had been yesterday and she blushed.

How did they do that? It wasn't like she hadn't been around the block a time or two. Hell, she'd been married to a lusty man. And yet both brothers reduced her poise to breathless sighs and flushes.

"I checked on the chili," Lonny said.

"Save us some?" True said, a hint of wry humor in his voice.

"There's plenty left." He leaned toward Honey. "The secret ingredient's beer."

Honey chuckled as True lifted a hand and chucked Lonny behind the head. She didn't have any siblings, but felt an instant envy for their obvious affection.

"Let me get your coat," Lonny said, reaching for her zipper.

True cleared his throat and dropped the overnight bag she'd packed beside his feet. "Anyone does any unzipping it's gonna be me."

Honey and Lonny locked gazes then dissolved into laughter.

"I'm so glad you are two are enjoying yourselves," True said, his tone dead even.

Honey wiped away a tear and tugged down her own zipper. When she slipped off the sleeves, she surrendered it to True, who hung it on a coat tree next to the door. He pulled off his own then bent to peel down his snow pants.

She was so hyper-aware of the slide of clothing that the act of shedding the cold-weather gear was a nearly erotic act. She was breathless by the time she straightened and handed everything over.

Her mind leapt straight to the bedroom, barreling forward to the moment they'd both shed the rest of what hid their skin from view. Something of what she was thinking must have been written on her face, because when she looked up, True's eyes were smoky, his jaw set.

"Since I've had dinner, I'll retire...with a good book," Lonny said, giving her wink.

She barely heard him. Couldn't take her eyes off True. She'd written this scene today—with the older brother taking the lead—easing Helen past her inhibitions until she moaned like a wanton.

"You hungry?"

She sucked in a deep breath, deciding that playing coy would be a complete waste of a perfectly good hard-on. The hard-on was impossible to ignore—long and thick and pressing against his pant leg.

"You're staring again."

"Can't help it," she said, feeling suddenly breathless.

"What are you thinking?"

"About choreography."

His snort sounded suspiciously like a laugh, but she wasn't going to look to be sure. "Choreography?" he murmured.

"Yeah, I think those pants have to come straight down. You'd never get enough room to work it out of the front."

This time he did laugh, deep and rich.

Heat crept up her neck and flooded her cheeks. When she glanced up, her gaze slammed straight into his.

He held out his hand. She slid hers along his work-roughened palm and shivered because she knew she'd feel the scrape in a hundred delicious places.

He led her through the house, to a staircase that curved up to the second floor. Their footsteps were hushed by thick beige carpeting.

He opened a door and flicked on a light, then tugged her inside the room.

Once there, she spared a glance around his bedroom. A blue and white quilt covered a king-sized mattress. Heavy navy curtains covered the window. The furniture was dark maple—plain, but sturdy.

True tugged her hand, reeling her in like a fish on a hook.

Her head dipped toward her chest, because she felt suddenly shy, suddenly unsure. It had been so long, and she'd thought she was ready for this. But a shiver struck her spine, shuddering downward.

A hand cupped her cheek, and a thumb tucked beneath her chin to lift her face.

True's expression was impossible to read. "I thought you wanted this."

"I do." She licked her lips. "Guess I'm a little nervous. This part's always a little scary."

"I scare you?"

She nodded. "It's different for a girl," she whispered. "We have to surrender, have to open. I guess I'm feeling a little vulnerable."

"Would it make you less nervous if I got naked first?"

That little hint of a smile turning up one corner of his mouth fascinated her. She gave in to a whim and came up on her toes to press her mouth against his. He didn't try to embrace her, just held himself still while she pressed one kiss then another against his mouth.

His lips responded, softly molding hers, reassuring her silently that he would let her take the lead if she needed it.

She lowered herself again, pulled her hand from his and then took a step back. Without glancing at him again, she unwound her scarf then lifted her sweater over her head and held out both to him.

His breath held as his gaze raked over her lacy white bra and the bare tops of her breasts. His fingers curled around her clothes.

She rested a hand on his arm and bent to tug off her silly boots, and then she went to work on her jeans, laying open the belt and unzipping her pants.

When she pushed them down and stepped out of them, she glanced up again, wanting to see his reaction. She hadn't been naked with a man in three years. Kenny had thought her perfect, had told her a thousand times how beautiful she was, and she'd believed him. Standing in her white bikini panties and bra, she wanted to be beautiful and alluring.

Instead, she felt awkward. She wanted True to say something to break the silence that stretched because she felt foolish, thinking maybe she should have let him take the lead because then she wouldn't be waiting for him to react.

"I'm not on the pill," she blurted.

"I've got it handled," he said in his gruff tone.

Still, he didn't move. She turned away and walked toward the bed, wanting to dive beneath the covers and hide, but his hand reached out and snagged her wrist. She froze while he stepped behind her and unhooked her bra. Then his long, callused fingers gripped her hips and rubbed downward, pushing her panties down her legs.

They fluttered to the floor, and she was nude. Standing with her back to a fully clothed man with an erection.

His hands settled on her shoulders. "What's wrong, Honey?"

She shook her head. "I wish you'd do something."

"Not until you tell me what you're thinking. Your face closed up while you stripped. Like you were a hundred miles away."

"It's not you. I want to be here. I swear I do."

"Then what's wrong?"

She bent her head, unwilling to tell him because she didn't think it was any of his business. This was personal. More so than getting naked with the man. "I'm cold."

He sighed. "Go get under the covers." He released her hand.

She knew she'd disappointed him. She'd disappointed herself. Just minutes ago, she'd felt so carefree, so aroused.

However, a thousand miles hadn't distanced her from her memories.

The rustle of clothing reassured her she hadn't completely

blown it. She lifted the quilt, pulled down the sheets and slipped into the bed, shivering because the crisp cotton was chilled.

Bare feet padded around the bed, and True entered her vision.

She sucked in a breath as she watched him remove his watch and set it on the nightstand. His chest was broad and lightly furred with dark brown hair that stretched between small brown nipples. His belly was taut, muscled, a study in shadow and light that tempted her fingers to explore the ridges that defined his washboard abdomen.

Everywhere she looked was so masculine, so hard, that her fingers tensed and her mouth grew dry.

But it was his cock that made her want to weep. Thick, long and so aroused it lifted proudly from his groin—it reminded her of everything she'd lost. She missed sex, missed feeling a man thrust deep inside her body. Missed the heat, the gentle violence.

"You're doing it again."

His gruff tone coaxed a smile from her. "I'm sorry."

"For what?"

"Killing the mood."

He sat on the edge of the bed. "Does it look like I'm worried?"

"Nope." She flipped back the covers, inviting him to lie beside her.

He eased into the bed, coming to his side, facing her, but not touching. "So tell me."

Honey drew in a breath, fortifying herself to say it. "I was married."

He nodded, but held silent.

She took another breath, but this time her chest didn't feel quite so tight. "He was a school teacher, but joined the Guard. Army Guard. His unit shipped to Iraq."

True scooted closer and clasped the hand that lay between them. His thumb swept up and down the back of her hand, soothing her as she breathed deeply, trying to put to words the pain of her loss. She cleared her throat. "He died three years ago. Shot in an ambush. I usually spend my winters holed up at the beach house I bought with the insurance he took out. I couldn't face it this year. Thought I needed to get away. It's so different here. The air's fresher. The cold...it's nothing like home."

"It sounds like you're not over him, Honey. You sure this is what you want?"

She met his gaze, but tears caused her view of the hard edge of his jaw to waver. "I have to let go sometime. And I have. Mostly. I thought if I could stay busy, maybe I wouldn't dwell on it. I felt so happy, moving in, meeting you and Lone...I felt ready."

True let go of her hand and combed his fingers through her hair, pushing it behind her ear. "We don't have to do anything."

She sniffed and shook her head. "That's not it. I want you. It's just the getting naked part that freaked me out a little. I haven't been with anyone else. And then Lonny kissed me and I felt happy, *horny* again." She wrinkled her nose, knowing she shouldn't be talking about his brother when she lay next to him in bed, but hey, he'd wanted to know. "He made me laugh, made me forget about how awkward it can be."

True's brows lowered. "I made it awkward?"

She swallowed hard, recognizing that something about his quiet intensity was actually turning her on. In fact, every spike in her arousal appeared to be directly linked to his increasing tension. "It's awkward only because I'm realizing how badly I want this to be good."

"Are you sure you should be in bed with me?" he rasped.

Honey quivered at the raw sound. "I'm attracted to you both. I've already admitted that. Can't stop thinking about some really naughty things, but I need you, True. I need you to be the first. And I know how that sounds. But I can't help what I feel, what I need."

He nodded, but his expression didn't close up, didn't look disapproving. He moved closer, pulling her flush against his body. His cock was there between them, hard and pulsing. She tilted her hips to rub her belly against it.

A muscle flexed at the edge of his jaw; his nostrils flared. "I'll tell you what, sweetheart," he whispered. "I'll be your first.

And then we'll talk about what's next. I thought I was the only one with issues. Makes me feel like a selfish bastard that I got so wound up about you choosing me. I had a wife, but she's still alive and kicking. Married to someone she likes a whole lot better than me."

She gave him a weak smile. "I can't believe that."

His mouth curved. "I'm not the easiest person to live with."

Her smile widened. "Imagine that. Did you bark at her too?"

"Never." His smile dimmed. "But then again, I didn't talk to her much either. She hated the silences, hated being alone when I was out working cattle. What was his name?"

She didn't have any trouble following his segue. "Kenny."

"What did he think about what you do?"

"Are you kidding?" Her smile didn't dim, but his face shimmered in the tears welling in her eyes again. "He was my biggest fan."

The tears did it. He couldn't be jealous of a dead man, but the fact she cried over him, the fact she'd really loved him, made him ache. For her.

He reached out slowly, slid a hand around her waist and pulled her closer. When her head settled on his arm, he breathed easier, taking in the sensations—the scent of her hair and skin, the softness of her cheek on his arm, her tightening breasts against his chest. Yeah, he was hard, but he could stand the discomfort. It was her sadness that nearly killed him.

She sighed and snuggled closer, easing her thigh higher over his hip. Her hand made a tentative glide over his belly then stopped liked she'd realized what she'd done. Her breath held for a long moment.

And he couldn't help it. He swore silently to himself, because his cock surged, nudging the back of her hand.

He held his breath, counting, wanting to be strong, willing his body back under control, but she turned her hand and glided her fingers down his shaft. It was just a light skim of her fingertips, but it was enough to make his pulse leap.

Her hips moved, surging against him. "True," she whispered.

He kissed her forehead. “Baby, be sure.”

“I am. I swear. Please.”

He cupped her cheek then curled his fingers under her chin. He slid his lips along her skin as he tilted her face higher. When his mouth touched hers, she sighed and melted closer.

Slowly, he moved away, just far enough to give them both room to look. He stared down between them, at her hard, cherry nipples, at her soft belly that quivered against his rock-hard cock.

Honey raised her thigh, setting her foot against his leg, opening herself. She watched him just as avidly as he smoothed a palm over her hip, rubbing her thigh to knee, then slid to her inner thigh and trailed his fingers upward to search between her legs.

She was wet, her sex steamy. He thrust two fingers into her and watched her eyelids dip, her nostrils flare.

He dragged in the steamy scent of her and swirled his fingers inside her.

“True,” she groaned.

He thrust deeper, rubbing the pad of his thumb over her clit, relieved to discover it was hard.

“True,” she said, her voice higher, more urgent.

He kissed her forehead again, smiling softly to himself. “What, baby?”

She nuzzled his cheek then whispered in his ear, “Got a condom?”

He pulled his fingers free and rolled to his back, stretching to reach the drawer to the nightstand. He pulled it open and fished for a packet, cursing when the drawer slid farther out and tilted downward. But his fingers closed around a small square just before the drawer crashed to the floor.

He came back to her, bit the foil and ripped it open. “I need two hands.”

“Let me?”

He gritted his teeth, wanting to cloak himself, because her hands were shaking and her fingers were cold, but he gritted his teeth and waited, watching while she plucked the center of the circle to stretch the tip, then placed it over the head and began to slowly roll it down his length.

Either she wasn't very skilled or she was nervous. She only rolled it halfway down his shaft.

"Been a while," she said, then bit her lip.

"You're doing fine."

Her fingers were too tentative and the latex stubborn.

Finally, he pushed away her hands and gripped himself, gliding the condom downward until he was sure it wouldn't come off when he began stroking her. Then he rolled and came over her.

Her breaths gusted in shallow huffs. Her hands gripped his shoulders.

He nudged her apart with his knees, but rested on his elbows so he wouldn't overwhelm her with his weight. "Put me inside you."

She fisted him. This time her fingers closed tighter around his shaft. On his knees, he reared back a little, gave her room to position him, then he flexed his hips and thighs, pushing forward and finding her center. He thrust slowly inside.

Her hand drew away, slid over his side, scooped at his lower back then traveled lower. Her fingernails scraped over his ass and dug into his flesh.

"True..."

"Yes, sweetheart." He pulled back, leaving just the crown inside her.

Her head tilted back, digging into the mattress. "Fuck me," she said, her voice deepening. "God, I ache for you. Please, don't tease. Don't be gentle."

Pulsing forward once, he bent to rub her lips with his. "You sure you're ready?"

Her nails dug in harder, her head rolled side-to-side, her hips surged upward, trying to capture him as he pulled away again. "Bastard, just do it."

He almost smiled, but his desperation made it a grimace. He sank, sliding deeper and deeper, and then hooking at the end to force her hips to move with his. When he was as far as he could go, he ground hard, moving side-to-side, stretching her, drilling—needing to be as deep as he could go, wanting to force her to recognize how well he filled her—giving in to the primitive, primal urge to imprint her with his masculinity.

Honey didn't seem to mind. Her body shivered against him, her hips bucking under him. Her thighs crept around his waist and held tight, giving him a glimpse of her own possessive urges. She pressed her lips against his shoulder then bit him there. "Move, please," she groaned. "I need you to move."

He came up on his arms, peering down at her, his gaze raking her spiked breasts, her undulating belly, then staring down at where their bodies joined. He eased from her, watching his cock, reddened and glazed pulling from her lips, before stroking in again, screwing her slowly.

Honey's features blurred, her cheeks reddened, her breaths became jagged. "Talk to me," she gasped.

True shook his head. "What?"

"Talk to me. You're staring, but what do you see?"

"Beautiful. Baby, let me talk...after."

"I need you to talk, to help me relax. I'm hot...hurting even...want to come, but I'm too tense."

"Not a good time." He bent and skimmed his mouth along her jaw, but she turned away and her fingers curved around his shoulders, holding him back.

He leaned his head on her shoulder. "This something he did?"

"Yes."

"I'm not him."

"I know that. But I'm..."

"Are you scared?"

"A little. I want this so much, but I can't let it happen."

He drove into her again, but her legs weren't squeezing around him now. She wasn't lowering them, but she wasn't participating anymore. "*Dammit.*"

"You say that a lot."

He grunted and slowed his motions, trying to gather back the frayed edges of his control. If she needed him to comfort her, he'd give her that. However hard it was for him to do this. He wasn't used to talking during sex. Didn't quite know how to start. "I'm not an easy man."

"I think that's one of the first things I noticed about you," she said breathily. "The fact you weren't easy. I thought you didn't like me much."

"I didn't not like you. I just didn't want you on my mountain."

"Because I'm a girl."

"Yeah. It wasn't anything personal."

"Do you still feel the same?"

"Guess I do. It's a hard place in winter."

"And yet you're fucking me."

True snorted and ground into her. "I'm a man."

"And I'm available."

He pulled out and thrust in again. "It's not like that."

Honey's lips thinned. "Yeah, maybe we shouldn't talk."

"You promised you wouldn't get bent out of shape."

"I wanted something I've been missing, something you can't give me. Obviously. Let's just fuck. That's all you want anyway."

"Dammit."

Her smile didn't hold an ounce of humor.

Feeling as though he'd failed a test, he pumped harder inside her. "Yeah, maybe we shouldn't talk too much. We can't manage to do that without having an argument." He'd bet she never had that problem with her paragon of a husband, but as soon as he thought it, he felt guilty. The man was dead. She'd loved him.

He was jealous of a dead man.

True pulled free and pushed her legs off his hips. "Turn."

Her eyes widened, but she did as he said, turning slowly onto her belly, then coming up on her knees in front of him.

This view of her body took his breath away, made him so hard he could barely squeeze a breath from his lungs. Round, peach ass, soaked, reddened labia. Her slender back quivered.

True tucked his fingers inside her, coaxing more of her natural lubricant down her channel then removed them. Fisting his cock, he fed it into her cunt, pushing deep. Finally, clasping her hips, he rocked forward and back, faster and faster.

When her head dropped between her shoulders, he reached around her and swirled his fingers on her clit, circling relentlessly while he hammered her.

Her back arched, her bottom thrust against him, backing up to take him deeper. He had it right now. Could give her this if he couldn't give her anything else of what she seemed to need from a man.

When her pussy clamped hard around him and she mewled like a kitten, he clutched her hips again and hammered faster, harder, not relenting until she gave a muffled scream.

True said his own hallelujahs in silence and pumped twice more before emptying himself inside her. He rocked in and out, milking every last sweet convulsion until she'd wrung him dry. Then he pulled free, settled on his side and dragged her into his arms.

He might not be the man she wanted, but he was the one holding her now.

Chapter Five

Honey woke just as dawn broke. In the gray light, she knew instantly that she was alone, and she didn't have a clue when True had left the bed.

She was glad he wasn't here because she'd made a mistake. How fucked up was she? True wasn't Kenny, and yet her husband had been here in the bed with them. She'd dragged him here, comparing the two. Asking True to fill the void Kenny's passing had left, if only for the short time they'd screwed.

She hadn't been fair to True. She should have kept her mouth shut, given him a smile and taken everything he'd offered. But she'd been greedy. She'd wanted it all—the closeness, the feeling of being cherished and loved.

God, she had to get out of here before she saw him again, but that was going to be difficult when she needed someone to take her home.

Honey showered in a hurry, dressed in the clothes she'd packed, and then silently crept through the house. Why? She wasn't sure. True and Lonny were ranchers and had likely been up for a couple of hours already. She wasn't going to wake them, but she didn't want to alert either that she was up, not until she had a chance to put on a happier face.

She'd have to brazen it out, pull H.A. Cahill's boldness around her, pretend that last night hadn't been earth shattering.

When she crept into the living room, her shoulders fell. Lonny sat on the couch, already dressed for the weather outside. He held a knit cap in his hands, twirling it in his fingers until he saw her. His glance looked her up and down, and he stood. "I'll take you home."

"True ask you to?" she said, her throat tightening in disappointment.

"Yeah, said you might need a little space." His lips thinned into a narrow line. "Are you all right? I thought you two would get along. Did he hurt you?"

Honey shrugged, not able to hold his gaze for more than a second. "He didn't hurt me. I…it was all my fault. But I really don't want to talk about it."

"To me?"

"To anyone. Not right now."

He nodded and strode to the door, lifted her jacket off the tree and held it for her as she slipped her arms inside. She zipped up and moved away while he lifted her bag and headed outside. She grabbed her snow pants and followed.

The temperature had dropped. A sharp wind rustled tree branches and stirred last night's snow. Lonny's vehicle sat in front of the porch and he climbed on then held out a hand to help her mount behind him. She tucked her pants under her bag and climbed on.

The trip was mercifully short. He pulled up to the porch and began to dismount, but she was already pulling her gear from under the bungee cord on the back of the saddle. "Don't bother, I can manage."

"But you'll need help with the stove."

She didn't want him inside. His presence would only remind her of how she'd let down her guard and invited him to touch her the last time. "I'm an expert now," she said, giving him a tight smile.

"Look, if you need anything…"

"There's the phone. I'll call. Promise."

He didn't look happy, but nodded and pulled away.

She climbed up the steps and opened her door. Inside the air was freezing, and she hurried to the stove, adding kindling and striking a long match. When the kindling caught, she fed the fire a couple of the logs.

The stove was lit, the air slowly warming. She took off her coat and hung it on the peg. She'd give her computer a chance to thaw before she opened up her story and started back to work.

While she waited, she shuffled through the kitchen, starting coffee and eating an energy bar. Anything to keep busy and not think about how True had looked when he'd tipped up her chin and asked her what was wrong.

He'd just tried to be kind. But she'd melted. And she hadn't been able to admit it to herself at the time, but he'd scared her, because she'd wanted to latch on to that hint of tenderness and make it into so much more. She'd fought her instincts and had muddled everything up. He had to be confused. He'd thought he was getting a sexpot writer in his bed, and instead he'd gotten a basket case.

That her emotions were so close to the surface disappointed her. She was ready to move on and take a new lover. That part of her life couldn't be over. She hoped he'd give her another chance because she remembered how'd he'd been, how gentle and gruff, how masterful and how well he'd filled her.

The sound of crackling logs stirred her from the counter, and she strode toward the furnace, ready to add enough wood to last the morning. She bent and opened the door.

Yellow-orange flame billowed out and she jumped back, but the fire caught the scarf she'd forgotten she was still wearing, causing it to crackle and curl. Frantically, she pulled it from her neck and flung it away, then stepped back.

Christ, how many times had Lonny told her to be careful opening the door?

Crackling behind her, louder now, drew her glance. She looked back and her heart stopped. The scarf had fallen on the sofa beneath the window. Flames licked at the throw and raced up to the curtains. Smoke was beginning to fill the room.

She lurched toward the table, grabbed her thumb drive and bent to get beneath the smoke near the door. It was her only exit, she didn't have much time. The fire was running across the walls, scorching the ceiling. She didn't have time to reach for her coat. She swung open the door, cool fresh air rushed into the room, fanning the flames. She ducked, raised both arms to protect her head and plunged through the door, coughing. She fell down the steps, and scurried away on her hands and knees, not halting until she was several feet away. Gasping, she climbed to her feet and turned back to see flames in the window catching the wood frame, licking up the roof and igniting the cedar shingles.

Fascination kept her rooted to the spot even though her boots sank deep into the snow. Flames, yellow, orange and red, could be seen through the window. The whisper of the fire as it consumed more fuel grew into a roar.

Shivering in the snow, she watched in horror as the fire leapt across the roof to the lean-to beside the house, the one where the gasoline for the generator was stored.

That realization, at last, pushed her to move. She turned and ran as fast as she could, feet sinking in snow, down the road toward the Wyatt brothers' house. Shock receded from her mind and she realized how much trouble she was in. Already shivering hard, without a coat or gloves, she stood a good chance of freezing to death before she reached safety.

Honey shoved away that thought. She wasn't going to die. She wasn't going to lose a single finger either. She needed those to type. Shoving her hands under her arm pits, she slowed and concentrated on putting one foot in front of the other. She'd get there.

No way in hell would she die and let True have his final proof that she'd never belonged here in the first place.

True gunned the engine, enjoying the burst of power and speed, not even minding the frigid wind that blew past him. He'd needed to get away from the house, from the woman sleeping in his bed.

Once she'd fallen asleep, Honey had snuggled up close against his side. He'd enjoyed her mingled scents—something floral, feminine musk and sex—and had decided not to bathe before heading out because he'd wanted to let Honey's smell linger just a little longer on his skin.

Not that he needed any reminders of what it had been like to be with her. She'd fit just right, her head on his shoulder, her hip snuggled against the side of his, her hand lying on his belly. He'd lifted it cautiously, not wanting to wake her, and measured the length of her small fingers against his. She was small and delicate, and yet she'd taken everything he'd given her.

Shame washed over him. He hadn't been as patient as he should have been. She'd had things on her mind, memories so haunting he'd seen the shadows in her eyes, and he'd wanted to obliterate every one of them. Wanted to imprint himself on her.

But she wasn't his to keep. He hadn't the right to expect her to cleave to him alone, to forget about any other man she'd known before. And did he really want that?

He'd only dozed after that, waking to think about what he ought to do for her, how he could make it up to her. He'd wrestled with his own jealousy, his own hang-ups, but had concluded he needed to have a talk with his brother.

He drew close to the crest of the ridge and considered heading to her place. However, he still wasn't sure what he'd say to her. Maybe he'd start by saying he was sorry.

The sound of another engine coming up behind him made him slow. Lonny pulled up alongside him.

"I took her home."

True nodded, ignoring Lonny's expression. His brother had a bone to chew, but True wasn't in the mood. "How was she?"

"Brittle," Lonny bit out. "She wouldn't look me in the eye."

True's stomach sank. "I'll go see her."

"If I were you, I'd give her some time alone."

True clenched his jaw. He didn't want to listen to Lonny's advice.

"Guess we should head back." True glanced up at the ridge. "What the fuck?" He twisted the throttle. The snowmobile shot forward.

It had to have been a branch, a shadow...something other than what he suspected, but already he could smell it on the air.

Smoke.

He turned to Lonny, who rode beside him. "Honey!" he shouted, punching a finger toward the plume.

Lonny's glance whipped toward the sky.

They crested the ridge. True's stomach dropped. The cabin was fully engulfed. He searched the clearing but didn't see a sign of Honey. *Fuck, fuck, fuck.*

He started forward, but Lonny cut in front of him, halting him. "The lean-to, bro," he shouted.

An explosion rocked the clearing. Burning timbers flew into the sky.

True ducked, raising an arm against the bright light, but as soon as the debris crashed to the ground, he was speeding down the hill, hell-bent for the cabin. Staring at the flames, at the smoke billowing out the broken windows, his heart thudded dully against his chest. No one could live through that.

He pulled up next to the house, killed the engine and swung his legs over the side.

"True," Lonny shouted over the roar of the fire.

True couldn't let his brother stop him. He lurched toward the steps.

Lonny tackled him, taking him to the ground. "Honey's not in there. Fuck, quit fighting me. She's not in the cabin."

That last bitten-out sentence got through, and True stopped bucking.

Lonny rolled off him, then grabbed his arm and helped him to his feet. Breathing hard, Lonny pointed to a set of tracks leading away from the cabin—tracks two small feet in ridiculous boots had made.

He climbed back on his the snowmobile, and sped down the trail.

Rounding a bend, he found her, walking with her head bent against the wind, hands tucked under her arms.

He cut the machine and climbed off. He unzipped his jacket and walked up behind her. She didn't seem to hear him, didn't flinch or react when he gripped her arms, one at a time and shoved them into the sleeves of his coat. He turned her.

Her face was smudged with soot. Her eyes vacant.

"Let's get her to the ranch house," Lonny said. "We can't warm her up here."

True zipped up the jacket then climbed onto the snowmobile. Lonny swept her up and handed her to True who draped her over his lap. The wind bit his ears and nose, but he couldn't worry about that now. Honey hadn't said a word.

The ride to the ranch house took only minutes, but felt like an eternity to True. At the steps, Lonny pulled her off his lap and carried her inside. True followed, shutting and latching the door, then headed straight to the fireplace. It took several minutes to build a fire, but by that time Lonny and Honey had disappeared.

He found the two of them in Lonny's bathroom. His brother had stripped her and set her in the tub. True hovered in the doorway, wanting to shove Lonny aside, but not knowing if he was what Honey needed right now.

Lonny glanced up and then rose from where he'd been kneeling beside the tub.

"I started a fire," True said, surprised his voice sounded hoarse.

Lonny nodded. "I'll hunt up something for her to wear. Warm up the water, gradually."

True stood aside while his brother left then turned all his attention to Honey.

She sat shivering in the bathtub, her shoulders bowed, her lips pale, and her head down.

He tipped the toilet seat closed and sat on it. Then dipped his fingers in the water. It was tepid. "Are you ready for me to add some hotter water, sweetheart?"

She nodded and wrapped her arms around her knees, hiding her body. "S-sorry," she stammered.

True shook his head then gave in to the temptation to touch her. He combed her hair back from her face then tucked a finger under her chin to lift it. "I thought you were inside," he rasped. "Nothing else matters."

Her lips curved downward, but he could see the relief in her eyes.

"Are you hurt?" he asked softly.

She shook her head. "Just cold." She tipped the stopper with her toe to drain more water. Then she gave him a pointed look.

He almost smiled at her show of spirit, small as it was.

"Yeah," he said, turning on the tap. "That was quite a fireworks display you put on."

"I fucked up. I swung open the furnace door..."

He nodded, pretending calm when he could picture it all too clearly. "You're lucky you didn't burn yourself."

"My scarf caught fire, and I flung it away. It caught the throw and the curtains. I didn't have time to get anything except my thumb drive."

"You saved your book?"

"Guess I should have gone for the coat instead, huh?"

"A coat might have been more practical." He tested the water and shut off the tap again. When he met her gaze, he drew a deep breath. "I'm thinking this is all my fault."

She wiped her nose with the back of her hand. "Because you didn't kick me off your mountain yesterday?"

"Because I didn't keep you in my bed."

"Oh." Her gaze fell away.

He cursed under his breath. He'd reminded her of what a bastard he'd been.

A knock sounded and Lonny stuck his head inside the door. "I'll leave the clothes on the bed out here."

"No," True said. "I'll see about getting some food heated up. Get her dressed." He lunged to his feet and pushed past Lonny, ignoring his scowl.

Behind him, Lonny said, "Honey, you ready to come out?"

His chest heavy, True moved through the house like an old man. Why did it matter to him that his brother was dressing a woman they both barely knew? Maybe he was suffering some sort of delayed reaction now that adrenaline wasn't spiking through his blood. He was relieved Honey hadn't been injured, or worse. He'd have felt guilt and remorse if she had been inside that house. Nothing more. They were strangers. Intimate strangers, sure, but she wasn't part of his life. Not part of his future. He'd do well to remember that.

Honey sat huddled under a blanket on the couch Lonny had moved nearer the fire. He'd found a pair of insulated leggings for her to wear that fit her well enough. Her ass kept them from falling off. The sweater was large, and fell off whichever shoulder she shrugged, but beggars couldn't be choosers. Her own clothing was salvageable and was in the laundry, but she'd save them for her trip off the mountain once the snowplows cleared the road.

Lonny had checked with the department of transportation and said it might be several days before she could leave. And she was determined to do just that—despite his assurances that she could stay and complete the work she'd come to do.

However, that seemed pointless. She'd saved the thumb drive, but she didn't have the heart to finish the new story. She was supposed to write something sexy and flirty, but all she had the urge to create was a tragedy.

She knew she was feeling sorry for herself, and she should pull up her big-girl panties and get on with it. But she didn't have any panties on.

"I have soup."

She jumped at True's quiet words. The man could creep up on a ghost. And was that all he had to say? *Seriously?*

Honey bit back a retort, recognizing that what she really wanted was to start a fight—with him. She held out her hand and waited while he turned the mug to present her the handle.

A small gesture, but one that fucked with her head. Why be gentle? Why pretend to care whether she burned her fingers? She'd burned down his entire cabin—his quaint little hunting cabin that his father had built years ago. Why wasn't he furious?

She gulped down a sip of chicken soup and blinked.

"Couldn't you tell it was hot?"

She blinked away pain-filled tears and aimed a blistering glare his way.

True's jaw clenched. "I'll leave you to finish." He began to turn away.

She bent to set the cup on the floor. "Why are you avoiding me?" If she could have bit her own tongue and swallowed it whole, she would have.

True hesitated. "You've been through enough."

"Don't give me that crock of—" She glanced away. She wasn't going to cuss at the man. Wasn't going to make herself look any more pathetic than she already was.

"I'm guessing now's not a good time to check on our girl."

Both Honey and True turned to glare at Lonny whose mouth moved like he was biting his lip. Was he laughing at them?

"Don't disappear," True said. "I can't seem to get anything right."

"No kidding," Honey muttered.

Lonny walked deeper into the room, glancing from Honey to True. "I take it you're feeling more yourself, Honey?"

"I've never been less myself," she snarled.

"I don't know about that," he said amiably. "The color's back in your cheeks."

Honey hit her thigh with her fist. "I don't shout at men. I don't ever want to shout at men. But he—" She glared at True. "He manages to push every last one of my buttons."

"And that's a bad thing?" Lonny asked softly. He took a seat beside her. "Quit hovering, True. Take a seat."

True looked reluctant but took up the space on her left side. Wedged between the two brothers, Honey blew out a deep breath. The temperature in the room had skyrocketed. She flipped back her blanket.

True reached for the edge and shoved it over her shoulder.

"I'm warm enough," she muttered.

"You'll get sick."

"And that would be a huge inconvenience on top of the hundred other inconveniences I've caused, wouldn't it?"

True nodded, but her searing glance had him buttoning his lip and glancing away. "I should head out to check on the horses in the barn."

"They'll wait," Lonny said flatly.

Honey flung up her hands. "I can assure both of you that I'm fine. No need for you to worry. If you'll just show me where I can sleep..."

Lonny laid a hand on her knee and leaned toward her.

"That's part of what we're going to talk about, sweetheart."

She narrowed her eyes to give him a mean glare even though inside her heart was thumping loudly in her chest. "Oh, yeah?"

"True mentioned what you're writing."

True muttered a curse under his breath.

Honey's cheeks burned. "Anyone ever tell you that you two are big fat gossips?"

"Not ever. Don't change the subject. A ménage, right?"

"I changed my mind," she said, folding her arms over her chest. "I've decided to scrap the book. Now I'm going to write a post-apocalyptic story—lots of blood and guts. I'm feeling pretty violent at the moment."

"I think you need to do the right research."

"Oh, really?" She wouldn't admit it even on her dying bed, but just the thought of doing a little *research* made her heart flutter madly.

"You can count me out," True said forcefully.

"Not to your taste, I know," Lonny said, so cheerfully he made Honey want to scream. "You mentioned that before."

Honey kept her gaze on Lonny because she was way too chicken to look at True. "You two talked about doing a ménage with me? Is anything sacred?"

"Don't get your panties in a twist."

"You know damn well I'm not wearing any."

"Dammit."

That did it. Honey swung toward True. "Do you know any other cuss words?"

"His vocabulary's limited," Lonny quipped.

She lifted her chin when True's gaze narrowed. "So I noticed," she said, keeping her tone even.

"Be nice," Lonny chided.

She grunted and faced forward again. "Sorry."

"Back to the ménage..."

True stirred beside her, and she felt his thighs tense like he was going to rise. Without looking at him, Honey laid her hand on his thigh and pressed down.

"There ought to be a few rules," Lonny continued. "Things each one of us won't do."

"Like swords never crossing," she quipped.

"For fuck sake," True ground out. "Did either of you hear what I said? *Not interested.*"

"If I believed that for a minute, I'd lay off." All humor was gone from Lonny's voice.

Honey held her breath, waiting...

True stayed tense beneath her hand. His breaths deepened.

"Personally, I'd just as soon not 'cross swords' as Honey suggested," Lonny said slowly.

Honey drew in a deep breath. "I'd just as soon not be tied down."

Both men pinned her with a glance.

She shrugged. "I like to touch."

True jerked but didn't try to rise.

"You got any aversions, True?" Lonny said.

True stayed silent for a long moment. "I'm the only one who fucks her pussy."

Honey bit back a groan.

"Crude, but to the point," Lonny murmured. "Leaves lots of fun stuff still on the table."

"I haven't agreed," she said. She wanted to say yes, wanted to so badly she was squeezing her thighs together. However, more was on the line than a simple sexy romp. She could feel the undercurrents stirring in the room. "I'm not a whore. Doesn't matter what I write."

True's hand covered hers resting on his thigh. His thumb swept over the back. He breathed a deep sigh. "Just once then. Because you're curious. Because I owe you."

"You don't owe me a damn thing."

"Yes, I do. When we're done, you and I are gonna talk."

Honey swallowed at his quiet intensity. "What if I freak out again?"

"You didn't freak out. You were a little scared is all. Lonny's good at chasing away shadows."

Honey darted a glance True's way and their gazes locked. Something hot and fierce raged in his eyes. "I don't want us to be over," she whispered.

His expression softened, and he leaned toward her. "Baby, I promise we're far from done."

Chapter Six

Lonny had chosen True's bed, saying he'd be the one to leave when they'd finished. Like he was leaving a table after a meal. And maybe this really was just his idea of a midnight snack.

Honey found some comfort in that thought. At least he didn't have any expectations beyond this day. She had enough for all of them.

Entering True's bedroom for a second time might have made her feel awkward, but Lonny grabbed her hand and walked in backwards, pulling her along with a tug and the wicked glint in his eyes.

She didn't have to look behind her to know True was likely glaring daggers Lonny's way. The thought made her grin. Lonny halted in the middle of the room and dropped her hand only to tug her sweater off one shoulder and nibble at her neck.

His tongue flicked over her skin, his teeth bit gently along the curve.

She giggled when he found a ticklish spot and drew back.

Humor was evident in the crinkled skin beside his green eyes, but his nostrils flared as well, his jaw hardened.

Her breath hitched in response to his arousal and heat melted her core.

His hands lifted the bottom hem of her garment and dragged it upward.

Since she was braless, the nubby cotton scraped her nipples into peaks that tightened in the cool air.

True had walked farther into the room and leaned against

the wall, watching silently as she stood with her arms at her sides and her breasts bared for both men. She should have felt a little shame, but instead, her nudity unleashed her desires. She reached for Lonny's buckle and slid the leather through the loop.

Lonny laughed and eagerly rucked up his shirt, dragging it over his head. She had his belt off and thumbed open the top button. When she couldn't tug down the zipper, she knelt in front of him and used both hands to coax it down.

Lonny's hand petted her hair. Then his fingers dug into her scalp. She grabbed his waistband and pulled his pants down, along with his boxers, not stopping until his cock sprang free in front of her face.

"Might have been easier if you'd started with the boots," Lonny murmured.

"Easier for whom?" she said, glancing up through her eyelashes. Holding his gaze, she gripped his shaft and pointed his thickened cock at her mouth.

From the corner of her eye, she watched True stir against the wall, uncrossing his feet and muttering.

Feeling powerful and sexy, she rubbed Lonny's cap over her lips, enjoying the softness. Then she stuck out her tongue and tasted him, lapping playfully around the head and curling her tongue to lick the underside of the ridge surrounding it.

Lonny's fingers pulled her hair. "Baby, you're killing me here."

"But I've only started," she said, giving him her best little Miss Innocent glance.

He growled and flexed his hips, driving his cock against her mouth, and she opened, letting him glide inside. He stroked over her tongue, forward and back, his breaths deepening.

She reached one hand around him to cup his ass and with the other, she palmed his balls, tugging them in rhythm with her forward bobs. He fucked her mouth—she met his strokes, beginning to suction around him the deeper he came.

The sounds they made were lewd—wet slurps, deepening moans. All the while they played, she knew True was watching, listening. She wanted to goad him to do more.

Wrapping her hand around Lonny's shaft, she began to pump, squeezing hard, her hand moving easily in the moisture she left. She pulled and stroked, faster and faster, suctioning harder until his fingers dug hard into her scalp and his thrusts became desperate jerks.

"Baby, pull away," he whispered. "I'm gonna blow."

Her mouth full, she gurgled, shook her head and pumped faster.

He gave a throaty laugh then groaned. The first spurt of semen lashed over her tongue, and she pulled free, still pumping him with her fist and closing her eyes as he striped her face, one hot spurt at a time.

When he stood trembling, breathing hard, she let go of him and rested her ass on her feet, her face still tilted toward him. Cloth brushed her cheeks, rubbing away his sperm. A kiss landed on her mouth and she opened her eyes to find Lonny smiling softly. "Does he have a clue how good you are?"

Honey grinned. "Not yet."

True's whole body was so tight, his cock so hard he was ready to drive a fist or his dick into something solid to relieve the tension.

Watching Honey swallow his brother's cock down had been hard enough. To watch the tender scene between them now made his stomach ache.

Lonny kissed her one last time then helped her to her feet. He lifted his chin toward True. "Go undress him while I get the rest of my clothes off."

Honey didn't hesitate, turning on her heel to approach him.

True straightened, dropping his arms, wanting to retreat because he didn't want this, didn't want an audience, didn't want to show them both how near to violence he really was.

Her body flowed like honey, hips swaying suggestively, her blue eyes dark and mysterious.

When she stood in front of him, the hard little cherries of her breasts near enough to scrape his chest, he stiffened.

She cocked her head to the side, studying his face. He knew he had to look hard-edged and angry. But she didn't hesitate, reaching for his belt, tugging the tongue free from the buckle and sliding it slowly from the loops. When her fingers went to work on his buttons, she had to break away and watch what she did.

He stared at her bent head, at the sticky cream in her hair that his brother had left as a taunt, and he wanted nothing more than to take her to the ground and fuck her raw.

Instead, he held still, letting her repeat the process of opening and lowering his pants. She knelt in front of him and looked up his body, her cheek sliding along his shaft.

Something in her eyes, something soft and pleading drew his hands from his sides and he cupped her cheeks. His fingers slid into her hair and centered her on his rigid cock.

The first glide of her tongue was heaven. Nothing less. The second caused him to stab forward, impaling her hot, wet mouth. She breathed loudly through her nose and sucked on him, her tongue and mouth squeezing around him.

True couldn't tear his gaze away from the woman working his cock so sweetly. His wife had done it because he'd asked. Honey loved it. He could tell by the soft moans she made, by the dreamy lowering of her lids as she suckled.

He'd never felt anything like her soft wet mouth. Never been loved so thoroughly. Watching her, feeling every stab and stroke of her tongue, his balls hardened, drawing close to his groin. His toes curled inside his boots.

True glanced up and found Lonny lying on his side on the bed, his hand around his dick. When his gaze rose to True's, he smiled. "She's something."

Something straight out of heaven.

Honey came off his cock, but continued to pump her fist. "Want me to swallow your come, True? Or do you want to paint me with it?"

"Fuck."

She smiled. "So you do know another cuss word, or was that just a statement of your intentions?"

Lonny chuckled, but True was way beyond verbalizing what he wanted. He pushed her hand away from his shaft, fisted himself then gripped her hair hard and pulled her face toward him. He slid his cock back into her mouth and fed it, inch by inch, until he had to drag his hand away. Then he rocked forward and back, watching his shaft slide into her pink mouth.

She cupped his ass and came up a little higher on her knees, aiming her mouth straight over him and swallowing him down, using the back of her throat to caress him.

It was the sweetest fucking kiss, and he felt it all the way to his toes and back. But she wasn't through surprising him.

Honey moaned around him, her jaw widened, and then she forced herself farther down his cock.

He'd never been deep-throated. Never heard the likes of the gargling groans she made as she took him down. He stroked once, twice, then felt his balls explode. "Fuck...*fuck*!"

His come blew through his cock in steady pulses, and she swallowed it greedily, suctioning and pulling more from him, until he finally lowered his heels to the floor and tried to drag her off him.

When his cock slipped from her mouth, she continued to lick his shaft, his balls, tongue-stroking him, lips gliding along his length, until she finally pulled away. Wiping the back of her hand over her mouth, she sat back on her haunches and stared up at him.

She wanted praise. He could see it in her expression.

He didn't know the words to express how he felt. Instead, he hauled her up, hands beneath her arms, and then held her against his chest until his heart slowed. "That was so damn good," he whispered against her hair.

"Glad you liked it," she said, laughter in her voice.

"I owe you."

"You said that before, but I'm not keeping score," she whispered. "Promise I'm not. Whatever you want of me, I'll give it. It's my pleasure."

Her pleasure. How the hell did he get so lucky? "I don't deserve you. I was rough with you last night."

"I thought I blew it, going all weepy on you. It embarrassed me, but you...the way you looked..." She nuzzled against his neck.

He hugged her harder against him. "How'd I look?"

"Like you cared," she said, her words muffled against his skin.

True closed his eyes, remembering the sick hollow feeling in his chest when he'd seen the cabin consumed by flames. "I do care. I swear I do."

Her head lifted and she pressed a kiss beneath his ear. "True?"

"Yes, baby?"

"I want to fuck."

Her words, gusting against his neck, made him shiver with delight. However, he was spent for now. The little witch really had wrung him dry. His gaze went to his brother. He didn't want to glance down, but Lonny's erection was too impressive to ignore. Taking a deep breath to fortify himself, he set Honey away from him, turned her and slapped her butt to get her moving toward Lonny.

She gasped and glanced over her shoulder. Her cheeks flushed. "Didn't know you had *that* in you."

True grunted. He hadn't known either, but he'd liked the sound his palm made against her soft flesh.

Honey slid a knee onto the bed.

Lonny reached for her and pulled her over his body as he lay back. At least he couldn't see his brother's dick anymore. It bothered him more that he was comfortable admitting that.

Lonny glanced over Honey's shoulder. "True, get on over here. We're ready to play and need another set of hands."

True closed his eyes. He could do this and not make an ass of himself. And truthfully, he was more than a little intrigued about how Honey was going to handle two men. She talked big, but he'd seen her less than confident.

Lonny had her draped over him, his hands planted on her soft ass, kneading her as he kissed her mouth.

Her feet stretched, her toes curled, her bottom sank as she ground against Lonny's cock.

True climbed onto the mattress and pulled her toes.

She chuckled and looked back. "You wanted my attention?"

"I want a sight more than that," he ground out.

She turned back to Lonny. "Did I tell you how much I love

it when he growls at me?"

Lonny smiled and lifted his head to kiss her again, and then he rolled, coming over her body. He straddled her waist and grabbed her wrists, holding them above her head.

A frown wrinkled her forehead. "I told you I don't like being restrained."

"Maybe you never had the right guys making you stay put. We'll give you plenty to touch."

She bit her bottom lip and glanced over at True.

He sat, one arm around a bent knee, pretending he wasn't ready to grab Lonny by the scruff of the neck and pitch him to the floor.

"We owe you a turn," Lonny said. "No matter what you told True." He climbed off her then crawled toward the head of the bed. He pulled Honey up until her back rested against his belly. His hands slid over her abdomen and swept upward to cup her breasts.

When he raised his head, he dared True to make the next move.

True knew exactly what he wanted to do. Taste every inch of her.

He grabbed Honey's ankles and forced apart her legs and climbed between them. Smoothing his hands up and down her soft thighs, he watched her skin rise in gooseflesh. Watched her sex clasp and open. She was wet, ready to be taken.

He bent and cupped her belly, skimming over the fine hairs, and dipped a fingertip into her belly button.

Lonny smacked her breast, causing her to gasp and squirm. True aimed a glare at his brother, but was caught by Honey's expression. Her eyelids dipped, her pink mouth formed an "O".

On his hands and knees, he climbed up her body, nestled a knee beside her hip and dipped to mouth her nipple.

Lonny cupped her, plumping up her breast, and held still while True latched onto the quivering tip and drew it into his mouth. He sucked hard, stretching the nubbin, then chewed gently, enjoying the sounds she made, low, pain-edged moans, loving the way she writhed and fought Lonny's restraint as he clasped her wrists again and held them out to her sides.

True rooted at her breast, nuzzling his face into the soft cushiony globe and then worked his way over to the other breast to torture her some more.

Honey let out a breathy laugh. "I didn't know you two were sadists."

"That pleases you?" Lonny said slyly.

"I didn't know it would, but...*fuuuck*..."

The last word stretched as True bit her nipple and tugged it, pulling it outward then releasing it to spring back.

Her one thigh he didn't have bracketed rose, hugging him, and she rolled her hip side-to-side, as though trying to comfort herself.

True gripped her upper thigh and lay it down, opening her wider beneath him, and scooted down the bed, nibbling and licking his way across her ribs, along the gentle curve of her belly. He tongued her belly button then gave her sharper flicks as he made his way to her soft mound.

"Jesus," she whispered. "Lonny, let me go."

Lonny stretched her arms upward, forcing her back to arch, pulling her belly taut.

True pushed apart her thighs and laid his hands against the tender insides to force them wider still until her inner lips opened, revealing her entrance.

He sank his face into the crease between her right labia and thigh and licked along the line, then the side of her smooth feminine fold. "You shave?" he murmured against her.

"Wax...it lasts longer," she moaned.

He fingered the soft bristles she'd left clinging to the edges of her outer labia. "I think I'd like to see you completely bare."

"I'll mention it to the attendant at my salon."

"Maybe you'll let me shave you."

Lonny chuckled. "Her pussy's wet, True. Quit teasing her. She's rubbing her butt so hard against my cock I might not last."

"I don't give a fuck about your hard-on, brother."

His own cock was thickening, but he concentrated on Honey's geography, spreading her outer lips and running a finger along the pink flesh he bared. Then he ruffled the edges of her inner labia, noting how they resembled flowers petals. But they didn't smell as innocently sweet. He dragged in the scent of her musk, stroked his tongue between her delicate lips and caught the cream oozing from inside her.

He'd never thought much about oral sex. He knew his way around a woman's pussy, but he'd never been this fascinated. Her response to his exploration, the breathy moans and subtle pump of her hips, fed his own arousal. He sank two fingers inside her, testing the fit, learning the texture of her inner tissues, rubbing around until he stroked over the spot that caused her to cry out and jerk upward.

"That it, baby? Did I find it?"

"Again...right there...please, True."

He rubbed her again, memorized the depth then slowly withdrew.

Her mournful cry made him smile. When he glanced up, Lonny smiled too, although his face was tight and strained.

True had had enough.

He came to his knees, laid his hands on her thighs and stroked her with his thumbs while he waited for her eyes to open.

When she peeked between her lashes, he said, "Just how far do you want to take this?"

Chapter Seven

Honey's eyes widened. He expected her to say it out loud?

"Not a fair question, bro," Lonny said, his thumb stroking over her wrists. "Despite how this seems, Honey's a lady, through and through."

His touch soothed where just True's hard expression made her pulse jump. She wanted it all. Wanted to be stuffed so full of cock she couldn't breathe, couldn't think. She wanted this to be different from anything she'd ever experienced—she needed it to be *more*. "You don't have to defend me," she said under her breath.

True rasped his thumb over her folds again, and her belly quivered. She was open, vulnerable. Couldn't he see how much she wanted to be taken? By both of them? She sucked in a breath to slow her heart rate and center her thoughts.

True bent over her and rubbed her mouth with his thumb, painting it with her cream. She licked her lip, touched his thumb then sucked it into her mouth, her gaze never leaving his.

He leaned closer and kissed her forehead, pulled away his thumb and kissed her mouth, then hovered there, his breath mingling with hers. "I know how strong you are. How sexy. You aren't afraid of the words. I've read them."

She swallowed hard. "It's different when it's in my head. I'm free to be however I want."

"You're free here, baby. To do anything you want. To have us do anything that'll please you. You only have to say it."

Her eyes filled and she blinked away the moisture. He'd

called her strong and all she wanted was for Lonny to let go of her wrists so that she could wrap her arms around True and hide her face when she said it.

But they weren't going to let her hide. "I want your cocks," she said hoarsely. "Both of them."

True kissed her mouth. "How?"

"You, in my...pussy," she paused because she'd almost tripped over the word. "I want Lonny..." Fuck, she couldn't say it.

Lonny's cheek glided against her hair. He freed her hand and squeezed her breasts. "Say it, baby, and I'm there."

She gave a choked laugh and shook her head. True's eyes glinted with heat, and maybe just a little jealousy. She didn't mind a bit that he felt possessive. "I want Lonny up my ass."

Lonny's chest shook beneath her.

Her cheeks flooded with heat.

The corners of True's mouth twitched. He kissed her hard and pulled back.

"Up you go, sweetheart," Lonny said, pushing her off his chest.

Honey sat up as Lonny slipped from behind her.

"Have to find the lube."

"Oh, hell," she whispered. She hadn't thought it through, knew intellectually there was a process to the preparation. Kenny had taken her on her virgin drive, but it had been a long, long time ago.

True lay down on the bed beside her. She rolled to face him, slipping her hands under her cheek. He smoothed a rough palm over her hip. His fingers tightened, pulling her in.

When they lay facing each other, their hips snuggled close, she gave him a shy glance. "I'm truly sorry about your cabin."

True grunted. "I'll rebuild. I have plenty of timber. Don't worry about it."

"You say 'I' not 'we'."

"I run the ranch. Lonny's pretty much ceded everything to me. We share profits, but he doesn't like the day-to-day. He only comes back during the winter to lend a hand. He prefers rodeoing."

"He mentioned that when we met." She lowered her lashes, wanting to ask more because he was talking to her. She enjoyed the low timbre of his voice. "I'm sorry about last night."

"I told you before, you shouldn't be. We were both there. I pushed a little too hard."

"I didn't mind that. You unnerved me a bit, but only because..." She bit her lip.

"Because, why? What did I do? I won't do it again."

She shook her head. "It was me. I liked it, when you were...tender. I was melting, and I didn't know how to handle it. I thought it would just be fun, you know?"

He combed back her hair then cupped her cheek. "It was never just fun. Not for me. Since we're being honest, I was a little confused too. I want more than this, more than sex, Honey. I didn't want to feel like this, but I do."

She blinked and raised her gaze. The banked heat was still there; his arousal painted his cheeks a rosy hue. But there was warmth in his green eyes. Words became a barrier, and she drew closer to rub her mouth on his, telling him the best way she knew how that she loved what he'd said.

His tongue darted out, slipping between her lips and he growled as he threaded his fingers through her hair and kissed her hard.

"Stay like that," Lonny said, his voice filled with dry humor.

True growled again, and broke the kiss to give his brother a hot glare.

Lonny chuckled.

Honey glanced over her shoulder.

Lonny held up a tube of K-Y. "Since I know True won't stand for me coming over the top of you two, side-by-side will work just fine."

She turned away, gave a moan and hid her face against True's chest. She felt the tension in his body.

He kissed her hair. "Sure this is what you want?"

"Only if it doesn't affect us," she whispered.

True hugged her closer. "Just the once then."

"Just this. I'm really not looking to be the middle of a threesome. But I'm..."

"You're curious."

"I want something I've never had before."

He tugged her hair to raise her face, and studied her expression for a long moment. The hard edges of his face relented and he kissed her forehead. "Lonny, quit hovering. We're doing this."

Honey stiffened as the bed dipped behind her. She flinched when a cool hand cupped her bottom.

"True, she's a little nervous," Lonny said quietly.

True slid his thumb along her cheek and leaned in to kiss her again. "Put your arm around me, sweetheart. Forget he's there. For now."

His kiss was soft and sweet, surprising when she could feel how hard he was, how his cock jerked every time her belly moved against it. True wasn't a naturally gentle man, but he restrained himself for her.

"Condoms, brother."

True pressed her lips again, then muttered a curse. He rolled to his back and reached for the nightstand drawer. "Dammit."

She smiled, remembering that he'd pulled it out in his rush to cloak himself last night.

He rolled up and bent to stretch toward the floor, and came back with two packets, one he tossed at Lonny. With his back to her still, True bit the foil. She heard the sounds of latex stretching, snapping. He cursed again then lay down, gathering her against him.

Her smile was wide because he was sweating and his scowl dug a furrow between his eyes. She smoothed a finger over the dent. "I wish we didn't have to bother."

"Why aren't you on the pill?"

"I haven't been since Kenny. Haven't needed it." She said her husband's name, and this time the ache it caused wasn't quite so painful. Nestling closer to True's chest, she ran her lips over his collarbone and slowly lifted her thigh to rest on his hip, opening herself to him.

His fingers traced down her belly, tugged the trimmed hair cloaking her mound. She tightened her thigh over him and gasped when his fingers slid inside her. He drew liquid arousal from inside her, exciting the secret spot he'd found, all the while watching her expressions.

She didn't hide a thing she felt. Biting her lip, she scrunched her nose and eased her hips closer, rubbing her abdomen against his erection. Her womb clenched, heat curling around and around inside her, and she gave a moan when his thumb scraped her clit.

"Put me inside you," he whispered.

Her hand slid down him, fingernails scratching. His belly leapt and tightened, and then she was there, gripping his thick shaft, centering his cloaked head at her entrance. She curled her hips and took him inside.

His fingers parted her folds, easing his entry, stretching them around his cock as he pumped in shallow thrusts.

His hand snagged her wrist and moved up to thread his fingers between hers and then squeeze. Holding her hand, he began to stroke deeper, his breaths sharpening along with hers, her channel melting around him, clasping him to invite him deeper.

Lonny came up against her back and caressed a buttock. "Don't jump," he said softly. His hand smoothed over the globe, massaging her. And then he traced the crease, a single digit circling on her tiny hole.

She moaned and bucked against True, while her whole body began to quiver. They were going to do this. It was really going to happen, and she didn't know if she could take it, but couldn't stand the thought of putting a halt to it.

Lonny's finger disappeared for a moment then returned coated in gel, which he rubbed around and around her little hole, exciting her so much her breaths grew ragged.

When a single finger pushed inside, she held still, a long breath squeezing from her lungs. He pushed another inside and began to pump, swirling his fingers around and around, screwing into her slowly, stretching her deliciously.

Yes, there was burning, but her pussy was heating too with the friction of True's quickening thrusts.

When Lonny withdrew again, he came so close his breath gusted against her ear. "You've done this before. You know how.

I'm coming into you now. Relax, baby."

The smooth blunt knob of his cock pushed against her opening, and she hissed between her lips at the pressure.

True kissed her. "Relax, Honey. Let him in. I'm right here."

She slipped an arm around his back and clutched him close, nuzzling her face into the corner of his neck while Lonny pushed, finally breaching the tight ring and sliding deeper.

Lonny's groan was loud and so filled with relief, she gave a nervous laugh.

"Not funny," he muttered. "You're so goddamn tight I feel like my dick's being chewed right up."

True cupped her face, pushing her hair off her cheeks where it stuck to sweat. "We're going to start moving. You okay with that?"

"Yeah, don't do a thing, Honey," Lonny said, his voice tight. "You'll kill us both if you do."

Again, she chuckled, and then groaned as first True then Lonny began to stroke deep. Any thoughts of embarrassment about what they were doing, what True and Lonny thought, burned away in the heat of their passion.

Caught between two strong, relentless lovers, she mewled and groaned, whimpering as the two men surged in tandem inside her. The coil twisting in her belly wound so tight, she squeezed her eyes shut, dug her nails into True's back and chest and keened while she splintered apart.

"Jesus, Honey," Lonny groaned, then buffeted her ass with several forceful lunges until he stroked one last time, stayed deep and shuddered through his orgasm. His groan was loud. His hands closed around her waist then cupped her breasts. His body writhed against her back until at last he relaxed, huffing, his lips trailing along her neck and shoulder. "Fuck!"

Honey smiled and met True's hard gaze. He was still lodged deep, still hard. Nowhere near a climax of his own. She could see in his face that he meant to leave the last, best impression. She liked that about him. How deliberate he could be in his lovemaking.

So while she was trembling in the aftermath of her own orgasm, already she felt a stirring, another coil of arousal building. Lonny had only stoked the fire.

Lonny eased from inside her and gave her one last hug. “I’m making myself scarce now.” He kissed her hair. “That was un-fucking-believable, sweetheart.”

Then he rolled away and his footsteps padded to the door.

Instead of gathering her closer, True disengaged, sliding his cock from her and peeling down his condom. She lay on the bed in a sprawl, watching, wondering what was next, because there was no way in hell he was leaving her. She let out sigh when he reached for her, lifted her in his arms and strode toward the bathroom.

Being a possessive kind of guy, she figured he didn’t want the scent of another man, even if it was his brother, on his lover’s skin. And she was okay with that.

He set her down on the rug in front of the shower, pushed back the glass door and turned the handle to start the water warming. Honey smiled to herself, content to let True do things his way.

When he glanced back, his eyes narrowed. “Don’t get too comfortable.”

She lifted her chin and placed her hands behind her back, pushing out her chest.

As expected, his gaze dropped to her nipples, which were hard and dimpled.

“They liked the way you gnawed on them.”

“Gnawed?”

“Mmm-hmm. Like a chew toy.”

Although his eyelids stayed narrowed, a smile twitched at the corners of his mouth.

She was starting to figure him out. The more she learned about this taciturn man, the more she liked and admired. True wasn’t exactly rigid or set in his ways, but he did like order. Did think that people belonged where they were put.

Lonny’s wanderlust confused True. He worried about him when he wasn’t around where he could keep a watchful eye over him. He’d worried over Honey, even before he knew her, not because she upset his schedule or inconvenienced him, but because he couldn’t protect her.

The longer they stood gazing into each other's eyes, the warmer she felt, the more sure she was that she wanted to pursue a relationship with this man—if he'd allow it. If he wanted her beyond this day, beyond the winter.

She wasn't sure she was in love, not yet, but she felt with a certainty that grew stronger with every moment she spent in his company that it would happen.

"The water's warm."

Which meant he wanted her to move. A man of few words who got his message across loud and clear. He should be her editor.

Smiling, she stepped into the shower and moved back to make room for him. Inside there was a seat, a ledge really, and a nice expanse of smooth slate gray tiles that made the shower seem like a cave with a waterfall splashing against the walls. It was a fanciful thought, but she liked the romance of it.

When he picked up a folded washcloth and indicated that she should face away, she bit back the embarrassment, because she knew what he wanted to wash. Thankfully, he didn't go straight for her ass.

He soothed her with a soapy massage and scrub that eased the muscles of her neck and back, before kneeling behind her. He parted her buttocks and washed her thoroughly, arousing her along the way, so that when he finally stood, she was leaning her hands against the wall to keep upright.

His arms encircled her from behind, the hand holding the washcloth opened and it dropped to the floor. He smoothed his soap-softened hands over her belly and breasts until she was rubbing her butt against his groin, trying to give him a hint she was ready for more.

True's hands gripped her shoulders and turned her to face him, then slid down her back to her bottom and gripped her hard. She gave a little jump to help him lift her, not that he needed any, and wound her legs around his slippery waist.

"Shower sex," she whispered. "My favorite. Makes everything slick."

"I don't think you need any help in that department."

"Guess I am constantly wet around you anyway."

He shook his head smiling. "I don't think I'll ever get used to the way you talk."

"Do you think you might want to?"

He didn't answer, but his gaze locked with hers and he lowered her onto his cock. He didn't need to center himself, didn't need nudge or tap to figure out where he was. His cock honed in on her pussy and slid right up in one lusty plunge.

"You're pretty good at that," she gasped.

He gave her a lazy grin. "What? Fucking?"

"Finding my pussy," she purred.

"The boy knows where he belongs."

"In my pussy?"

"Lady's got a dirty mouth."

She arched a brow. "Guess you'll have to keep it busy."

True snorted, and then began to move her with his big, capable hands, up and down his shaft. Too slowly to suit her.

She bit his shoulder. "Faster, bastard."

True tsked. "I like the pace just fine. Don't want it endin' too soon."

She tightened her legs around him and tried to bounce, but he held her steady. "We can do it again."

Up and down, up and down. The air warmed around them, growing mistier and hotter. She wasn't sure if she was dripping from water streaming over them or from her own sweat. Damn, the man was going to drive her crazy.

She licked the side of his neck, tasted his shoulder, and then lapped up the side of his cheek.

Dimples sunk into his cheeks as his smile widened and she marveled that she'd never known he had them.

True backed her up to the smooth wall and began to pump faster, his legs braced wider for more leverage.

She appreciated the extra force and squeezed hard around him, a little reward to encourage more progress.

"You're not big on patience," he gritted out. His face was reddening, his cheeks tightening to show the sharp, high-set bones beneath his skin. He was close. Not close enough to let go, but he only needed a little more incentive.

She laved his ear and stuck her tongue inside the whorls,

rimming him over and over. Ending with a nip at his earlobe, she whispered, "Fuck me harder and I'll let you do anything you want. I'll give it to you so good."

A laugh disguised as a snort shook his chest, but he tightened his grip on her ass and hammered up her channel. She'd have bruises, but she didn't give a damn, the friction he built was burning her up. Each powerful, sharp surge rubbed her raw inner tissues. He was big, thick, more than she should be able to handle, but fuck he was so damn near godlike when he fucked, all she could do was hold on and try to catch a breath.

True was relentless. Pounding so hard, so deep she felt each tap against her cervix, and she realized with a start that neither of them had remembered protection.

Not that she was concerned. Not really. He wasn't a player. Neither was she. And there would only be the sweetest consequence of all if their mistake bore fruit.

The thought of a child from a man like True filled her heart with warmth. No matter how long this lasted, she couldn't be sorry. She'd cherish every damn second she spent inside his arms.

True's strokes shortened. She let go of her hold around his waist and strained to lift her legs just little higher, a little wider. The angle caused the hairs around the base of his cock to abrade her clit and Honey rocketed.

Her back arched and her legs stiffened. Her whole body spasmed as her orgasm rushed over her.

Faintly aware, she heard his muffled shout and felt the melting spurts of his come bathe her womb in hot, rhythmic pulses. His hips slowed and his hands eased.

She wrapped her legs around him again, hugged him with her arms and let him rock them together. The moment stretched and she groaned when he eased her legs off his hips and set her on her feet. She swayed, but he swept an arm around her back to steady her.

He kissed her forehead. "You okay?"

She rubbed her cheek up and down his chest in assent.

He chuckled, turned off the water then opened the glass to reach for a towel. He dried her off, rubbing until her skin glowed.

"Leave me some skin," she groused.

He popped her with the end of the towel. "Go get under the covers. I need to shave."

"Don't."

"Baby, you haven't seen your face."

She gave him a lopsided grin. "Do I have stubble-burn?"

"Yeah."

"I don't mind, really. And I have a plan for that beard of yours."

"You're nearly legless with exhaustion. Why don't you rest? I swear, we're not done, Honey. Not by a long shot."

Honey blinked. Understanding at last that he wanted a minute alone. Maybe more than a minute. She nodded, gave him a smile and headed to the bed. He'd said they weren't done. But that didn't mean he didn't see an end to their relationship.

Telling herself not to dwell on thoughts of the future, she yawned, dropped the towel and crawled between the cool sheets.

True scraped a hand over his newly shaved face and stepped into the bedroom. The light shining from the nightstand glinted on the dried tangled strands of Honey's brown hair. She'd have knots in her hair when she woke up, but he guessed she'd pretty much fallen into the bed the second the door closed between them.

He almost felt guilty about disturbing her again, but he'd come to some conclusions while he'd shaved.

First and foremost, no way in hell was she leaving his mountain.

Second, well, he'd take care of his second concern right now, before he woke her up to talk.

He knotted his towel around his hip and went in search of Lonny. A cool draft swept up the towel as he walked with purpose to the kitchen. Lonny sat at the counter eating another bowl of chili.

Lonny glanced up and arched a brow at his attire. "Didn't

expect to see you so soon."

"She's sleeping."

"We wear her out?"

"We did. But you're not gonna mention it to her. Not ever."

Lonny's lips pursed, but he nodded. "Agreed. It never happened. But is that so you can feel better or for her?"

"I want her to feel comfortable here with us."

"You want her to stay."

"I do."

"Have you asked her?"

"I will. Just as soon as we finish here."

Lonny pushed back his bowl. "All right, shoot. What's on your mind?"

"You're my brother. I want you here. Working beside me. But I get that you're not ready to commit. If you're eager to head out come spring, I won't try to stop you."

"You never have before. What's different now?"

"I'm giving you my blessing. If you don't want to come back, you don't have to. If you find something out there you want more than this place, don't worry about me."

"Think I do?"

"Yeah, I think you don't like the thought of me being alone."

Lonny let out a breath. "This place is home. But I've never felt tied to it like you. I want to see more of the world."

True's eyes misted, but he blinked the moisture, the weakness away. "I'm ready to let go."

Lonny's jaw flexed, but he nodded. "If you need me, you know I'll always come back."

"We'll always be family."

True strode closer to Lonny and looped an arm around his shoulder to pull him in for a hug.

"No crossin' swords, dammit," Lonny muttered, but he was grinning when True let him go.

"I'll say goodnight," True said, tipping his chin, then turning to stride away.

"I'll handle the livestock tomorrow," Lonny called after him.

True lifted a hand to let him know he'd heard, but he was

already thinking about what he had to say to Honey. He better make it good.

He tossed his damp towel onto the tile floor in the bathroom then walked softly to the bed. She still slept, on her stomach, her legs and arms stretched out, covering half the bed. For such a little thing she managed to take up a lot of room.

Kind of like the way she'd crowded her way into his heart. Hell, they'd only known each other a couple of days, but already he couldn't imagine not having her underfoot.

She fit. Sure, she was stubborn, mouthy, didn't know she needed someone to watch over her. He'd have to be careful not to let her know that. She had a lot of pride.

He picked up the covers and slid in beside her, nudging a leg to make room.

She stirred and snuggled in next to him.

One eye shot open. "You're cold," she grumbled.

"You snore." She didn't, but he wanted to see her reaction. Teasing her might become his favorite sport—especially, if he could get her to let loose with that hot temper of hers. The consequences were always interesting.

"Don't snore," she said petulantly and snuggled closer. "But you're a damn iceberg."

"Warm me up."

"You saw what happened the last time I lit a fire."

True grinned and stuck an arm beneath his head. Talking to Honey wasn't so hard.

Honey's hand swept over his belly then rested over his heart. She let out a deep sigh.

"You going back to sleep?"

"How can I? I have a horny cowboy yammering in my ear."

He caught her hand and held it cupped inside his. "I want you to stay."

She came up on an elbow and blinked. "Lonny already offered to let me stay to finish my book."

"And you said you were leaving. Do you still plan to go when the roads are clear?"

"I guess it depends..."

He swallowed and kept staring at their hands. "On what?"

"Whether it's just for the winter. Or whether you think you might want me to stay longer."

His gaze met hers. Her expression was closed. Her features set. Like his answer might hurt her.

"I don't want you to leave. Not ever."

Her lips parted. Her eyes filled. "It's crazy, you know that? How fast this is happening."

True had enough of the distance, even if she was snuggled up to his side. He pulled her over his body until they were perfectly aligned.

Honey rested her chin on her hands. "I think I'm falling in love with you."

"I'm not thinkin'. I'm already there."

A tear slipped down one cheek, and he wiped it away with his thumb. "I'm not an easy man."

"You've said that before and you still don't scare me."

True tucked his hands under her arms and pulled her higher. Their mouths met in a slow, steamy kiss.

When they drew apart she was smiling and her eyes held a wicked glint.

"What's going through your mind?"

"Ways to keep my dirty mouth busy."

He laughed and felt a blush flood his cheeks.

Honey's chuckles didn't stop. They gusted against his chest and then his belly as she disappeared beneath the covers. As her hot, *dirty* mouth went to work on warming the parts of him she seemed to like best, he lay smiling at the ceiling, wondering just when he'd let his control slip—for he'd ceded it completely to the woman mouthing his shaft. He might bluster and shout. And he was sure he'd have to take a firm hand to her backside now and then, only because she'd demand it, but he was pretty sure he knew exactly who'd rule this roost. Not that he would complain.

He wouldn't mind that she probably couldn't cook, didn't know how to stoke a furnace, or that he was going to have to follow her up slippery stairs for the rest of their lives.

Honey Cahill was the cure for his loneliness. A ray of the

sweetest, brightest sunshine. He smiled at the flowery language and wondered if she might be rubbing off on him.

A slim, warm hand stroked his sex, coaxing it to lift and thicken. A wicked, hot tongue laved his balls and shaft. He reached beneath the blankets, sank his fingers in her hair and guided her over the tip. Only when she sank her mouth on him and began to suck could he find the words to express what she gave him.

Her pure, true heart.

About the Author

Until recently, award-winning erotica and romance author Delilah Devlin lived in South Texas at the intersection of two dry creeks, surrounded by sexy cowboys in Wranglers. These days, she's missing the wide-open skies and starry nights but loving her dark forest in Central Arkansas, with its eccentric characters and isolation—the better to feed her hungry muse! For Delilah, the greatest sin is driving between the lines, because it's comfortable and safe. Her personal journey has taken her through one war and many countries, cultures, jobs, and relationships to bring her to the place where she is now—writing sexy adventures that hold more than a kernel of autobiography and often share a common thread of self-discovery and transformation.

To learn more about Delilah Devlin, please visit www.delilahdevlin.com. Send an email to delilah@delilahdevlin.com or join her Yahoo! group to enter in the fun with other readers as well as Delilah: DelilahsDiary@yahoogroups.com

Look for these titles by *Delilah Devlin*

Now Available:

Saddled
Stone's Embrace

Lone Star Lovers series
Unbridled
Unforgiven
Four Sworn
Breaking Leather
A Four-Gone Conclusion

Dark Frontier series
Undeniable

Delta Heat series
Five Ways 'til Sunday

Print Anthologies
Captive Souls
Cowboy Fever

CPSIA information can be obtained at www.ICGtesting.com
Printed in the USA
BVOW08s1116171013

334012BV00001B/60/P